The eagle let forth with one of his horrendous screeches.

Startled, Barbara slipped and braced her hand against the front of Orville's cage.

Stephen grabbed her wrist and pulled it away from the cage a second before Orville's beak struck the wire. He kept her wrist and spun her to face him. "You okay?"

Her eyes were wide with fear and he heard her breathing speed up. He held her close. Those flecks in her eyes drew him to her as though he were a miner who'd discovered a seam of gold a foot wide.

A moment later they were closer still. The kiss came without thought or even volition. It started out as a friendly peck. A moment later it changed into something deeper.

It was one heck of a kiss before breakfast!

Dear Reader,

Losing a beloved spouse, the person with whom we share memories no one else shares, can feel as though we are stuck with a leftover life to live. The very idea that we could find another love feels like a betrayal. Yet, even when we turn our backs on love, it can sneak back into our hearts and our minds.

Barbara Carew, a veterinarian with a small practice by the Tennessee River, is too busy to think about love. The sudden death of her husband left her with complete responsibility for herself, their two children and all the animals that desperately need her help.

Stephen MacDonald, a history professor, not only lost his wife to cancer, but nearly lost his leg in an automobile accident. After a year in rehab, he still uses a cane. He seems to be functioning, but in reality he's forgotten what it's like to laugh, to love, to take chances.

Barbara and Stephen are brought together by a shrieking, angry, desperately wounded bird that Stephen names Orville. And through Orville's journey of healing, Barbara and Stephen find their own hope.

This second book in the animal rehabilitator series Williamston Wildlife Rescue is also in praise of the wonderful people who take in and care for wild animals, raptors included. These people devote their lives and frequently their money to help the wild creatures that so often are in trouble because of human beings in the first place.

Watch for the third book in the Williamston Wildlife Rescue series, available in 2019.

Carolyn

HEARTWARMING

Tennessee Vet

Carolyn McSparren

HARLEQUIN® HEARTWARMING™

Recycling programs
for this product may
not exist in your area.

ISBN-13: 978-1-335-63384-2

Tennessee Vet

Copyright © 2018 by Carolyn McSparren

Printed in U.S.A.

RITA® Award nominee and Maggie Award winner **Carolyn McSparren** has lived in Germany, France, Italy and "too many cities in the US to count." She's sailed boats, raised horses, rides dressage and drives a carriage with her Shire-cross mare. She teaches writing seminars to romance and mystery writers, and writes mystery and women's fiction as well as romance books. Carolyn lives in the country outside of Memphis, Tennessee, in an old house with three cats, three horses and one husband.

Books by Carolyn McSparren

Harlequin Superromance

The Wrong Wife
Safe at Home
The Money Man
The Payback Man
House of Strangers
Listen to the Child
Over His Head
His Only Defense
Bachelor Cop

Williamston Wildlife Rescue

Tennessee Rescue

Visit the Author Profile page
at Harlequin.com for more titles.

This book is dedicated to the US Fish and Wildlife Service at Reelfoot Lake State Park in Tennessee, who watch over and protect our bald eagles. Thanks to them, the number of breeding pairs is increasing every year.

You go, guys!

CHAPTER ONE

"The closest service station that has snacks and drinks is eight miles away in that direction," Emma Logan said and pointed out the window down the two-lane road to her left. "And it's twelve miles in the other if you want to drive into Williamston. Can you stand to be so isolated? Seth and I live right across the road, but I'm either helping out down at the veterinary clinic or looking after whatever animals we've rescued. And in this condition—" she pointed down at her sizable belly "—I can't pick you up if you fall."

Stephen MacDonald thumped his Malacca cane with the silver wolf's head against the floor between his knees. "I do not fall, Emma. I limp. I am not an invalid."

"Then why hide out here? I've known you and your daughters since you all moved into the neighborhood years ago. I know you're hiding. Takes one to know one. I came out here to hole up and lick my wounds when I lost my job and my fiancé, and look what happened." She waved her hand at the living room of the farmhouse. From behind the back wall came the thud of nail guns and shouts of men. "It's already nearly October. With Kicks almost here, we have to finish the nursery and the kitchen and the new bathroom fast before he, she or it arrives."

"Kicks?" He gave her the barest flicker of a smile. "I remember my Nina nicknamed our Elaine *Salsa* when she was carrying her. Anne was quieter. I can't remember Nina's name for her." He turned away quickly, but not before Emma caught the flash of pain in his eyes.

When Anne had called to make the appointment for her father to view Emma's rental house, she'd warned her that she might not recognize Stephen.

"He looks even taller now that he's lost so much weight—like Abraham Lincoln without the beard. He's also angry," Anne had told her. "It's almost as though he blames Mother for dying on him."

"I'm sure he does," Emma had said. "She protected him from the world. I was terrified of him when I used to come to your house after school, until Nina showed me what a pushover he really is. And then his accident—

it's no wonder he's bad-tempered. Pain makes everybody angry."

"Not like this. I hope he does rent your cottage, Emma. He's not teaching until spring, and he's driving us all nuts. Maybe writing his new textbook will pull him back into life."

Sitting across from him now in her living room, Emma saw what Anne meant. Stephen was perfectly polite, but he wasn't quite there.

"I assume you are calling him, her or it Kicks because it does?" Stephen asked as he nodded toward her midsection.

"Does it ever. The doctor assures me it is not twins, which is all I cared about. Seth and I decided not to find out, which means the nursery will be your basic buttercup-yellow. Okay, enough about me. Why are you coming up here to hide out? I thought you were still in rehab. And you have a perfectly good house in Memphis. You could lock the door and turn off your phone if you want to write, couldn't you?"

"I do not intend to spend a day longer in rehab, Emma, even if our government would pay for it—which they wouldn't. And I refuse to allow either of my children to become caregivers. If I were where they could get to me, I'd be up to my ears in casseroles and being 'checked on' a dozen times a day. I would get nothing done. Anne usually calls ahead when she comes to see me. Elaine always 'just happens to be in the neighborhood.' Nina…" His voice caught. He took a deep breath before he was able to continue. "Nina was my guard dog at the gate. No one disturbed me when I was working. Or if I was simply feeling curmudgeonly.

"The official story is that I am moving to your cabin in the wilderness to work on my new textbook. You know, publish or perish? I already have tenure, but it doesn't hurt to keep one's name out there."

"Be careful. This place will suck you in. You'll discover all sorts of interesting ways to take up your time that are not academic."

"Fine. I need a quiet place where I am totally alone or surrounded by strangers. I am fed up with everyone I know commiserating with me over the accident. Nobody mentions Nina any longer. After three years, it is assumed I have gotten over my wife's death. I have not. I'll never be fully alive again without her, but that's nobody else's business."

"I suspect she would have kicked your butt if she thought you used her death as an excuse to stop living yourself."

"No doubt. Up to now I could hide in rehab and in hospitals. Since that is no longer an option, I am hiding in your rental cottage. At least I can avoid being checked out to see whether my limp is any better as I walk across campus."

"What do you expect?" Emma said. "You nearly lost your leg, Stephen."

"I know. I was there."

"If that truck had been any bigger, you probably wouldn't be here to complain about your leg."

"No doubt. But I am here and I do complain on a regular basis, and I intend to finish my rehab out here in what my daughters call the middle of nowhere. My dean says 'write, write, write that blasted textbook.' The doctor says 'walk, walk, walk on that leg.' I'll probably always have to use a cane, he says. No way, say I. I've already missed teaching the spring semester, I dropped my classes for summer school and I'm being allowed to take the fall semester as a sabbatical to write. By next spring I expect to be back a hundred percent.

"Now, about the rent on— What do you call it? The Hovel?" He pointed across the street toward an old-fashioned Tennessee farmhouse sporting a fresh coat of pale gray paint and dark red shutters. "Doesn't look very hovel-like to me."

"Not now, maybe, but you should have seen it before my stepmother, Andrea, came up and redecorated."

"I'm sure Andrea did a good job. She always does. So, how much rent? I may only be here for a couple of months full-time, but I will probably continue to use it on weekends, so I'll be happy to sign a lease for six months with automatic renewal for another six."

"I wouldn't dream of charging you rent."

Stephen cut her off by raising his hand. "No. Unless I pay the going rate, I cannot come. I am hardly destitute, Emma, and Andrea said you had redone the place *to* rent. So, how much per month?"

"What do you think of this for rent?" She gave him a figure.

"Much less than it would be in Memphis or Nashville. I accept. I'll drive back up this evening with the rest of my stuff and move in, if that's all right," he said.

"And I'll feed you dinner."

"Give me a rain check for tonight. I'll be back much too late. How close to the stove can you stand?"

"Now, was that a nice thing to say?" Emma patted her belly and chuckled. "Close enough. In a sense we're both invalids."

The smile he gave her was real. Fleeting, but real.

"Your problem will disappear in a few months," he said, still smiling. "Mine will last a good bit longer. My doctor says the knee will never be perfect. Maybe not, but I refuse to dodder into old age with a cane in my hand. I'd have to grow a beard and wear glasses with a little chain attaching them to my jacket so I don't lose them. I don't *think* so."

"Do you need to go look at the house again?" Emma asked.

"I have to drive an hour and a half back to Memphis to pack." He set the ferrule of his cane on the floor between his feet, then began to lever himself up.

Across the coffee table, Emma grabbed the arm of the sofa and began to hoist her heavy body to a standing position.

Halfway up, they caught sight of each other's predicaments.

And fell back grinning at one another.

Five minutes later, as she waved him down her gravel driveway to the road in the Triumph Spitfire sports car he had owned as long as she had known him, she wondered how on earth to drag him back into life.

Well, it might be kicking and screaming, but she'd manage somehow. She owed it to Nina and his daughters. Nina would have wanted him to find someone else wonderful to spend the rest of his life with. Emma knew a dozen women who would jump at the chance.

CHAPTER TWO

Dr. Barbara Carew, DVM, large and small animals, finished stitching the torn ear of Hubert, a French lop rabbit that had played too rough with his housemate, Louis, the Belgian mastiff. According to Louis's owner, the big dog was miserable and missing his buddy. Usually Hubert—pronounced *you-bear*—ran Louis ragged. This was an unfortunate accident, but Hubert was going to have to be guarded from that sort of rough-and-tumble play for a couple of weeks, at least until the stitches were removed. Then the pair would have to be supervised, because unfortunately Hubert thought he was more than mastiff-size and a whole lot tougher.

"All right, my little French friend," Barbara said as she scooped up the giant bunny. "Off you go to your cage and nighty-night." She settled the rabbit down, checked to be certain that everything was in order in the clinic's office and reception area, walked out the back door and across the parking lot. Outside, Mabel the lame goose was securely caged with her current crop of goslings.

"No foxes tonight," Barbara said and tossed the big goose a handful of grain. Not that Mabel wasn't a match for most creatures that wanted to devour her. But she couldn't protect her goslings if she was busy protecting herself.

Mabel snapped up the grain but didn't even chuckle a response. The goslings snuggled deeper under her. Actually, no fox in his right mind would challenge Mabel, although it might make an attempt to snatch a gosling.

Barbara walked across the grass to the barn and through it to her apartment, built at the far end. She was so tired, she was not certain she could bend down to take off her boots without falling over. She prayed the clinic answering service could handle any calls until morning.

She needed sleep more than she needed food, but she tossed a frozen diet meat-loaf dinner into her microwave and started the timer. She'd still be hungry afterward, but she'd try to endure without ice cream or cookies. She tossed her scrubs into the laundry hamper and slipped into her largest, oldest, softest T-shirt and a pair of Bermuda shorts, then poured herself a diet soda.

"I would kill for a glass of wine," she said aloud. "But sure as I do, I'll get called out to some cow that can't calve."

She stayed on her feet until the microwave dinged. "If I sit down, I will wake up in my chair tomorrow morning. And why am I talking to myself?"

Because there's no one else to talk to.

The dinner was anything but delicious. The meat loaf tasted like cardboard and the mashed potatoes were one congealed lump. Still, it was food. Not enough, but food.

She jumped a foot when the gate alarm at the road sounded as the gate opened, and the motion-sensor lights flashed on in the clinic parking lot as someone drove around the building and stopped at the back door. "What the heck?" She yanked on her boots back over her bare feet, grabbed her big flashlight and went to see who in Sam Hill was coming in this late without calling ahead.

"Is Dr. Carew available?" A male voice, deep baritone. He was standing at the back door of the clinic, silhouetted against the lights. All she could tell about him was that he was tall and sounded as though he had some education.

"I'm available," Barbara said. "And the only Dr. Carew there is."

"I've got an emergency. Emma Logan told me your clinic was down this way but didn't give me your phone number. I couldn't think of anything to do but search you out." Behind him the very bright lights of some kind of fancy sports car shone directly into Barbara's eyes. "It may be too late to help him, but he was moving, and this is all I could think of."

"You hit something on the road." Probably a deer.

"It hit me," he said. "Flew smack into the front of my car."

"So you squashed an owl?"

"Not quite. Take a look."

He stood aside. Barbara turned on her powerful flashlight and walked up to the front of the car. "You mind turning your lights off? I can't see squat."

A moment later the headlights went out. Barbara allowed her eyes to adjust to the lower light of the motion sensors under the eaves before she looked at the damage to whatever it was. She fully expected it to be dead.

It shrieked. A hair-raising, enraged and I'm-alive-here-people shriek.

"That's no owl," Barbara whispered.

She dropped to her haunches two feet from the grille of the car and shone the light on… "Lord save us," she whispered. "You hit a bald eagle."

"Indeed I did not. It hit me. I wasn't driving fast, not on these roads, when I've barely moved in to The Hovel after driving up here this morning, then back to Memphis to pick up my stuff and right back here. I thought some kind of pterodactyl was about to yank me out of the car. One minute nothing, the next this thing appears in front of me and *whomp*!"

"Take off the grille," Barbara said.

"I beg your pardon?"

"These cars carry fancy toolkits, don't they? Let's see if we can keep him alive long enough to get him out of there." She stood and walked back toward the barn.

"Where are you going?"

"To get some towels and heavy gloves. If we do get him loose, we'll have to wrap him up tight. He's going to come out of there fighting like a dragon, no matter how badly he's hurt. You have any heavy driving gloves?"

"In the glove compartment."

"Get 'em." She pointed at the car. "Unscrew that grille, please. Carefully. Stay out of talon or beak range. He'll take your head off as soon as he looks at you. He's certain this is your fault. Eagles aren't noted for forgiveness. They prefer punishment, preferably death by devouring."

Wearing leather gauntlets, Barbara returned with an armload of heavy towels. "Whoa!" she snapped as the eagle screamed again. "Calm down, you. We're trying to help."

The eagle stared at her with insane black eyes, but stopped thrashing momentarily, almost as though it understood. Barbara knew it did not. More likely, it was gathering itself to try to break free and savage the people who were attempting to save it.

"I think the left wing is broken—see how twisted it is hanging between the struts on the grille?" she asked.

"There is no way I can unscrew this grille. The grille has not been off since it came from the showroom years ago. This car is a genuine antique. It's as rusted as I am."

"Can you actually cut those struts? Ease it off him?" She expected horror. In the lights, she could tell the car was a classic, beautifully maintained.

That grille would cost a fortune and probably take weeks to replace.

Instead, the man said, "Do you have some heavy-duty bolt cutters?"

"Be right back."

Not one howl of complaint from him. Hmm. Even if he did drive a silly car and hit birds with it. She handed him her largest bolt cutters.

"Show me where to cut," he said.

"I'm not altogether certain. Need to get him loose but keep hold of him so he doesn't flap himself to death." For a long minute vet and eagle stared one another in the eye, then Barbara nodded. "Yeah. I'm going to try something that should work for the short haul." She took a small towel and tossed it over the eagle's head, covering its eyes. Instantly it stopped fighting. "Now, cut here and here. Fast. It'll take him less than a minute to realize he isn't actually hooded. Can you manage alone?"

The man actually growled at her, as if she'd impugned his masculinity. "Hang in there, big guy," he whispered. "We're trying to help you." He grunted with the effort of snapping the grille. "We're not about to let you die on us."

The grille snapped and snapped again. Possibly all to the good that it was old.

Man's got muscles, I'll say that for him. And
it almost sounded as though he was command-
ing the bird to survive. "Hold the feet, avoid
the talons," Barbara said. "I don't want to have
to sew you up, too. With luck I'll get him out
fast and swaddle him tight."

Getting him actually loose didn't prove to
be as difficult as Barbara had thought. "I wish
I had a real raptors' hood," she said as she
held the bird, snugly, under one arm, while
she kept the towel taut over the eagle's head.
"If I can keep his head covered until we get
him on the table, I can give him a little gas.
Then we'll see what's going on. Come on. We
need to move fast."

CHAPTER THREE

STEPHEN MACDONALD GLANCED at the pieces of his grille lying on the tarmac of the parking lot. Small price to pay to save this living creature. He now understood what an eagle eye was. The bird had glared at him as though to say, "This is your fault. Fix it!" He was already too involved, as though his life had become intertwined with the eagle's. He'd been helpless to save Nina, watching her fade away. And he hadn't been able to heal his own injuries, either. Somehow, he had to help this wounded creature. That was nuts, but it was the way he felt.

He followed Barbara toward the back door of the clinic.

He'd managed to hold the eagle's feet until the doctor had the bird free. He gave thanks for his fancy driving gloves. The thing's talons looked as long as a grizzly bear's and twice as sharp.

The motion-sensor lights stayed on, so they could see where they were walking.

"Hey," Dr. Carew called, "I need a hand here. Open the back door of the clinic, turn on the lights on the left, open the door to exam room one and help me get this sucker on the table. Now! Before he kills me."

And he thought his daughters were bossy. He hobbled as fast as he could and opened the back door of the clinic, then realized he'd left his cane in the car. He felt for the light switch, found himself in a hall with doors on either side, opened the first one, turned on that light and got out of the vet's way.

"I had no idea they were this big," Stephen said. The eagle wasn't fighting at the moment. It was, however, dripping blood from a gash in one of its legs—what would have been the drumstick in a turkey.

"Here, hold him still." Barbara brought up some sort of plastic mask and stuck the eagle's beak into it. Amazingly enough, it had not dislodged the towel covering its eyes, so it was lying quietly.

"These guys are not as tough as you'd think," Barbara said. "When people talk about bird bones, they aren't kidding. We need to x-ray that wing and see if anything else is busted. Internal injuries, fractured skull. I'm amazed he made it this long. Come on. Help me carry him to the X-ray room. He's heavier than he looks."

Together, they managed to get the bird situated on the X-ray table. Barbara pulled an X-ray shield over her shoulders and handed one to him.

"Do we have to wait while you develop the pictures?" Stephen asked as he settled the shield in front of his chest.

"Comes up on the screen right here. Animals don't wait while you develop anything. Want to see what you did?"

"I keep telling you *it* hit *me*."

"I know. You're the innocent victim. Hold him down. I have to stretch that wing out far enough to see the bones. We don't dare let him go. See that?" she said and pointed to the screen. "Looks like a clean break to that left wing. I'm not seeing any other breaks, but that cut on the thigh needs to be cleaned and stitched. He needs antibiotics. Too soon to talk about internal injuries, but I don't see anything obvious. Maybe a concussion, but apparently not a fractured skull. You, sir—" she nodded to the eagle "—are one lucky bird."

"How do you fix the wing?"

"I'll straighten it as much as I dare, try to line the bones up, fold it correctly and tape it tight to his body for tonight. Then tomorrow, if he makes it, we'll see whether he can get by with a splint or whether we'll need to pin it. Come on, he's waking up. We need a trifle more happy gas, then we stitch, give him antibiotics, strap that wing in place, put him down in a nice tight cage so he doesn't flail and worry about him all night."

"Isn't there anything else you can do to stabilize the wing right now? You have the X-rays. Can't you at least splint it?"

She glanced at him from under her eyebrows. "Ever hear of swelling, *doctor*? Birds are notorious for going into shock and dying on you. I'm not about to put more pressure on him until we're sure he's going to survive the night. How many eagles have you worked on?"

"None. But…"

Barbara turned to him. "I would suggest you say a few earnest prayers he survives, because, if we lose this eagle, you owe the United States a big fat fine for hitting him." He started to speak, but she held up her hands to forestall him. "Who *are* you, anyway? And how do you know Emma?"

CHAPTER FOUR

"I'M STEPHEN MACDONALD," he said. "Emma and Seth's new tenant. And why should I owe the government anything? It hit *me*."

"It's a bird. And you're a human being—the one with the big brain and the opposable thumbs. Heck of an introduction to the neighborhood."

Stephen watched Barbara clean and close the eagle's cut with small, neat stitches. He'd never been fond of the sight of blood, but then usually it came from a scrape or a bloody nose on one of his daughters. This was different. This woman was obviously good at what she did. His own blood hadn't bothered him after the accident that had nearly cost him a leg, but then, he'd been in shock and unconscious for the worst part—the part when the surgeons had worked to keep him alive and with both legs attached to his body.

He realized that he didn't even know what this vet looked like. At first, she'd been behind her flashlight, then he'd been paying so much attention to the eagle he hadn't even glanced at her, and now she was wearing a surgical mask.

She finished her stitching, and between them they moved the eagle—already stirring—into a cage. "I have to clean up the mess," she said. She pulled off her mask and tossed it into the trash receptacle, then turned to look at him.

He felt a jolt go through his solar plexus. She was probably five foot five and not model-thin. He guessed in her thirties. Chestnut-brown hair was pulled back in a scrunchie, but escaping in tendrils around her face.

Those eyes. Extraordinary. The color of Barbados rum with flecks of what looked like 24-carat gold in them. They were wide eyes, as though she could take in the whole world without turning her head the way that eagle could. Wise, aware eyes, as though she'd seen it all and knew she could handle it. He had a feeling that she didn't simply look, she *saw*. Not a beautiful face, exactly, but he didn't think he'd forget those high cheekbones or that broad forehead. His first impression was that she was a person of value. Worth knowing. He also noted that she had great legs.

"I don't know about you, but I'm spitting cotton and hungry as a coyote," she said. "You do with some sweet tea and a pimento cheese sandwich? It's homemade."

"I could probably eat the coyote. I was headed to the overnight gas station to get some snacks when I hit our friend in there. I didn't have sense enough to go to the grocery before I drove back up here from Memphis this afternoon. I'm not used to having to think about those things ahead of time. In town I'm five minutes away from a supermarket. Here, the closest place is eight miles away."

"You get used to planning ahead." As she chatted, she straightened, cleaned, put instruments into the sterilizer, scrubbed down the table and tossed her trash. "I can go over all this again and scrub the floors tomorrow morning. Come on."

"Shouldn't we stay with him tonight?" Stephen asked.

Barbara shook her head. "We've done all we can do before morning. He needs to rest." She turned out the lights, locked the clinic and flashed her light on Stephen's mauled grill. "Sorry about your car. I think you can drive it, though. He doesn't seem to have punctured the radiator or slashed any hoses. After I feed us, I'll follow you home to be sure you get there."

"You don't…"

"All part of the service. Sorry, my apartment's off the back of the barn."

He followed her out of the clinic, across the parking lot, through the barn and to a door at the end. With all but a couple of lights off, he couldn't see much of the animals in the stalls, but he heard a couple of horses snoring. "I'll be glad to stay with him and let you get some sleep. I can call you if—"

"If what? You don't know what you're looking at. I promise you there is nothing more I can do tonight. It's up to him. He's alive, which is amazing. 'Course, he may never be able to be released back into the wild..."

"After you fix his wing and he convalesces, of course you can release him."

"Not necessarily. Come in." She turned on lights in her apartment. He followed her in.

"Bathroom's down that hall past the bedroom," she said and pointed. "Look, I have no idea at this point whether I can fix his wing or not. It may not knit properly or at all. It may have to be amputated."

He was halfway down the hall, but he spun to look at her. "No! You can't do that. He has to fly again. Be whole again."

"Don't freak, Mr. MacDonald. Even if he can't fly, he'll live a comfortable life in one of the zoo's animal training programs. He'll be well fed and possibly even find another mate."

"*Another* mate?"

"Bird his age will almost certainly have a mate. I assume he belongs up at Reelfoot Lake. No idea how he got down here. He and his family are probably nesting in the same nest they've used for fifty years or longer."

"You're kidding, right?"

"Not at all. Eagles keep their nests. There's a nest on a river in the Grand Tetons that they think has been there a couple of hundred years."

"He's hurt, broken, possibly disabled, not knowing where his mate is or whether his eaglets are surviving, unable to care for them and he may spend his life in a cage. Being stared at and pitied, unable to fly free. What kind of life is that for him? I should have let him die." A wave of depression washed over him. He'd learned to fight it most of the time by refusing to feel anything at all, but this depression was for another creature, one whose situation was too close to his own. How did he guard against that?

"You do know what anthropomorphism means, don't you?" she asked.

"Of course I do. It's giving human characteristics to animals. The more research is done, however, the more we find there is precious little difference between us and them. He has to fly again. Find his way back."

"So he can land and say, 'Honey, I'm home?' All I can do is my best, Mr. MacDonald. Now, about that sandwich."

OF ALL THE crazy ways to spend an evening, Barbara thought as she spread mayonnaise on slices of the French baguette she'd picked up at the bakery in Williamston. She was always as ravenous after a difficult surgery as if she'd bicycled twenty miles or run a marathon. Her body had long since used up whatever energy she'd gained from that second-rate diet meat loaf.

She glanced up from the kitchen island where she was working. MacDonald was pacing around her living room staring at the books on the shelves. Lots of shelves, lots of books. Not in matching leather bindings. Not alphabetized. Her books and John's were as intermingled as they had been the day he died.

Barbara had a simple filing system. Total recall.

When she and John had built the barn and created their apartment, they'd planned to give themselves plenty of room for books. Originally, they'd planned a big deck off the back, but after John had died she'd never gotten around to it. Or to anything else domestic for that matter. Who had the time? Or the interest when there was no one to share it with.

She saw the room as Stephen saw it. It was squeaky clean, but all it needed was a thick layer of dust and a bunch of hanging cobwebs to turn it into Miss Havisham's wedding feast in Dickens's *Great Expectations*. And she acknowledged the truth—that she hadn't yet built the deck because finishing a project alone that she and John had planned together seemed like a betrayal. She'd never admit to a soul that she felt that way. Her friends, her clients and even her children talked about how well she had coped with John's loss, how she had kept growing and changing. She knew better. Emotionally, she was as empty as she had been the day John died. She told herself she was happy being alone with no one to answer to except her children and her clients.

But sometimes in the night, when she reached for the place beside her where once she had felt John's chest rise and fall, she hated knowing that she'd never love again.

Her fallback position was physical and mental exhaustion. She considered herself meticulous when it came to keeping the clinic immaculate. But when half the time she fell into bed after working flat out for twelve or more hours, it really didn't matter when the coffee table had last been dusted. She managed to keep the kitchen and bathroom clean and the papers and magazines at least in separate piles, but that was as far as it went.

She wasn't exactly embarrassed to have Stephen MacDonald scrub up in her bathroom, but this MacDonald guy in his vintage Triumph and polo shirt with the proper logo on it did not belong either in Emma's rental cottage or Barbara's apartment.

When he came back from the bathroom, she saw he had run water over his face and hair as well as scrubbed his hands and forearms.

She took her first good look at him. Oh, boy. Talk about the wolf in Little Red Riding Hood! *Grandmother, what big eyes you have. And how bright blue.* She didn't think his eyes were the result of those fake colored contacts, but you never knew.

Further perpetuating the wolfish image was his short gray hair and what Shakespeare would have called a "lean and hungry" look. Actually, she seemed to recall Shakespeare was talking about an assassin. He stood a bit over six feet tall and had kept his stomach flat. Golf, maybe. Barbara sucked in her own stomach on a big breath, but she couldn't hold it in for long.

"Sorry, I made kind of a mess," he said. "I tried to get the blood out of my khakis. Unsuccessfully."

"When you get back to The Hovel, put everything into the washer on cold. If there is anything I know about, it's how to get blood out of cloth."

"Does it ever bother you?" He propped himself up on the wall beside the refrigerator and stuck his hands into his damp pockets.

"Blood?" She picked up a wicked kitchen knife and sliced the sandwiches crossways, then slid two halves apiece onto plates and added pickles and potato chips. "I grew up on a farm. I was pulling piglets out of sows when I was five or six years old. Gangrene bothers me… Sorry, not the proper social chitchat over snacks. Death bothers me. Creatures in pain bother me. Damage I can't fix bothers me. If it can live a happy life, then whatever I have to do to get the animal to that point is merely repair work. The same thing your mechanic will have to do with your radiator grille—I just do it with flesh and bone instead of metal."

"Did you always want to be a vet?"

She laid out silverware and napkins and handed him a plate. "I wanted to be an Olympic three-day event rider. Jumping incredibly large and athletic horses over humongous fences at death-defying speeds." She looked down at herself and let out a rueful sigh. "That was twenty pounds ago when I was seventeen. I was a good enough rider for local over-fences horse shows, but even if my pop had been able to afford a million-dollar jumper or the training and travel to go along with it, I wouldn't have been good enough."

"Why not?"

"Most three-day eventers at the Olympic level are certifiably insane. I have too much imagination. I could always visualize what would happen to the horse if I crashed."

"The horse? Not you?"

This time she laughed. "Human doctors say 'First, do no harm.' We say 'The animal always comes first.'"

"So my eagle took precedence over my antique automobile grille?"

"Of course it did, as you knew at the time.

A lot of people would have sliced up the bird to avoid nicking their chrome. You didn't."

"As dearly as I love and baby that car, it is not alive. That bird, as he told us in no uncertain terms, *is*. No contest."

"I have to keep warning you. He may not make it."

"I did. He will, too."

At the back of the kitchen was a banquette breakfast nook. He took his sandwich, slid in to one of the seats and stretched his right leg out to the side. "Be careful of my bum leg. I can be a hazard to navigation."

"Beer, wine, water, soda?"

"I WOULD KILL for a beer." What Stephen really wanted was a handful of opioids to cut the ache in his right leg and knee. That was what he got for being macho. He'd left his cane on the front seat of the car. And he didn't take opioids. It would have been too easy to get hooked on them in rehab. Even if reality sucked, he preferred it to living in cloud-cuckoo-land.

"What's with the leg?" Barbara said as she started on her sandwich.

"Hey, you're not kidding. I know Southerners and their pimento cheese. This is exceptional."

"Thank you. All my own work, as the street artists say in London. So, do we not mention the leg?"

"Most people don't. They avoid staring, but I can tell they're dying to ask about it. That's part of the reason I'm at Emma's. Sometimes I feel as if I am one gigantic leg with tiny little arms, legs and head sewed on around the edges."

"I'm sorry..."

"No! Please. I don't mind talking about it, if you don't start every conversation from here on out with 'And how are you *today*, Stephen?'"

She chuckled. "Promise."

"Okay. I was headed home from a faculty dinner. I had not touched a drop of alcohol. I was driving a small SUV that had belonged to my wife, and a guy in a gigantic diesel pickup truck T-boned me when he ran a light. He, by the way, had three DUIs pending already. They used the Jaws of Life and several miracles to get me as far as the trauma center at the Med Hospital Trauma Center. Very much the way we got our eagle disentangled from my grille. I spent the next year getting operated on, going through rehab, getting operated on some more, more rehab, lots of titanium pins in my bones, skin grafts, yada, yada, yada. In the end, I kept my bionic leg and knee, and I'm down to a cane after a wheelchair and a walker. But I still limp, more when I'm tired."

"And you hurt."

He nodded. "They say that more exercises like walking and swimming will help diminish the pain. That's one of the reasons I'm here."

"Good luck with finding a public swimming pool this side of Jackson. Even this late in September, it's still warm enough to take a dip in the little lake where Seth and Emma have their cabin, but not for much longer. And if you walk on our road out there—" she pointed toward the front of the clinic "—watch out for crazy drivers, and the occasional deer in your face."

"Boy, are you Miss Comfort!"

"Just sayin'. I have nothing to offer you for dessert," she said.

He took a final swig of his beer. "That was wonderful. I can make it to morning without hunger pangs."

"I can front you breakfast stuff—eggs, bacon, bread for toast, even coffee."

"Not necessary. Emma is taking me to Williamston so that she can introduce me to the denizens of the café. I feel as though I'm being presented at court."

"Around here, you're pretty much right. What are you planning to do about your poor car?"

"Call my mechanical genius in Memphis to come get it and try to locate a grille for it. In the meantime, I'll have to rent a car. I assume there is some place to do that in town?"

Barbara waggled a hand. "If you're lucky, our esteemed mayor, Sonny Prather, will rent you a baby truck. I assume you can't borrow one from your wife. Obviously, her SUV didn't survive your accident."

He caught his breath. "Slight miscommunication. Nina, my wife, died several years ago of cancer. The night of my accident I was driving her SUV because the Triumph was in the shop. It often is. I just kept her old car as a backup for me and my daughters to use in case one of our cars was out of commission. I decided to drive my Triumph up here today instead of the sedan I bought to replace the SUV. At the moment, my younger daughter, Anne, is driving that while her car is being worked on."

Her hand flew to her mouth. "Oh, I am so sorry! I thought your wife was in Memphis."

He reached out and laid his hand on her other arm. "Don't be. You had no way of knowing from the way I talked. Took me a couple of years to be able even to say 'cancer.' Now, I think I've turned that last year into a kind of myth. It's as though every time I mention it I add one more layer of scar tissue I can use to protect myself."

"I know exactly what you mean. John—my vet partner in the clinic as well as my husband and the father of our two children—died several years ago. One of those young heart attacks, unsuspected and nearly always fatal. I felt as though someone had turned off the sun like flipping a light switch. The only thing that saved me was that I had to take over the clinic alone to support the family or starve. I had good friends who helped keep me sane. Apparently, I did a decent job, but I have almost no recollection of the first two years after John's death. The children helped. I have a son and a daughter, Mark and Caitlyn. Those are their pictures on the mantelpiece. Suddenly, I was the sole support of the family."

"Must have been tough. I managed to act sane until my accident, then I was doped up until I was aware enough to refuse anymore opioids, and being *rehabilitated*—a synonym for attempted murder. Anyway, I've been planning to buy a new car. This may be a good time to go ahead and do it. Let's face it, the Triumph is my toy, but it's not practical. I had to have the entire transmission replaced with an automatic so I could drive it safely with one completely functional foot and leg. I've about made up my mind to buy a small truck, except I have no idea what to buy or where to buy it."

"You are deep in the land of the pickup. After breakfast, get Emma to take you shopping and introduce you around. Tomorrow is not one of her days doing receptionist duty here, so she'll be free."

"I can't drag Emma around, the shape she's in."

"Don't tell *her* that. Now, how about we see if you can drive your car to your house. I'll follow you."

"You don't have to do that. It's only a couple of miles. If I get stuck on the side of the road I can walk home."

"This is the country. You do not want to be walking down this road in the middle of the night or *you'll* be the one stuck on somebody's grille."

"Let me at least help you clean up the dishes."

"That's what God gave us dishwashers for."

"May I check on our patient before we leave?"

Barbara sighed. "I'd rather check him myself after I come back from following you home. I want him kept as quiet as possible. Hey—my clinic, my rules."

Stephen drew himself up but did not actually protest. He was not used to being questioned about his decisions. No doubt she knew her business, but she hadn't a clue how invested he already was in the eagle. It was obvious she wanted him out of the way.

Climbing into the Triumph always took some doing. Before he attempted it, Stephen checked to see that there was no coolant leakage behind his radiator and collected a couple of small pieces of grille he'd missed earlier. The little car started and ran smoothly. The headlights of Barbara's truck came on, and their small convoy eased out of the parking lot onto the road.

Accompanied by worrying clinks, he drove slowly and carefully, but the car ran smoothly. He pulled into the driveway in front of his new abode, shut off the engine, levered himself out from behind the wheel, grabbed his cane from the passenger's seat and limped up to Barbara's truck. "Thank you for everything. I'll come by to check on him as soon as I can after breakfast."

She leaned out her open window. "Here's my card. Numbers for me, the clinic, my cell and my email. I'll let you know if something changes. Mr. MacDonald—"

"Stephen, please."

"And I'm Barbara. Try to get some sleep, and don't worry. He obviously wants to live. Now we have to hope his will is as strong as his bones." She pulled away and waved through her window as she drove back onto the road and turned toward the clinic.

He stood in the dark and watched her taillights until she turned the bend and disappeared. Heck of an introduction to the country, he thought. And a heck of an introduction to the most interesting woman he'd met since Nina died.

Though she was a bit too sure of herself…

CHAPTER FIVE

"AN EAGLE? REALLY?" Emma Logan swiveled as much as she could to look at Stephen in the passenger seat of her SUV. It was clearly a challenge to get the distance she needed between her stomach and the steering wheel while still being able to keep her feet on the pedals. "Have you talked to Barbara this morning? How is he?"

"I called at six thirty this morning. That was as late as I could wait. She told me she's calling in one of her colleagues from the raptor center in Memphis to give her a hand in case she has to pin the wing. I'm glad she decided to bring in another vet. She seemed excellent, but it never hurts to have a second opinion."

"She's a gem, but she's going to kill herself unless she can hire another vet to take some of the pressure off her. There is a vet south of Williamston, but he's only interested in small animals. The closest large animal vet is in Somerville, twenty-five miles away. Seth says she and John picked this location because nobody else was practicing here. And now the locals love her, so everybody calls or just shows up when they have a problem. Some days when I'm working for her I can barely find a place to park."

"I suspect you need earplugs."

She laughed. "The big fancy kind. The dogs and cats aren't the worst. It's the pigs. Ever hear a pig squeal when it's being restrained?"

"Probably the way that eagle screamed last night."

"Oh, I'll bet Little Oinky can top that eagle's decibel level. Pigs have no defense mechanisms except flight and noise."

"Not Olympic sprint speed, right?"

"Right, although under pressure even a full-grown domestic pig can put on a surprising turn of speed for a short distance. When anything or anyone tries to restrain them, their instinct is to squeal and run. Preferably knocking you down and stomping on you in the process."

"I thought they ate people."

"I think that's an old wives' tale. I do know, however, that hogs keep growing until they die. I rode along with Barbara to see a pig with an abscessed hoof the other day. I swear the hog, Arnold, was the size of a camping tent—and not for one person, either." She looked down at her belly and sighed. "I know how he feels."

"I didn't ask last night," Stephen said, "but if it's not a rude question…"

"When am I due? First week in December. Perfect time. After Thanksgiving and before Christmas. Assuming good ol' Kicks here can read schedules." She patted her tummy. "Actually, I have tons of energy, unlike the first three months, when all I wanted to do was sleep and eat. Barbara says all mammals tend to do that. She's warned me that when I start rearranging the linen closet and cleaning out the kitchen cabinets I need to watch out for labor. Sometimes I wish I was a sea horse. The daddy has full responsibility for the offspring.

"Here we are at the café. Prepare to be checked out." She turned into the parking lot of the brick building. A small sign over the door read Café, and a sign on the window said Open. Other than that and the large number of cars in the lot at seven thirty in the morning, nothing shouted that this was the place everyone in town came for meals, if they ate out at all.

The minute Stephen opened the glass front

door for Emma the noise poured out. People noise. Not jukebox or even radio. "Ah," he said with a grin. "Nothing but conversation and cutlery."

"Oooh," Emma said. "I'll have to remember that the next time my sometime boss Nathan wants me to come up with a title for a new restaurant."

"You're still working for Nathan? I assumed you quit when you married Seth and moved up here from Memphis."

"Long distance via computer and cell phone. I'm not leaving the county again until Kicks is a separate entity. Between doing special projects for Nathan and running the appointment scheduling for Barbara three half days a week and supervising the addition to the house and—"

"Having a baby."

"It's crazy, but what would I do if I stayed home? Play video games? Listen to the men who are working on the addition to the house? They all speak Spanish, so our conversations consist mostly of smiles and charades. I'll be glad when they are finished, so I can have my house back. Hey, my word! Here's Barbara."

Stephen felt his heart stop for a moment as he swiveled to look at her. He assumed she'd come to tell him the bird had not survived the night. Well, she'd warned him his rescue was unlikely to survive. He grabbed a deep breath and prepared for some new psychic pain.

She waved at them and wound her way through the restaurant to their table, speaking to nearly everyone she passed. She slipped into the seat across from him and said, "Morning, Emma, Stephen. Mind if I join you?"

"You already have," Emma said, though she nodded and smiled. She raised a hand to catch the eye of Velma, the waitress.

"I had to come tell you personally," Barbara said to Stephen.

"You don't have to tell me. He didn't make it, did he?"

Her eyes opened wide. "No, no. I should have realized you'd think... He made it through the night and swallowed a mouse whole an hour ago. Tried to devour my fingers, too. He hated the mouse, because we had to give him one of the frozen ones we keep for emergencies. I did thaw it. He grumped a bit, but he ate it eventually. At the moment, he's trying to figure out how to remove his neck collar so he can tear off his bandages."

"But he's alive?"

"So far. One of my best vet buds from Land

Between the Lakes park is driving over his morning. We may have to pin the wing, although checking the X-rays, I don't think we'll need to. If he survives that, we start the healing. Then, if that works, we start rehabilitating him—if we can figure out where to do it."

"How can you do that without a flight cage?" Emma asked.

"We can't. We may have to move him up to Reelfoot Lake before he heals. It's crazy that we can't have one closer than that. We desperately need it for all the birds we rehabilitate. In the meantime, Stephen, since he's your responsibility…"

"I should have mentioned that last night. I'll be totally responsible for your charges. I do have a book to write. I intend, however, to monitor his progress closely. Anything you need, I will attempt to provide for him. I plan to see him fly away without a backward glance."

"No charges. He's part of my work with the animal rehabilitators group. If we could clean up the outdoor cage Seth and his team built for Emma at The Hovel when she first moved here and was raising her abandoned skunk babies, we could move the bird down there once he's out of the woods and ready to rehabilitate…

It's not adequate for a flight cage, but it will do to start off with once we dare to give him that much space. But as to responsibilities, if you want to avoid a big fine for hitting him…"

Stephen started to protest.

"I know, I know. *He* hit *you*. Tough to prove it. If you work with me on him, the law will probably cut you some slack. Killing an eagle could mean not only incurring a massive fine, but—if it could be proved it was done on purpose—you could get jail time as well. There are even restrictions about possessing an eagle feather."

"I would hope you could testify on my behalf."

She cut her eyes at him. "I believe you, but I did not actually witness the accident. Let's hope the eagle heals completely and is released back into the wild. We'll give him the best possible care."

He hastened to assure her that he appreciated her professional skills. Although, he had only last night's experience to rely on. He had the feeling she was not used to being questioned.

"Emma's cage won't be adequate for long, but we have time before a larger cage is a necessity. You could look after him between writing chapters of your book." She turned a beatific smile on Stephen.

He felt himself being dragged into her aura. Then he caught Emma staring at him.

He stopped short of agreeing to babysit the eagle 24/7 and picked up on Barbara's remark. "Emma has a cage? Where?"

"Quite a nice one. Didn't you see it around the corner of your porch under the trees? Seth and his buds built it for the baby skunks Emma raised."

"I heard about those in Memphis. The tale of Emma and her baby skunks was a seven-day wonder. Her old boss Nathan is still disgruntled because she wouldn't allow him to bring them to town for a photo shoot for one of his public-relations projects. Why can't it be used as a flight cage?"

"It's tall enough, but not nearly long enough. It would have to be extended twenty feet at least."

"Isn't there enough room to extend it?"

"Oh, there's enough room, but somebody has to do the work. Nobody has time or money or interest."

Stephen realized he had all three—money, time and interest. With the eagle right around the edge of the porch from where he lived, he actually could watch out for him most of the time.

What he did not have was the physical capability to build a cage. With his leg, he would be unlikely ever to climb a ladder again and could hardly drive a nail with one hand if he held on to his cane with the other.

Velma laid down heaping breakfast plates before them, then hovered, obviously waiting for an introduction.

"Velma, this is Dr. Stephen MacDonald. Stephen, this is Velma. She will remember your breakfast order and give it to you whether you order it or not, so don't try to change it." She turned to Velma. "He's moving into The Hovel for six months."

Stephen stood and shook her hand. Hers felt rough and strong, although her nails were nearly as long as the eagle's talons and painted bright turquoise. Her smile, however, was nearly as brilliant as Barbara's. "I will too let you change your order. Just tell me when you come in. Otherwise you're stuck with your usual, whatever you decide that is. I'm glad you're gonna be across the street from Emma and Seth, Doctor. Half the time Seth's gone way into the night and out of cell-phone range.

Emma needs somebody close by to get her to the hospital."

"Not that kind of doctor, I'm afraid," Stephen told her. "I teach history at the university."

"I'm perfectly capable of driving myself," Emma said with a grin. "I'm just having a baby. My OB-GYN says first babies take a long time to come."

"Huh. I got three, Miss Emma. Didn't none of 'em take but a little minute. Near about didn't get to the hospital with any of 'em." Velma turned to Stephen. "You give her your cell-phone number, and don't go wandering off anywhere without it, you hear."

She whirled toward the back of the café. "All right, Darrell, hold your horses. I've got the coffeepot in my hand."

Turning back to their table, she said, "Nice to meet you, Stephen. Next time I might even be willing to give you an actual menu, but don't count on it." She wended her way through the tables and back to the counter.

"I'd never try to go on a diet with Velma around," Barbara said.

"The way you work," Emma said as she buttered a piece of toast, "you need the calories or you'd pass out."

"Velma," Barbara called, "has the mayor been in yet this morning?"

Velma nodded toward the wide front window. "That's his truck pulling in now. He's late."

"Here comes the purveyor of rental cars and everything automotive in Williamston," Barbara said.

The man who toddled in was a couple of inches shorter than Stephen and outweighed him by at least a hundred pounds. The bib overalls he wore were immaculate and looked as though they had been tailored for him, then starched and ironed. Stephen glanced at his boots. A marine in boot camp would be proud of the spit shine on the cordovan leather. He'd be willing to bet they also had been made for him.

"Mornin', you all," the mayor boomed from the doorway. "Velma, honey..."

"I got it, Mayor," she said and reached a gigantic coffee mug across the counter to him.

"Mayor," Barbara called to him. "Come meet Emma's new tenant. This is Dr. Stephen MacDonald."

Again, Stephen stood and shook hands, then sat down again.

"Another doctor?"

"Not that kind. I teach at the university."

Stephen saw him eye the cane beside his seat, but he didn't comment.

"Stephen pretty much murdered his car last night," Barbara said.

"You want us to fix it?"

"It's a vintage Triumph," Stephen said. "The parts will have to come off the internet or out of some salvage yard. I have a guy in Memphis who can do it. He's going to tow it in this afternoon and try to find everything he needs. In the meantime, I can't keep catching rides with Emma."

"I can't rent you a car, but a truck—sure. Little bitty or big honkin'?"

"I've never owned a truck. I have no idea."

"Well, Steve, how 'bout you come on down to the place after breakfast, and I will flat out *sell* you one? You can't make do with a sports car up here." He clapped a hand on Stephen's shoulder and came close to knocking him out of his chair.

Steve? Nobody called him Steve, Stephen thought. Not even Nina when she was furious with him. It suddenly hit him that he had crossed the threshold into another universe. He didn't know the language or the customs. Thank God for Barbara—and Emma, of course. Why had he put Barbara first? He'd known her less than twenty-four hours. But then maybe wallowing in blood together, or something approximating wallowing, gave them a kind of kinship he didn't have with his daughter's friends or even his academic friends.

"Join us, Mr. Mayor?" Emma asked.

"No, darlin', I got to get on down to the showroom. Just came in to pick up my coffee and a couple of sweet rolls." He turned to Stephen. "You let Emma drop you down at the showroom. I'll rent or sell you wheels. And if I don't, I'll have one of my people run you back to your house."

"Thank you."

Sonny took the sack Velma handed him in one hand and his mug in the other, did a 360-degree wave to the patrons and staff with the sack hand, then toddled back out the door.

Interested to see what the major drove, Stephen stood, then nearly fell over again at the decibel level of the horn that blasted as the man drove out of the parking lot.

"That thing has more chrome on it than an eighteen-wheeler," Stephen said. "And it's nearly as big."

"He owns the dealership," Emma said.

"As well as the feed store, most of the rental property in Williamston and heaven knows how much more," Barbara added. "In the country, Stephen, a man's truck is a symbol of his place in the community."

"Like a knight's armor or the caparison of his warhorse?" Stephen asked.

"Pretty much. I've got to get back to open the clinic," Barbara said. She reached for her check, but Stephen got there first.

"This is for the pimento cheese last night and for keeping Orville alive."

"Orville?"

"Better than Wilbur."

Barbara said over her shoulder, "Emma, explain to him about naming rescues, will you? Don't do it, Stephen. If you don't keep your distance, keep your objectivity about your rescues, it's a disservice both to the animals and yourself. Besides, it can break your heart."

He felt as though Barbara had taken a tiny bit of peace with her when the door shut behind her. Ridiculous. But he made a mental note to call her in the afternoon and offer to drive back to Williamston in whatever new vehicle he would be driving to pick up a pizza for their dinner. After all, he needed to check on Orville. Orville? When had the blasted bird become Orville? Just happened. But Orville he was, for better or worse alive or, heaven forbid, dead. So much for not naming your rescues. Please, let Orville not break his heart.

"Stephen," Emma said and laid a hand on his sleeve. "Everybody hates advice, but I'm going to give you some anyway. Barbara is a wonderful person and a great veterinarian. She is also a one-man woman, and that man died five years ago."

He felt as though she'd slapped him. "And that has to do with me how?"

"Come on. I saw the way you looked at her. If you'd been a puppy, you'd have rolled over to have your tummy scratched."

"Don't be ridiculous. I was impressed at the way she handled Orville."

"There is not an unattached—or in some cases attached—male in the county or beyond who has not tried to court Barbara since John died. She ignores them. She works too hard, and when she relaxes, it's with friends like Seth and me. She's never moved on from John and has never shown the slightest interest in doing it. She says she's comfortable with the life she has and hasn't room for any compli-cations."

"Fine. We should do well together, then. She

has her John. I have my Nina. Never the twain shall meet. Shall we go? I need wheels. Then I need to go check on Orville."

As he climbed into Emma's SUV, he admitted that he didn't want to lose touch with Barbara even if Orville died. She didn't want to move on from her John, just as he wouldn't ever move on from Nina. Nothing wrong with a friendship.

Maybe offering to build an extension to Emma's cage, making it suitable for Orville's flight training, might lift his credit with Barbara a hair.

Two hours later, he drove out of the mayor's automobile dealership in a bright red crew cab pickup with every bell and whistle the mayor could cram into it. Remembering their discussion about status and trucks at breakfast, he figured this particular truck would qualify as "honkin'" and give him the status of a knight in the good-ol'-boy hierarchy.

He was used to sitting in the confined quarters of his Triumph, freezing in the winter and roasting in the summer. This particular truck could no doubt reverse that—it was capable of freezing him in the summer and roasting him in the winter. For the first time since his accident, however, he could actually stretch out his bum leg and not have to stop every twenty miles or so to rub the pain out of it.

Silly to pay so much attention to a truck, but he felt as though he'd stepped through a portal into a weird new era in his life. How Nina would have laughed! She'd have presented him with a straw farmer's hat and a pair of mirrored sunglasses.

God, how he missed her! All those years she had kept him on an even keel whenever he was exasperated about his students' lack of interest or annoyed at the frequent idiocy of his colleagues. His former dean had once warned him that the smaller the academic fiefdom, the harder the faculty fought for control of it.

Until Nina had died he'd been right up there on the front lines, battling as hard as his colleagues for the optimum teaching schedule, the best teaching assistants, the most lucrative contracts for writing textbooks. Even the closest parking space to his office.

Since she'd died, none of it meant anything. He understood for the first time what it meant to want to swap places to save a loved one. He'd always thought Sydney Carton in Dickens's *A Tale of Two Cities* was an idiot to go to the guillotine to save someone else. To save Nina, however, he'd have chased that tumbrel down the Champs-élysées and jumped on board.

Rather than drive straight back home, he decided to wander along the back roads. He and Nina used to enjoy driving out and getting hopelessly lost on Sunday afternoons. Not so easy to do in the familiar environs around his house in Memphis. Here, however, every road was new to him. And beautiful. In southern fall, the trees were finally changing colors. He drove past his new house without turning into the driveway and on down past Barbara's clinic. He hadn't seen it in daylight and had not expected to see the parking lot filled with trucks and vans.

The mayor's advice had been right on. The Triumph would have stood out like a Roman chariot. He wanted to turn in and told himself it was to check on Orville, but Barbara would be working, possibly saving some other animal's life. Without Emma's holding down the phones, he had no idea how Barbara coped. From the number of vehicles in the lot he could see her need for an additional vet.

He would certainly need a break from his writing. Maybe he could offer to walk down— emphasis on the *walk* part—to add his volunteer efforts to Emma's.

Down the road a bit farther he caught the sparkle of water off to his left. Seth had said there was a good-sized lake over there that emptied into the Tennessee River. Maybe he should see if he could rent a canoe.

He drove for over an hour without crossing the same path twice. For him driving was a method of getting from one place to another, but in this behemoth he was actually having a pleasant time.

He stopped at the convenience store that he'd been headed to last evening and discovered it also served takeout. Not what he was used to in the drive-throughs in town, but fried chicken, barbecue, fried catfish and steamed vegetables. Heavy on the fried, but it all looked delicious. He left with enough supplies to provide lunch, dinner and tomorrow morning's breakfast. Dinner for Barbara as well, if she'd agree to join him. It would be better than pizza. If Emma was correct, Barbara probably would not agree to have dinner with him unless he could convince her that he wasn't intruding on her solitary lifestyle. Both of them had to eat. Why not together?

He turned off the main road by a sign that read Marina, found the lake and ate lunch at a picnic bench in the trees.

How many meals had he eaten alone since Nina's death? How much of it had been tasteless hospital food, eaten while staring at blank walls in rehab?

Here he didn't feel alone. A cheeky crow landed two feet from him and, after alerting every creature in the vicinity that there was a human being around, stalked back and forth demanding that Stephen share.

He did.

He was preparing to toss his last morsel of biscuit to the raven when he heard a voice behind him.

"Better watch it. He'll mug you for that biscuit."

"He's getting up his nerve to attack," Stephen said as he turned. "Well, Seth Logan. Won't you join me? I have an extra ham-and-cheese sandwich, some potato chips and a couple of sodas."

"Already had lunch, thanks," Seth said as he took the seat along the other side of the picnic table. "I'll take one of those sodas, however. Diet, if you have one."

"Yep, diet, and no longer terribly cold. My fancy new truck has a built-in cooler, but I have no idea how it works. I may actually have to read the manual—something I avoid doing if possible."

"There speaks a college professor," Seth said as he popped the top on his soda. He took a long swig. "So, this is your replacement for the Triumph? Rented or bought? And before you tell me, remember I know our esteemed mayor."

"If you guessed bought, you'd be correct. Isn't it outrageous? I do not have an 'ooga' horn like the mayor's, although he lobbied long and hard to add one. My next stop is the local boot shop. These very expensive trainers don't seem appropriate."

"You can't do all that walking you're supposed to do in cowboy boots, my friend. You'll be back in rehab in a week."

"Ah, but there is method in my madness. The boots will live in the truck for when I want to show off the new good-ol'-boy Stephen. Or, according to the mayor, 'Steve.' I will break them in slowly."

"Don't use neat's-foot compound, use the oil."

"Amazingly enough, I know that. My youngest daughter, Anne, is a horse trainer. I have scrubbed my share of tack.

"Anne reminds me of Barbara. She has the

same sort of connection with animals. They are more important to her than people. She can get annoyed when anyone interferes in her relationship with them. I suspect that's why there are no current men in her life. Not that I am aware of, at any rate."

"Speaking of relationships, how's your eagle?"

"Alive. In a permanent state of fury at his confinement. Last night when I saw him, he had already perfected the guilt-inducing glare. I never considered that human doctors have one set of anatomy to learn, while Barbara treats everything from a bald eagle to somebody's pet Gila monster with dermatitis."

Seth laughed. "Somebody around here owns a Gila monster?"

"I have no idea. The example is sound, however. She seems to have constructed a way of life that only works if nothing except an animal emergency interferes and throws off her schedule."

"Nothing?" Seth asked. "Or no one?" Seth tossed his empty drink can at an open trash container some distance away. The can landed precisely in the center without touching the sides. "Three points," he said and stood. "Back to work."

"What are you doing out here anyway?"

"Never-ending checking. Sam, who runs this marina, keeps an eye out for suspicious characters. Couple of the big marinas down on Kentucky Lake have had some break-ins lately. I need to see if he's had any trouble or noticed anything suspicious." He picked up his clipboard. "Thanks for the soda. Emma says you're coming for dinner this evening, correct?"

He'd completely forgotten. So much for asking Barbara to join him for dinner. He considered asking Seth whether Emma had invited Barbara, but he didn't want to show untoward interest in someone else's guest list.

"Barbara's supposed to show up if she gets finished at the clinic and doesn't get called out on an emergency. She doesn't often go out except to our house," Seth said. "She's usually worn out at the end of the day."

"I'll look forward to it," Stephen said, with a shiver of pleasure that he tried to ignore. No big deal. Just friends. "Should I bring something?"

"Not a thing. Emma is a great arranger. Just show up." He walked down toward the marina office at the end of the small pier.

Stephen collected, bagged and deposited his

trash into the bin. Interesting that Seth had not said his wife was a great cook.

The crow flew off with a final caw that expressed its disappointment at not being given more treats.

Stephen watched the main and jib sails being raised on a small cruising sailboat in the cove. It was late afternoon. The wind was almost nonexistent, but the boat managed to glide through the water toward the exit from the inlet and out into the lake beyond. A man stood at the helm while a woman lounged beside him.

He and Nina had owned and sailed a twenty-four-foot boat when the girls were young, but they'd sold it once the girls grew to the age where they resented being away from their friends and their preferred activities on the weekends. Maybe he should invest in a small day sailer while he stayed up here close to the water. Compared to ski boats, day sailers were relatively inexpensive and didn't need a slip at a marina. They could be towed back and forth to a house.

As he watched the pair on their small boat relaxing together, content with one another, he felt one of those sudden pangs of grief that hit him like a boxer's jab in the gut. What did any of it matter without Nina?

He would hate sailing alone. How could he thrill to a coral-and-peach Southern sunset without being able to share the experience with her? He'd always considered himself a loner, a man who enjoyed his own company. His writing and research were a solitary occupation. He'd been surprised to discover how lonely he was.

Working alone in his study while Nina read a book in the den—when he could share some arcane factoid he had just discovered simply by calling out to her—was different from working alone and knowing that no one would answer or care.

Did everyone who had lost a partner find that the little things brought his loss home to him most poignantly? The odor of peaches from her shampoo in the shower; knowing that the special orange marmalade for his toast would be sitting on the breakfast-room table; reaching for a clean shirt and feeling the extra starch she always had the cleaners iron into his collars; the way she rolled his socks—a million small things she did for him he'd taken for granted as a part of his life. The small things he'd done for her in return, he'd often griped about. When he was forced to drive her car, he invariably had to fill up the gas tank or risk running out of gas on his way to the college. Every morning he continued to make their king-size bed because a made-up bed had been important to her. How he wished she was still around to fuss at him if he left it a tangle of sheets.

This was no way to live.

Is that the way Barbara felt about the loss of her husband? Was she as lonely as he was?

He loved his children, but they were building their own memories. He wasn't building any new ones with anyone at all. Well, he supposed he had built a new memory last night with Barbara.

But for her, professional challenges seemed sufficient. Clients, not friends—except for Emma and Seth. But was that enough to base a life on? There was more to life than work. More than being alone at the end of the day.

Deep within him something stirred.

"Enough with the pity party," he said as he climbed into his new truck. "I've got a life to live, and by God, it is not going to be made up of leftovers.

BARBARA STRIPPED, DROPPED her bloody overalls into the hamper, jumped into the shower and scrubbed her whole body with the face soap with the exfoliator in it. It scratched a little, but it would remove the lingering scent of cow's blood she'd gotten covered with when she'd pulled out that doggone oversize Brahman calf. He would have killed himself and his mother if he'd stayed in her womb much longer.

She could live on a diet of miracles like this. It was enough fulfillment for one lifetime. It had to be.

She badly needed a big miracle to get Orville up in the air again. Orville? At least it was better than Wilbur. And the Wright brothers did finally get up in the air.

She leaned against the wall of the shower and realized she was sobbing. Miracles were no longer enough. She was desperately lonely for someone to share a high five with after a win, like she'd had with that healthy calf. And just as lonely for someone to share the grief and pain of losing against her old enemy, death.

She told herself she was simply exhausted. Pure release of tension. But it was more than that. The way the cow had licked her wet, new baby so gently, she could nearly touch the love. She couldn't go on making do with second-hand love. But could there ever be anything else for her? Did she dare to reach for it?

She had never been as frightened in her life. Staying the same, protecting the borders of her life and her heart was safe. Did she even know how to change? Did she want to?

This was Stephen's fault. Before he strode into her life, she'd thought she was content with the status quo.

She finished drying off and ran a comb through her wet hair. Then she raced into her bedroom to don clean underwear, a red polo shirt and ironed jeans. No time for makeup— just moisturizer and lipstick. She had to go to dinner with wet hair. She ran a comb through it again, plumped it up with her fingers, put on clean sneakers, grabbed her handbag and ran down the barn aisle to the parking lot. She refused to think. She hardened her heart against the soft, pleading eyes of the latest crop of abandoned fawns she was fostering. They hung their heads over the stall door. Hard to resist, but she knew they'd already been fed.

"You have been fed, knock it off," she said as she ran by. "You, too, Mabel. Don't you hiss at me, you goose. I'll smoke you for Christmas, see if I don't."

Mabel, used to empty threats, hissed and flapped her wings but retreated. Her goslings fluttered back under their mother.

SHE PULLED INTO Seth's driveway only twenty minutes late. An animal emergency always trumped dinner plans, but she tried to keep to a polite schedule. Across the street, in front of the house Stephen MacDonald was renting, sat a shiny red truck. Even from here, she could tell it was an outrageously overdressed monster. So, Mayor Sonny had seduced the good professor into a sale. He'd never allow anyone to rent that chariot.

Seth opened the door to her. She was surprised to hear two voices from the living room—Emma's voice and a baritone male.

Her heart gave a lurch. Stephen MacDonald. And here she looked like she'd been rode hard and put away wet. Which she had. He would probably be dressed as though he'd helicoptered in from Savile Row in London, where the bespoke tailors hung out. No woman liked looking like a rag doll with a strange man around. All that emotion that had hit her so unexpectedly while she was in the shower did not mean she wanted to open the gates and let him or anyone else into her life. She had no intention of taking so much as a baby step outside her comfort zone.

Face it—she was scared. Better not to care than to care and lose again, the way she'd lost John. But she was finding it difficult to remain cool and detached around Stephen. He definitely made her heart speed up.

What on earth could interest a man like Stephen in a woman like her? Okay, so they had shared a life-and-death moment with the eagle. They had a connection, but only as doctor and client.

Her defenses were thin at the moment. High time she beefed them up.

When she came in to the living room, Emma turned to smile at her, but made no attempt to climb out of the leather recliner where she sat with her feet up. Twisting even that far didn't look easy.

Stephen stood. He was nearly as tall as Seth, but thinner. He wore pristine chinos, a gray polo shirt and a pair of cordovan loafers that looked downright burnished. Not Savile Row, but not from a discount store, either. A dark wood cane topped by a wolf's head leaned against the arm of the sofa. Not the plain aluminum cane he'd used at the café. A formal cane? Maybe he had one to go with every outfit.

"White or red?" Seth called from the kitchen.

"White, thanks," Barbara said as she came forward to shake Stephen's hand. It felt smooth, unlike her hands, eternally rough from too much soaking in horse liniment and antiseptic. "Remember I warned you about naming him, but I find myself calling him Orville, too, so I guess Orville he is. He's settling down, although he is still irate and blaming you," she said to Stephen.

"I am innocent, Your Honor," he said. "How come you escape the blame?"

"Oh, he'd probably tear a strip off me, too, if he could reach me. But maybe he's smart enough to know who hit him."

"I keep telling you…"

She grinned.

After a second, he grinned back at her. "Is he doing all right? I've been worried, but I hesitated to keep calling your office for updates."

"He's holding his own. Thank you for not calling back every five minutes the way some of my clients do. We're just too busy to field all the calls. Things do slow down a bit in the fall and winter. Breeding season is over for many species, like horses, and dogs and cats seem to stick closer to home, so they don't get hit by cars quite as often."

"How is the search for Mr. Right coming?" Emma asked. She turned to Stephen. "Barbara is finally on the hunt for another vet to help share the load. She's needed one for donkey's years."

"*Dr.* Right, please. I'm open to somebody fresh out of vet school, to either a male or female associate veterinarian. And, yes, I've had several inquiries, but I haven't scheduled any interviews yet. This is quite a ways to drive for an interview, so I'm trying to take care on the front end. I don't want to interview somebody that doesn't look good on paper." She held up a hand. "But—and this is a good *but*—I've had a promising answer to my ad for an office assistant. I'm seeing her tomorrow morning. You can help interview and choose if she'll do."

"Yeah!" Emma said. "I don't know how long I can keep working without having someone trundle me around in a wheelbarrow. I really can't manage anything but paperwork without help. I'm so ready to have this baby I'm considering driving down bumpy roads to hurry things up a tad."

"You still have two months left, tiger," Seth said.

"And first babies frequently come late," Stephen added.

"The bumpy-road thing is an old wives' tale," Barbara said. "My first was three weeks late, and I hit all the potholes I could find. They come when they want to. You will never be more out of control. Relax and put up with it."

"Ooh, aren't you a little ray of sunshine," Emma said with a grin. "No more baby talk. Tell us about Orville. How's he doing?"

"As well as can be expected. Maybe a little better," Barbara answered. "We ended up not having to pin his break, just immobilize it."

"At some point I have to take a statement from you, Stephen. It's the responsibility of us fish-and-wildlife game wardens," Seth said. "I have to write up the incident and fill out a bunch of forms. It's a good thing you drove straight to Barbara's and got help."

"I'm willing to stipulate in my professional opinion it was an unavoidable accident, in which Dr. MacDonald was in no way at fault," Barbara said. She lifted her glass to Stephen and took a sip, then winked at him.

So SHE HAD decided to back him up. Stephen would thank her later when they were alone.

"Good. Otherwise, Stephen, you might

wind up before a judge. The fine can be up to five thousand dollars with possible jail time."

"But wouldn't that be if you shot it?" Emma asked.

"I've already volunteered to pay any vet charges associated with the incident," Stephen said.

"And he's going to help with the rehabilitation," Barbara said.

"I am?" Stephen glanced at her quizzically. "I haven't any idea how to do something like that."

"You'll learn. There really isn't anyone else available without interfering with the work at the clinic. Write that as part of your report, Seth. And you, Stephen, smile and say 'of course I am.'"

Seth laughed. "My friend, I think you have just been expertly sandbagged."

"The main problem is that I don't have a flight cage," Barbara said. "The closest one is in Kentucky, and I don't want to move Orville out of Tennessee."

"Then you shouldn't," Stephen said. "We'd have no way of tracking his progress, knowing if he was getting the proper care…"

"It may be the only solution to the lack of a flight cage. In my professional opinion, he's better off where he is for the moment, but that could change. Dealing with the federal government over an accident involving a protected species and dealing with the state of Tennessee, too—I do not even want to think about adding another state's regulations and bureaucrats. More red tape that might interfere with Orville's healing, not good for Orville's recovery. I know what I'm dealing with in Tennessee, and I trust myself."

"With you he's getting the best possible care," Stephen said. "Why would anyone purposely hurt a bald eagle?"

"Men and their trophies," Barbara said.

"I have a theory that the only reason we have survived to evolve this far is because we taste bad." The others began to laugh. She held up her hands. "No, listen. Most young, healthy predators avoid killing human beings in favor of yummier meals for themselves and their young. When the hunters take out a man-eater, they generally find that it's old or diseased and too slow to run away."

"How about grizzlies?" Stephen asked.

"Animals basically want to assure their DNA is passed on to the next generation," Stephen said. "The same thing Orville wants."

"Orville probably has mated for life," Barbara said. "For tough birds, they can seem to be extremely romantic. When they mate, they lock their talons together high up in the atmosphere and fall and fall until you think they're going to plummet to the ground, before they break apart and soar again."

"We're going to send Orville soaring again to find his lady," Stephen said and patted her hand.

She withdrew it quickly. "Talk about counting chickens! Don't say things like that—it's bad luck."

"Then let's talk about you instead." He grinned at her. "Why did you become a veterinarian? And don't most women gravitate to small-animal practices? Dogs and cats?"

Barbara looked away and shrugged. She seemed casual, but Stephen had noticed that when she talked about something important to her, her earlobes turned pink. He thought it endearing and wondered what she'd do if he nibbled one.

Smack him, probably, or give him a what-on-earth? stare. Even the way she sat slightly turned away from him said "Keep your distance."

Fine. He intended to, but he rather enjoyed looking at her pink earlobes.

"I like animals," she said simply. "Even when I was little, if it breathed, I wanted to keep it." She turned the palm of her hand toward him. "See that little scar?" She pointed to a raised place beside the thumb. "When I was about five I tried to catch a baby raccoon. Its mother was opposed and bit me."

"Did you have to take rabies shots?" Emma asked.

"The old-fashioned kind in the stomach," Barbara said. "That should have cured me, but it didn't. More and more women are going in for large-animal practices. I met John at orientation the first day of classes. Neither of us ever looked at anyone else again." She stared into the fireplace, took a deep breath and squared her shoulders.

Stephen caught the glint of tears in the firelight. He'd done his crying where no one could see or hear him, but he knew what she felt. That big open hole that seemed unfillable. He would've liked to put his arms around her and let her cry on his shoulder.

If he no longer wanted a leftover life to live, maybe he could convince her she didn't want one, either. He knew Nina would have been furious at him for wallowing in grief for so long. From the little he had heard about the man, he strongly suspected John would have been just as annoyed at Barbara.

From the kitchen came a *ding*. Emma rocked her chair back into place. "Seth, darling, where have you hidden the forklift?"

The dinner was simple but tasty. Spaghetti Bolognese, a big salad, French bread and cheesecake. "The cheesecake is from the café in Williamston," Emma admitted. "Seth knows I am no great shakes as a cook. But I'm trying."

They all made appropriate complimentary noises. Without being asked, Barbara took over cleaning duties so that Emma could enjoy the company.

"May I help?" Stephen asked.

Emma shook her head. "I count as family. You still count as company. Go sit."

"Are you sure?"

"Go. How's the addition coming?" she called to the living room. "From here the kitchen looks pretty much finished."

"Nearly," Emma called back. "Seth's mother, Laila, is going to try to come over this weekend to help get it all put back in order. Seth, why don't you give them the grand tour?"

STEPHEN WAS SURPRISED how much of the construction had been finished fast. The nursery—buttercup-yellow, as Emma had said—was finished, complete with a crib and a roomy, plush rocking chair.

Barbara joined them as soon as she put the dishes into the dishwasher and scrubbed the counters.

"I never had a rocking chair that luxurious when John and I had our two," Barbara said. "There was no way I could breast-feed and set up a new practice at the same time, let alone build the clinic and the barn with our apartment. John and I split feeding duties, and our old rocking chair felt comforting to the babies whoever was on bottle duty."

"Where are your kids now?" Stephen asked. They clearly didn't live with her. He would have noticed the signs during their shared meal.

"They both live in Nashville," she said. "Mark works part-time as a sound engineer for some of the smaller groups that play there. It's a crazy job, but he loves it. He wants to travel before he thinks about settling down, though. My daughter is in sales at a boutique hotel in Nashville and very much one of the young social set. She shows no sign of settling down, either."

"Then we have something in common," Stephen said. "My elder daughter, Elaine, worked in sales at The Peabody until she married. My younger daughter, Anne, works as a waitress and bartender to make enough money to support her horse. She'd love to make a full-time career as a horse trainer eventually…"

"But very few people can," Barbara said. "My condolences. Horse-crazy daughters generally have fewer problems in adolescence, but speaking from experience, anything to do with horses is hard, expensive and time-consuming, and isolates you from the non-horse-crazy."

When they came back from the short house tour, Barbara took one look at Emma and whispered, "She's sound asleep. Time for us to go, Seth. Come on, Stephen." Seth followed them out onto the front porch. Barbara stood on tiptoes and gave him a kiss. "I hope this new girl will work out for me. It's time for Emma to cut her hours. And how about *your* hours?" she asked Seth. "Are you taking any more time off?"

"As much as I can, and I'm giving Earl most of the tough jobs that require traveling all over the county. Stephen, Earl's my partner," Seth explained. "We're heading into black-powder season for deer hunting. That means more, rather than less, work. I'm like you, Barbara, pretty much on call all the time."

Stephen waited on the porch while Seth helped Emma to move from the recliner to the bedroom, then walked across the street to his own little house. He'd considered inviting Barbara in for a final cup of coffee. But he assumed she'd decline.

He climbed into his truck and backed out of his driveway to follow her home. He'd never allowed a woman to reach her door unaccompanied in his life. His mother would have killed him.

He'd forgotten the motion-sensor lights. The moment he pulled his truck behind the clinic, the area was flooded with enough light to curtail a prison break.

An instant later, Barbara's door flew open.

"Stephen, what on earth?" she said as he climbed out.

"Sorry. I didn't mean to disturb you. May I say good night to Orville?" And maybe garner an invitation to come in for a cup of coffee?

Unlikely.

"Fine. Now that he's in a cage in the barn, you don't have to go into the clinic to visit him. Thank you, Stephen, for following me home. If you don't mind, I'm off to bed."

And she was.

He found Orville, who waked instantly and made a sleepy attempt at a squeal before tucking his head under his sound wing and subsiding back into sleep.

"Good night, big guy. May you dream of field mice scampering around just waiting to be gobbled up. I, on the other hand, will dream about being invited to Barbara's for coffee one day."

CHAPTER SIX

IT WASN'T TOO late for Stephen to call Anne at home in Memphis. Although she would love to get an apartment, her horse was a drain on her income, and Stephen had never charged her any rent. She had a separate apartment on the third floor. He'd been grateful to have someone in the big old place with him, someone to have breakfast with once in a while. Between horses and her two jobs, she had very little free time.

He only saw Elaine on the occasional Sunday. Now that he could no longer play golf, his Sunday afternoons were free. But Elaine's visits were pity calls—always short and usually boring. He and Elaine had never had anything in common. Nina swore that Elaine had been born judgmental, and he was most often in her crosshairs. He liked Roger, her husband, who was a lawyer for several large Memphis-based corporations, but again, they had very little in common. Roger tended to pontificate about

ideas that Stephen considered to the right of
Nero and spent as many hours of his weekend
as Elaine allowed him playing golf.

His own two had taught him that most
adults had no respect for children. They might
love them but refused to admit that sometimes
children had a right to be irate when parents
did things like get divorces. He often did not
agree with Anne and Elaine, but he had always respected their opinions, even when he
thought they were boneheaded.

Sometimes, however, it was difficult to respect Elaine's ideas. He had tried to teach both
girls that they could set forth any opinion, but
they must be willing to back it up. Anne could
always give him a backup for her opinions,
even if Stephen thought they were ludicrous.
Elaine, on the other hand, was of the because-
I-said-so school.

When Anne picked up her cell phone, he
could hear the noise of the bar she tended in
the background. "Are you too busy to talk?"
he asked.

"Daddy? I have time. It's quiet right now."

"If what I am hearing is quiet, I dread to
think what a crowd sounds like."

"Give me a second to get back to the office."
A moment later the ambient crowd noise went

away. "There, the door's shut. Are you sick of the country and itching to come home yet? Or, considering the bugs, just itching?"

"I'm barely settled in. I thought you'd be enjoying having the house to yourself. You are alone, aren't you?"

"You think I'm having wild parties?"

"I hope not. My homeowner's insurance doesn't cover raves."

"Well, I am not having any raves…or any dates, more's the pity. You need to return your calls to all your lady friends. They keep leaving messages inviting you to everything from dinner to the theater."

"Please do not tell them where I am or give them my new cell-phone number."

"I can't believe you changed your number when you got your new phone. Who does that? Members of a drug cartel?"

"I intend to keep the number when I go back into the classroom. In the meantime, a new number cuts down on nuisance calls. It's the number the department will give out to students who are about to miss deadlines to turn in their essays and beg for more time."

"Which you won't give them."

"Not for anything less than a meteor strike on all the computers in the world."

"Isn't there at least one of your recent dates you want me to give your number to?"

"Not so far."

"Are the pickings so slim?"

"So it would seem. I have not met anyone that intrigues me more than reading a good book in my own library."

"Boy, is that an indictment of the local ladies."

He realized he'd inadvertently lied to Anne. If he had a choice between reading a book alone or being with Barbara doing nothing special, he was surprised that he'd choose her over the entire *New York Times* bestseller list.

She had brought a new energy to his life. With Orville's help. "Anyway, one dinner date does not make a lady friend," he said, "I haven't had more than one date with anybody in three years. They've even slacked off on bringing over casseroles."

"I know. Some of them I miss. The casseroles, I mean. Maybe you should be working on a cookbook—*Casseroles to Seduce the Lonely Male*."

"I hate to say it, but that would probably sell better than *Effects of the Great Plague on Property Values in Britain*."

"Is that what it's going to be about?"

"Maybe. Probably. I haven't come up with anything better, but I'm still waffling between that and the impact of rampant inflation in Germany after the First World War."

"Daddy, anything would sell better than those. Boring. How is this great new tome actually coming? Have you even started it?"

"You remember Emma Logan is my landlady?"

"Sure. In school I thought she was wonderful. She was even nice to us little kids."

"She warned me when I moved in across the street from her that up here I would find a great many occupations more interesting than sitting at my desk borrowing inter-library research materials. She is being proved right. It has been an eventful couple of days."

"What sort of eventful?" Anne asked. "You have a stampede or something?"

Stephen told her about hitting the eagle and his surgically assaulted Triumph. He told her about Barbara. Just the bare facts.

His daughter, however, picked up on something in his voice. "Is she beautiful?" Anne asked.

"That is not germane to the situation."

"Sure it is. Beautiful, skilled, solvent. You interested?" Anne asked, wheedling.

"No, and even if I were, she is a widow and not interested in making any changes in her very comfortable single life."

"Are you protesting too much?"

"No!"

"If you say so. And, Daddy, it's about time the Triumph went to the sports-car graveyard." She sounded delighted when she heard about the fancy truck. "Your truck will pull my horse trailer better than mine."

"But it won't get the chance. A father may give up his life for his child, but around here, he'll think long and hard before lending his new crew cab to her."

"We'll see about that," Anne said, laughing. "Good night, Dad. Try not to attack any more wildlife."

"And you avoid raves."

"Right."

He plugged in his cell phone after he hung up and propped himself up in the comfortable king-size bed Emma provided in The Hovel.

He hadn't mentioned anything about spending time with Barbara, except for when she'd saved Orville's life. He definitely had not told her that he'd just spent the evening with her at Emma and Seth's house.

Anne's unwarranted assumptions would have been given more fuel.

Or were they unwarranted?

Anne would like Barbara. Barbara would probably like Anne. They had horses in common, if nothing else.

As he dropped off to sleep, he wondered what it would be like to cuddle up on Barbara's sofa with her.

It was unlikely he'd ever get the chance, when he couldn't even wangle an invitation for a cup of coffee. He had endured too many forgettable dates. Whatever she was, Barbara Carew was not forgettable. Not by him, at any rate.

STEPHEN SLEPT BETTER than he had in months. Sleep in the rehab center had been next to impossible. The nurses were always waking him in the middle of the night for meds or to take his blood pressure. Sometimes he thought they woke him up just to be irritating. With pain as his constant companion, he'd had trouble sleeping anyway. The rehab regime hadn't helped. That was why he'd lost twenty pounds he had not needed to lose.

He slept until eight o'clock. Unheard of. He wanted to call Barbara but decided instead to start his walking program today. He would use her clinic as his turning point. He could say good morning to her and check on Orville at the same time.

The clinic was about two miles away. Could he possibly walk there and back? Four miles total? He'd walked conscientiously on the treadmill at rehab and later around the lake in the grounds. The path around that lake was supposed to be a little over a mile. At the end of his stay he could walk it twice if he pushed himself and soaked his leg afterward.

What if he collapsed on the way to the clinic or, more likely, on the way back? What if he did damage to his newly repaired leg? He needed a backup plan. He called Emma's landline.

When she answered, he apologized for calling so early.

"We've already had breakfast. Seth's left for work. What's up?" Emma asked.

"Do you work at Barbara's today?"

"Yep. I'm getting ready to go. We open at eight thirty, and I try to get there a few minutes early."

"Could I ride to the clinic with you?"

"Something wrong with your fancy new truck?"

He really didn't want to explain, but he felt he had to. "I can't walk there and back, but I can walk one way. If I ride with you, I can make it back here on my own. Two miles is my limit these days."

"How fast can you put on your walking clothes?"

"I'm ready now. I'll breakfast when I get back."

"Give me five minutes," Emma said. "I'll pick you up at the road."

The morning was beautiful. For the first time, the breeze felt cooler. People from up north didn't understand that for Southerners, fall didn't signify the death of the year but its rebirth after the miserable heat and humidity of summer. The trees were finally turning. Leaves were touched with gold and red on their tips, while closer to the branches and trunks they were still green. Head-high goldenrod crowded the verges of the road, while late-day lilies punctuated the gold with lemon-yellow.

"Morning, Stephen," Emma said as he climbed into the passenger seat of her SUV.

"And a glorious morning it is, too. Thank you for ferrying me down to the clinic." Stephen gazed at the road and thought how pleasant it would be to walk home. Slowly.

Limp home, actually. And probably in pain. Not so pleasant, then. But it had to be done.

"Not like you took me out of my way."

Emma pulled through the parking lot that was half-full of cars and pickup trucks, drove around to the back and parked where Stephen had parked when he'd brought in Orville.

As he climbed out of Emma's SUV, he shrugged. "Probably silly to visit Orville like I'm visiting a sick student."

"At least you didn't bring him a potted plant," Emma said.

"He would have preferred a nice live mouse. Orville doesn't care that I'm here, but that doesn't make a bit of difference. Thanks, Emma," he said as he climbed out of the SUV. "Do you need any help getting out?"

"Nope. I can climb down once I get the seat back far enough. Come on into the office after you check on Orville."

As he walked toward the eagle's cage, he felt his daily worry until he saw the bird was still alive. He was invested in Orville's flying again. Even if Stephen spent the rest of his life limping, he wanted to see Orville do what Stephen would never do again—soar! More than soar. He felt certain that Orville knew he was earthbound and hated it. Open the door of that cage and he'd stagger out and try to flap his poor, wounded wing. He'd keep trying, even if he never flew again.

So, what gave Stephen the right not to try to build a new life? For that matter, what gave Barbara the right not to try her wings, leave her comfort zone? They might both fall flat on their faces. So might Orville, but he'd keep trying.

"Orville, big guy, I refuse to say you have more gumption than we do. So how do we do this? We take it slow, take it easy, don't push it, don't hurt or scare ourselves until we're strong enough to flap our wings and soar. It's not just you any longer. It's all three of us. You lead off. I don't know how, exactly, but somehow we'll follow."

He found Emma inside the office getting ready for the clients.

"I have to start the coffee," she said. "Then get the computer booted up and open the front door for the onslaught."

"May I help?"

"Sure. Do you know how to make coffee? In an urn?"

"I am a dab hand at brewing the big pot in the faculty lounge."

"Have at it." Emma pointed to a thirty-cup urn on a table against the wall of the reception area. "Water's over there. Coffee packets are under the table, so are the sugar and cream packets. Stirrers, napkins and cups are in that cabinet." She pointed. "If you'd get that started and then open the front door, we'll be good to go."

"Where's Barbara?" he asked. He'd been looking forward to seeing her, checking whether she continued to have the impact on him she'd had last night at dinner. He hoped there would be at least a bit of pleasure on her side when she saw him. He felt there was a connection growing between them.

"Her truck's here, so she's probably feeding the animals in the barn. You must have just missed her. You want to help? Check the cages in the back and make certain all the water dishes are filled for our in-house patients after you open the front door." She took a deep breath.

"You think Barbara will be bothered that I'm showing up out of the blue like this and taking over?"

"You're not taking over, you're taking orders. We do not turn down volunteer help, Stephen. Barbara is as touchy about her professional parameters as anyone, but she doesn't have time to resent help with the logistics. Oops, we're two minutes late opening. We may get mauled. So, Stephen, go open up and stand back."

CHAPTER SEVEN

ONLY SIX PEOPLE came in the front door when he opened it. He heard Emma give a sigh that was probably relief, not disappointment.

"Stephen? You here to visit our patient?" Barbara walked in the back door and came down the hall toward him.

His heart gave a jolt when he saw her. If anything, she had more of an impact on him now than she had last night. How could she work as hard as she did, yet arrive at the clinic on time, scrubbed and shining? She wore starched jeans and a crisp denim shirt. Those crazy dark rum eyes with their golden flecks drew him like a daiquiri on a beach in Aruba.

At eight thirty in the morning, he was not used to thinking about daiquiris or feeling drunk looking in anybody's eyes.

And that smile of hers made him feel as warm as though he had slugged down a jigger of French brandy instead.

"Morning, Barbara. I think the coffee's finished. May I bring you a cup?" he asked. He needed plenty of caffeine himself.

"Hey, the rule is, he fixes it, he fetches it," Emma said. "Why don't we hire him to be our new vet tech?"

"Above my skill level," Stephen said with a smile.

"Then I'll take that big mug over Emma's desk with one glug of creamer and two packets of sweetener. You did fine with Orville, Stephen. He wasn't above your skill level."

"I've already been out to check on him. How is he doing?"

"Better than I expected. We'll need to move him to a bigger cage sooner than I imagined. He's walking around grumbling. I borrowed jesses and a hood from my friend Jeremy when we set his wing. That should help us change his cage. Don't want him moving much right now, but it won't be long before he needs exercise. Birds like Orville either die on the table or mend fast."

"How soon do you need a flight cage?"

"I have a couple of cages by the barn that can be linked together and will give him room to hop around and flex a bit. Soon, he has to be able to fly so that he can stoop and kill. He definitely does not like his meals dead."

"How big an animal can he take down?"

"Good-size fish. He prefers them. Small rats, mice, snakes, even rabbits if he has room to lift off. Out west he'd go for trout or salmon, neither of which we have. So he goes for bream and crappie and the occasional catfish."

"I want to see him…what did you call it? Stoop?"

"He can spot movement from an incredible height, fold those wings and dive straight down. The prey doesn't stand a chance, but he kills clean and quick. Better than many humans do."

Better than life did, Stephen thought. Barbara's husband had died quickly, but he doubted Barbara considered it a blessing. With Nina, there'd been time for hope, then despair, then more hope, more despair.

But the loss was the same.

The entire room of clients had been listening avidly. Now a lady hanging on to a large, scruffy hound said, "Poor little rabbits!"

"Marian, honey," Barbara said, "Virgil there has killed a bunch more rabbits than Orville ever will."

"I just hate it! But he will do it. I can't keep ahold of him when he takes off after something. He pulls me right off my feet." She dropped her head and grinned. "Must say, he misses a bunch more than he ever gets close to. He's just a big ol' baby, aren't you, Virg?"

"What's wrong with him this morning?" Barbara asked.

"Just needs his shots."

"Emma, tell whoever's first on the list to go into the first exam room." She turned to the room. "I'll be right there, y'all. Come on, Stephen, time to visit the hospital ward."

One of the reasons Stephen felt such kinship with Orville was that he, too, felt put-upon and grumpy. In both their cases a motor vehicle had come out of nowhere and changed the course of their lives. Hopefully, Orville would take less time to heal and would heal completely. Stephen never would. Stephen crouched in front of the cage so that he was eye-to-eye with the eagle. "Benjamin Franklin was wrong," Stephen said. "You may be a good-for-nothing thief who doesn't even taste good like turkey, but you'll come out swinging and fight for what you believe in."

"Food and family," Barbara said with a laugh. "I don't think he has a clue about truth or justice."

Stephen stood up. "If you have to believe in something, there are worse things than food and family." She turned her head away from him. She was blushing. Those telltale earlobes were hot pink.

Orville, no doubt feeling neglected, let forth one of his horrendous screeches. Startled, Barbara slipped and braced her hand against the front of Orville's cage.

Stephen grabbed her wrist and pulled her hand away from the cage a second before Orville's beak struck the wire. "Hey! Watch it!" He kept her wrist and spun her to face him. "You okay?"

Her eyes were wide with fear. He held her and heard her breathing speed up. He couldn't look away. Those flecks in her eyes drew him to her as though he was a miner who'd discovered a seam of gold a foot wide.

A moment later they were closer still. The kiss came without thought or even volition. It started out as a friendly peck. A moment later, it changed into a full-blown arms-around-the-neck kiss. One heck of a kiss before breakfast!

Barbara broke the kiss first. Her pupils, when he was far enough away from her to see them, were large, and her skin felt warm where his hands held her arms.

"He almost nailed you," Stephen whispered. "He's fast."

She held his eyes for a moment, then she moved away. "So much for rapport with a wild animal," she said. She now sounded both casual and businesslike. He didn't think he was capable of changing course so fast. He wanted to kiss her again, keep kissing her, holding her, until he could absorb her into his very bones. And he badly wanted to cuss out Orville, even though he knew that was ridiculous. Orville had done precisely what he'd been born to do.

"You're welcome to visit Orville for a while longer, but I have to go to work." He watched her walk down the hall, open the door to the examining room, hesitate and actually brace herself against the doorjamb for a second. He grinned after her. So she wasn't so casual after all. Simply better at acting.

I have no idea what just happened, but that was one hell of a kiss, Stephen thought. *It may be the last. She might never allow me that close again.* He glanced behind him and caught Orville's interested eyes. "I ought to thank you, not blame you. Hey, how can I fail with an eagle for a wingman?"

He said goodbye to Emma at her computer station on his way out the front door. She acknowledged him with a quick wave before she went back to her conversation with a large man carrying a Yorkshire terrier that wore a red bow in its forelock.

For a heavily pregnant woman, she was handling the pressure of juggling Barbara's clients with aplomb.

Stephen didn't see how she could possibly work for Barbara much longer. Just carrying the baby must be exhausting. Once the baby came, she'd have her hands full at home. He didn't know whether Seth was allowed paternity leave, and if so, whether it would be paid.

Nina's temper had been touchy the last six weeks she'd carried Anne and Elaine. His dean, the doting father of five daughters, had warned him that if he didn't know how to duck and cover, he'd better learn, because women in the final stages of pregnancy and in labor tended to savage whichever male was responsible for getting them into their predicament. If Barbara was willing, he'd offer to help her. Writing his book seemed less and less important.

He'd brought his folding hiking stick with him. Better than a cane. Not so obvious. Plenty of people who did not limp carried hiking sticks when they went for a walk. He could lean on it as well as keep his balance with it.

He pulled it out of the capacious side pocket

of his windbreaker, stood on the front steps
of the clinic and opened it, then stepped aside
for some sort of fluffy terrier that was pulling his owner in the opposite direction from
the clinic.

Stephen always felt like an idiot doing his
stretches in public, but his doctor had made
him promise not to start one of his walks without stretching first. He found a spot behind a
horse trailer and went through his warm-up
exercises. Then he started his two-mile walk
home.

The glorious morning had begun to cloud
up. The breeze had stiffened and switched
from west to northwest. That meant rain.
Good thing he was walking early because he
hadn't brought his rain gear with him. He'd
been warned to avoid getting wet and chilled,
so he increased his pace along the road.

Big mistake. It wasn't just his leg that
needed exercise, but his lungs did as well.

By the time he'd gone what he considered
halfway home, he was breathing hard and his
knee throbbed. He'd only taken a few days off
to get settled up here. Surely that small hiatus
had not set him back.

He told himself he was struggling because
this country road was much rougher than the

track around the lake at his rehab facility. He stubbed his toe a couple of times and once had to catch himself with his stick to keep from stumbling and possibly falling.

He was trying to decide whether he wanted to cross the shallow ditch that ran alongside the road and find somewhere to sit for a few minutes, when he heard a car coming around the curve behind him. He stepped closer to the side of the road and turned to see Seth Logan in his official fish-and-game SUV. He didn't want to flag down Seth and admit that he could use some help, but he was glad when Seth pulled up beside him and stopped.

"Morning, Stephen. How's the walk going?"

"Better than I deserve for skipping last week, and worse than I'd hoped."

"How about a lift home? It's about to rain."

"I would very much appreciate a ride." He agreed with Orville. Pain was a brute. Orville could make an unholy noise about his. College professors, however, did not shriek at the wind without being locked up somewhere they couldn't hurt themselves. He walked around Seth's truck, climbed in the passenger side and leaned against the high headrest with a sigh that nearly turned into a sob. "Damnation, Seth, I can't even walk two miles on my own. I hate carrying that cane. If I use it long, my good leg starts to ache as well."

"You'll get there. You haven't been out of rehab that long, have you?"

"Less than a month. Before the accident, I played golf and tennis and ran ten-K races for charity. I rode a bicycle back and forth to school a couple of times a week when the weather was good. I could count on my body to do what I asked."

He could still probably ride a quiet horse, but golf and tennis were out for the rest of his life. "To make up for this rescue ride, I'll try checking out the rest of the property north of my house," he said. "Assuming it's not too muddy."

"Trust me," Seth said, "It will be. You should put that off until I can show you around back there. Here we are." Seth pulled off the road and stopped behind Stephen's red truck.

"I am in worse shape than I imagined," Stephen said as he reached for the door handle.

"That's why you're here, isn't it? To build yourself back up?"

"I am only now becoming aware of how far I have to go. My dean tells me I am here to write a book. My children say I am here to get away from them."

Seth laughed. "What do *you* say?"

"I came up here to discover whether I had any reason to continue living. I've about decided I do, but not how. I'm not sure if I should continue teaching or find something new." He shrugged. "If I had a clue as to what I want... Don't tell anyone that."

"So you don't feel pulled in a particular direction?"

"Indeed not. When some big executive gets fired, don't they tell the media they are exploring other options? I've often wondered what those options were.

"You wouldn't by any chance like a cup of coffee, would you? I haven't had breakfast. I might make toast and jam if you're interested."

"Of course I am." Seth climbed out of his SUV and followed Stephen to his house.

SINCE THE RAIN continued to hold off, they took their coffee out onto the front porch after they finished three pieces of toast apiece. Seth seemed impressed with the imported orange marmalade that Stephen had brought with him from home.

"Until fairly recently," Stephen continued, "I wasn't sure I had any options left. Except maybe to sit in a wheelchair and fight to remain sane. The doctors weren't certain my leg would ever be able to hold me. Long-term planning becomes impossible. I avoided my friends and family. I do understand Barbara's aversion to change. You decide that there is no such thing as a good change. Any change will result in more disaster. You fight for the status quo, as she is doing. But life can never be static. At some place in her psyche she understands that there is room for positive change. For hope of something better. Otherwise she wouldn't fight so hard for her animals. She'd walk away and let them die."

"Oh, she's a fighter for her animals, all right," Seth said and set down his empty cup. "Not so much for herself."

"Obviously she trusts her skills as a veterinarian. I can't see her second-guessing herself on that score. But she seems to want to keep the rest of her life in a state of suspended animation... Although, she is trying to hire people for the clinic," Stephen said. "That's change and growth of a sort. She hired Emma."

"So what else do you want her to do? Seems to me she's doing fine."

Stephen subsided. He couldn't put into words what he wanted. Maybe just trust that he wouldn't mess up her life by becoming her friend.

"I think we better show you some of those other options you were talking about, Stephen. Would you be interested in riding along with me to check deer stands?"

"How much walking is involved?"

"Not a whole lot. Deer are edge dwellers. They sleep in the woods, but they forage along the edges, where there is plenty of food."

"Ergo, deer stands are along the edges as well."

"Right. You do any hunting?"

"Good heavens, no. When I was a kid my grandfather lived on a farm. He tried to indoctrinate me into the hunting culture, but I generally had my nose in a book. I enjoy target shooting, though I haven't done it for a while, but actually aiming at a sentient creature and pulling the trigger? I might be able to do that if I was starving, or my children were starving. Otherwise, no. Intellectually, I know herds must be culled to avoid starvation for the remaining members, and I dearly love venison, but I want someone else to give it to me. That makes me a hypocrite."

"Not really. I gave up hunting years ago for much the same reasons as yours. As long as hunters follow the rules, which I am here to enforce, I don't allow my personal preferences to get between me and my job. As you say, herds must be culled or they all starve. I'm more concerned about saving Barbara's orphan fawns, whose mothers were either shot or hit by cars. They then grow up and become members of that herd that must be culled. So if you're a hypocrite I guess that makes me a hypocrite, as well. Can't help it. I'm not making war on God's youngsters."

"Barbara's fawns?"

"Didn't you meet the fawns in her barn when you delivered the eagle to her? She's the go-to lady for raising orphan deer. She's a licensed animal rehabilitator, including raptors, which is a higher category. That's why she is allowed to keep Orville. She's reared and released raptors before, but never, so far as I am aware, a bald eagle."

"We both want to get him into the air again, but she has no place to let him strengthen his wing and learn to fly. We need to solve that problem by getting her a flight cage, or she may decide to send him away to another facility. I am selfish enough to want him to stay where I can be part of his progress."

"The local rehabilitators need a flight cage

and more room to set up and rehabilitate all the critters they rescue. Get Emma to tell you about how she and I met." Seth set his empty coffee cup on the small iron table beside the stairs, thrust his hands into his pants pockets and narrowed his eyes at the encroaching dark clouds.

"Over skunks, wasn't it?" Stephen asked "That story made the rounds in Memphis along with the invitation to your wedding. Have you seen them since you released them?"

"Haven't looked. We took them far enough away that they can't find their way back. We kept our interaction with them to a minimum to avoid running into them in the woods."

"Would they recognize you?"

Seth shrugged. "Emma thinks they would. I disagree. We definitely want to avoid having one of our three skunks wander up to a stranger, looking for a handout."

"Would they use their scent glands on you?"

"If we annoyed them, you bet. That's what those glands are for," Seth said.

"I heard from Emma's father that he got skunked."

"Poor David," Seth chortled. "He smelled unholy awful. And he was simply trying to see what they looked like close up. They took exception to his being that near and *wham-o*. How do you know my father-in-law?"

"Our daughters went to the same school, and Emma showed horses for a while, so we saw one another at horse shows. David's wife, Andrea, was very supportive after my wife died. She warned me not to do anything substantive like selling our house and moving, for at least a year. I had no intention of doing that, then after my accident I spent more time in the hospital and rehab than I did at home. Having nothing change around me gave me a place of refuge when I did get to sleep in my—our—bed.

"Andrea said I would know when it was time to move on. Coming up here may mean I am finally ready.

"My daughters vacillate between wanting to preserve everything the way it was before Nina died and wanting me to 'get on with it' so they don't have to worry about dear old Dad alone in that big house."

"What do *you* want?" Seth asked.

"Damned if I know. I don't want to spend the rest of my life alone and doing the same thing day after day with the same people. But as to specifics?" He spread his hands and shrugged. Into his mind came an echo of Barbara's voice. She worked in blood and dirt, was always tired and frequently lost her battles against mortality, yet she managed to seem joyous. When was the last time he'd felt joy?

That kiss had been joyful. That was why he wanted more of her company. More of *her*.

CHAPTER EIGHT

"I HAVE TO get to work mapping deer stands," Seth said. "I've enjoyed this. I'm often down this way or at home for lunch to check on Emma." He reached into his wallet and handed Stephen a business card. "Here are all my numbers. I'll keep an eye out for you on the road if you'll check on Emma when she's home. I know she's fed up with being pregnant, but I worry about her having the baby prematurely and alone."

"As well you should. Thankfully both of mine came late. Nina was annoyed but agreed that late is better than early. I don't know which days Emma works with Barbara."

"Mondays, Tuesdays and Fridays."

"This morning over my coffee, I decided to offer to volunteer at Barbara's clinic for a few hours a week if she does not shortly hire someone full-time. And if she'll have me. Emma says they are always looking for volunteers. That way I may be able to help Barbara while

I keep an eye on Orville. I enjoy watching his progress, but I have to be careful not to hover like an overprotective father."

At the clinic he had the chance to spend more time around Barbara. He'd have to avoid getting underfoot, but it was obvious she needed more help. He was competent with computers and used to working with people. Granted, they didn't usually come attached to pets, but they weren't that different. With some instruction, he might be able to take some of the simpler decisions off her shoulders.

"I don't know why Barbara's having such a hard time finding someone to help in the clinic full-time, Seth. There can't be many jobs in this area over minimum wage."

"Her clinic is in downtown Nowheresville and can be a real madhouse when Barbara is there to see one client after another. Then you have to put off people who come into the clinic while Barbara is out on an emergency call. The nearest large-animal vet is in Somerville. There is a small-animal vet south of Williamston, but Dr. Kirksey prefers to work strictly with dogs and cats. Barbara takes on all comers as well as the rescues, so she's got more work than she can handle. Newly fledged vets who are anxious to work for a total practice are on top of the latest practices, eager and ready to work long hours, and are usually less expensive than older vets. Too many vets these days are going into small animal practices in urban areas. She wants a well-rounded country vet."

Stephen walked out into the yard with Seth. "Emma tells me that the pasture over there behind the barbed-wire fence belongs to this property."

Seth stopped with his hand on the door of his SUV. "Like I said before, don't go messing around there without me. Ask Emma to tell you what happened to her when she went exploring on her own. She wound up with a twisted ankle and a whole lot of scratches and bruises."

"The pasture looks as though all it needs is a good going-over with a Bush Hog. What am I missing?"

Seth raised his eyebrows and climbed into his front seat. "Between the water moccasins and the snapping turtles in the pond? There's a barn with a roof that's fallen in and has been reclaimed by all the wild critters who need a place to get out of the weather. Then there are the lethal wild rose thorns and thorny locust trees that will rip your clothes right off your body."

"But it's land, Seth. And it's yours. How big?"

"Just over ten acres."

"Why leave it fallow? Can't you rent it out to one of your neighbors?"

"Emma and I do want to reclaim it. We have plans to rent it, but at the moment it's not high on the priority list. I'm trying to find the time to run over it with the Bush Hog one more time before frost, so it will be ready to over-seed with Bermuda grass in the spring. Emma wants to clean out the old cattle barn, reroof it and let the rehabilitators use it as a base of operations for their rescues."

"With a flight cage?"

"So that is your plan? Sneaky, Stephen, sneaky. Listen, Orville will be long gone before spring. He'll either fly away or, if he can't, be moved to the zoo in Memphis to become part of their education program. Standard practice for wounded creatures that can't be repatriated to the wild."

"Trust me. He will fly. He has to." Or Stephen wouldn't be able to find fulfillment in his lame life. It was that old decision-making thing kids did. *If I do this and it works, then everything will all work out. If I do it and it doesn't, then nothing will.* "Thanks for rescuing me on the road today, Seth."

"Thanks for the coffee."

"Anytime. The pot is always on."

"You need to meet my partner, Earl. Next time, I'll bring him with me. He is a caffeine fanatic."

Stephen watched Seth's SUV until it disappeared beyond the curve, then strode over to the barbed-wire fence at the side of the yard. He assessed what he could see from this distance.

Judging from the height of the grass and weeds, it was indeed overdue for that second pass with the Bush Hog. Seth had managed to knock over the spindliest of the locust trees, with their two-inch-long thorns, and pushed them together to create a tall brush pile in the open area. It reminded Stephen of the preparations for bonfires in England on Guy Fawkes night. He'd attended several parties for The Guy when he'd happened to be in England on November 5th doing research. Once, Nina had been with him when they'd visited friends for the weekend in their small Cotswold village. She'd loved the minor mayhem in the village square, bagpipes and all.

Why not a Williamston Guy Fawkes bon-fire? Complete with The Guy, the effigy of the peasant leader who'd tried unsuccessfully to blow up the houses of Parliament in 1605? It was still a bigger holiday in the British Isles than Halloween, although Halloween was getting more popular every year. Nobody here even knew who Guy Fawkes was.

History was Stephen's job as well as his passion. It would be appropriate for him to stage a Guy Fawkes night bonfire. He'd be willing to bet Barbara would love it.

Only it was impossible.

He couldn't start a fire this close to a barn on someone else's property—not even a dilapidated barn built of concrete blocks—in the dry fall in Tennessee. Emma and Seth would never agree. It was their brush pile, after all.

But a bonfire would clear away the pasture debris and the rotten wood from the barn. The pasture would be clear to plant in the spring. The barn would be cleaned out and ready to reroof now. And clear, most importantly, to build a flight cage for Barbara. For Orville.

Maybe Seth didn't have time to run the Bush Hog over ten acres, but Stephen had nothing but time. He could write his blasted book—a book he was starting to hate when he'd barely begun it—in the winter, when the weather was too miserable to walk outdoors. West Tennessee didn't normally have but one or two good snowfalls a year, and the snow on the ground disappeared within days.

What it did have was cold rain, colder wind and ice storms that coated everything in sight with black glare ice that broke hundred-year-old trees like matchsticks. No driving in that, much less walking. He'd be grateful for his lone fireplace in an ice storm when the power went out.

No walking down to Barbara's for his exercise. He'd be forced to go get his treadmill from home and bring it back up here with him.

He had a beautiful, big new truck to carry it. Anne would be so jealous.

Even if this whole idea of the November 5th bonfire remained a pipe dream, he could do some preliminary research about how to get a permit to burn brush in this county. Seth must know. There had to be a procedure, a way to do it safely. He was good with bureaucracy. First, he would investigate. Then, he'd consult Emma and Seth.

He would wait for Seth's permission to walk out into that forbidden pasture. In the meantime, he'd walk over to check out Seth's tractor with its attached Bush Hog. It perched like a giant yellow prehistoric mantis behind their house, capable of knocking down all the brush in the pasture.

He ambled across the street, grateful that Seth had not yet found a new dog to replace the one that Emma said had died before they were married. A dog might take exception to a stranger in the yard.

He had not seen any construction workers in a couple of days. The addition to the house did look complete from the outside. This late in the fall they might be happy with such a simple project as a flight cage. He'd happily pay for it if Seth and Emma agreed. His rescued eagle, his cash. Seemed only fair.

The carport was open, although no one was likely to steal such a behemoth from a fish-and-game warden. In these parts stealing a man's car was a felony and stealing his truck was a travesty, but stealing his tractor was darned near a hanging offense.

This tractor was a beauty. Stephen itched to get his hands on the controls. He climbed up to stare in the window of the enclosed cab. Then he tried the door.

Unlocked. He felt a wave of the same motor lust that had kept him driving an antique Triumph. He loved his new truck, but this monster was something else entirely.

"I am capable of driving a tractor, even with a Bush Hog attached," Stephen said aloud with more than a hint of hauteur. How hard could it be? Less experienced people than he did it all the time. He had been driving cars since he got his license at sixteen. Actually, he'd gotten behind the wheel of his grandfather's station wagon on his twelfth birthday, not unusual in the country. By the time he would have been allowed to drive his grandfather's big tractor, however, his grandparents were dead and their little farm and its equipment had been sold.

Explain to him how all the gears and pedals worked, then give him a bit of hands-on practice, he'd be good to go. Or would he? Most of the controls on his grandfather's old tractor had been levers worked by hands, not feet. His wounded leg could now drive his new truck easily. Admittedly, Seth's tractor was a whole different animal from his grandfather's antique, or from one of those small lawn tractors the landscape service used to cut his lawn in town.

He'd always justified using their service because he was too busy, not because he hadn't a clue how to run a lawn tractor. Though he didn't.

He was acting like a fourteen-year-old boy out to impress a girl at school by jumping off the roof of his garage or skateboarding down the porch stairs. Pretty silly, since Barbara would undoubtedly be able to drive a tractor. She was a country woman. Surely, country feats would be more impressive to her than his ability to read galley proofs on his textbooks. He was actually trying something outside his comfort zone. That ought to impress her. Sure impressed him. He didn't consider himself Mr. Macho, but women seemed impressed by heavy machinery and power tools.

When he and Nina were first dating, he'd taken her to the skating rink. She'd been beautiful, a swan, a princess, gliding around like some magical being. He, on the other hand, had spent more time on his rump than on his feet.

But Nina had not laughed.

Where had he lost that sense of adventure? After they were married, Nina had been the one pushing him to take her dancing or snorkeling. With only the memory of her laughter, life was bleak.

He didn't even feel passionate about teaching anymore. But without teaching, what would he do? Travel? He loathed traveling without someone to share the experience with. Play bridge? Chess at the faculty club? Drink? His idea of drinking was a glass of wine once a year or so at a party.

One of his friends had walked the Appalachian Trail from the beginning all the way to Mount Katahdin in Maine at age eighty-two. Stephen was not much over half that age, but he doubted he'd finish the first day's hiking with his leg.

How did people move on? After her husband died, Barbara Carew had flung herself back into her career, if not precisely into a new life. She didn't realize that she'd inadvertently flung herself into *his* and knocked him as flat as that darned Mabel the goose that Barbara had introduced him to could.

The wild geese that invaded the campus every spring and autumn on their commute to and from Canada ran or flew away when he came near them. Mabel, with her lame foot, attacked first and asked questions later. She believed in close-quarters combat.

The two nonhuman creatures that had insinuated themselves into his life—Mabel and Orville—were lame like him, but they certainly weren't letting their infirmities stop them. They were brave. They figuratively stuck out their noses—all right…beaks—and attacked life. Stephen was beginning to rediscover living a little at a time. Barbara seemed to be afraid to try flying free. But he wanted her to find her way, as well.

The birds had one advantage. When walking wouldn't do, they could fly.

Eventually, Orville would fly again. Mabel would fly enough to teach her goslings to fly, as well. Stephen couldn't fly away and would always be lame, but he would learn to make do with what he had left.

He *would* drive Seth's tractor.

All he had to do was clear that pasture with the Bush Hog, build up the makings of a bonfire, get all the permits and regulations and have a Guy Fawkes party for all his friends.

He caught himself. "Yeah, and just what friends would those be?"

CHAPTER NINE

BARBARA WONDERED WHETHER Stephen had reached his house safely. The road that ran in front of the clinic wasn't busy, except in the summer when people drove to and from their cottages on the lake, but vehicles tended to speed down the center of the road, ignoring the lane markers. She would recommend that Stephen drive into Williamston to the municipal park and walk the two-mile-long trail through the woods there. Not as convenient, but certainly safer. She took out her cell phone to call him, realized she didn't have his cell number and was forced to worry instead. Emma would have his number, but Barbara hesitated to ask Emma to call. After that impromptu kiss, he might be embarrassed. She sure was.

Heck, he ought to be glad somebody cared enough to check that he wasn't roadkill.

She tightened the last stitch on the belly of

the cat she had just spayed—a yellow tabby due to come into her first heat any day.

Barbara considered her special low-cost neutering-and-spaying clinics her payback to the community. Any new vet she hired would have to continue the practice.

The percentage of kittens and puppies that were adopted into forever homes was even lower in the country than in the city. The farmers frequently allowed their barn cats to breed at will. The feral kittens generally lived their entire lives as wild as tigers. There were not enough mice in the world to keep them fed, and catching wild cats took humane cages and cat-whispering genius. Many farmers didn't bother.

She ran ad campaigns in the Marquette weekly newspaper every couple of months offering low-cost spaying and neutering, as well as rabies vaccinations. She also cajoled and browbeat her clients into taking advantage of her offers.

Stray dogs weren't so great a problem, although the number of human beings who simply tossed away dogs when they moved from the area infuriated her. She thought they deserved jail or worse. She did not consider them actual human beings at all but some sort of horrible mutant subspecies.

Every spring game wardens like Seth baited the animal trails with rabies vaccination powder. Since there had been no rabid animals in Marquette County for years, they seemed to have been successful. So far.

Now, however, with global warming forcing more animals out of their usual habitat, that could change in a minute. One rabid animal infecting others was worse than a zombie apocalypse and much more likely to happen.

And then there was the armadillo incursion. Whenever she told one of her clients that armadillos carried leprosy, she got the same horrified stare. No matter how carefully she explained that leprosy was very difficult to catch, was presently known as Hansen's disease and could be controlled medically, her clients still goggled at her.

"Leave them alone," she always told them. "You'll be fine."

She desperately needed help. Every day she seemed to get more and more worn out. She knew if she didn't get some rest—mental and physical—her body would ambush her and force her to take care of it. She'd thought she'd reached her limit, but that was before Stephen had walked into her life with that blasted bird.

Now, when she wasn't concentrating on stitching or operating or taking blood or worming or any one of the other jobs she did on a regular basis, one part of her mind was struggling with thoughts of Stephen.

His kiss had lit her up like fireworks. He was a complication that threatened the careful wall she had built to separate her professional life from her personal life.

Why couldn't he just leave her alone? Emma said he wanted to volunteer some time at the clinic. Just what she needed. More Stephen. He got to her, blast it.

She laid the groggy tabby back into her cage to recover from her surgery. She'd be much happier without babies and without being chased all over her owner's farm by every tomcat in the neighborhood.

The intercom beside the door beeped. "Doctor, the lady you're interviewing for the job is here," Emma said.

Barbara took a deep breath, peeled off her gloves and dropped them into the waste container. "Please, heaven, let her be perfect and actually take the job."

The woman wasn't all that young, although

she did look fairly fit, despite her suspiciously yellow hair. Maybe mid-forties or early fifties. Not a teenager looking for an after-school job, then. Good, the clinic already had one of those.

"Hey, I'm Barbara Carew," Barbara said and offered her hand.

"You're the doctor?" the woman asked. She sounded surprised.

"Yes, ma'am."

The woman brushed Barbara's hand for no more than a millisecond. "I'm Dorothy Miller." She dropped her eyes. "Everybody calls me Dotie. Not Dotty—Dotie."

"Nice to meet you, Dotie. This is Emma Logan. You can see why we need somebody right away."

"Lord yes, honey. When are you due?"

"Just after Thanksgiving."

"You didn't ought to be working around all these animal germs," Dotie whispered, as if the germs would attack if they heard her. She gave a glance at the four clients with their four dogs avidly watching and listening. "You could be hurtin' your baby. I hope you ain't changing no kitty pans. My doctor tol' me when I was pregnant with my first not to touch none of that."

Uh-oh, Barbara thought and rolled her eyes at Emma.

"No, ma'am. Your doctor was correct. Someone else comes in to do that."

You, if we hire you, Barbara thought. *Not that it looks promising.*

Barbara took Dotie into her office and started the interview. It largely consisted of what Dotie would not do if she were hired. She would not stay late or come early. Or work weekends.

"My Duane wants his dinner at straight-up six o'clock," she said.

"We can't always close the clinic on time. You'd have to handle rescheduling appointments when I am off on an emergency. How are your computer skills?"

"Oh, they're fine. I took me some courses down at the junior college when Duane thought it was time I got back into the workforce full-time."

Duane's voice echoed in Barbara's head. She remembered a biblical quote about no man—in this case no woman—could serve two masters. Given a choice, Dotie would probably always choose Duane over Barbara.

"Past few years I worked holidays down at Dress Pretty, but this year I decided I needed something permanent, not just before Christ-mas. Duane says I'm good with people."

"How are you with guinea pigs?" Mentally, Barbara slapped herself. *That was snide.*

"Pigs? In the office?"

"Not that kind. Usually. Although if we have a pig come in needing treatment, we treat him." Actually, if a Barbary ape wandered in needing treatment, he'd get it, but best not to mention that to Dotie.

Dotie's eyes grew bigger and bigger.

"Dotie, do you like dogs and cats?"

"Lord, yes. I got me two big ol' tabbies I keep in the house, and Duane has a coonhound he loves better than he loves his grandchil-dren."

Good. One for Dotie.

"Do you mind scrubbing and cleaning?"

"What kind?" Her eyes narrowed. "I thought this was about the computer and all."

"It's about anything that needs doing. If we see a mess, we clean it up. The actual cleanup person comes in every afternoon…mostly… but this is a small practice." That the cleanup crew consisted of one teenager who came in after school was not germane.

"I don't like blood," Dotie said with a shiver

and a sniff. "It's unsanitary. Not to mention those other bodily functions."

Which have names. "That's why we wear gloves and masks and scrubs and use lots of disinfectant."

"Can I ask a question?"

"Absolutely."

"Your ad said 'Dr. B. Carew,' not Barbara. Are you the only doctor?"

"I am in the process of hiring another."

"Man or woman?"

Barbara didn't know, since so far the *hiree* was a figment of her imagination. "Does it matter?"

"I'm not too sure about working for a woman, but if you hire a man, Duane wouldn't like me being here alone with a man if you had to go out. He worries about me."

"That's sweet, but if it can't be a man or a woman, I think we're pretty much stuck."

Dotie snickered.

After that the interview wound to its inevitable conclusion quickly. Barbara walked Dotie to the front door and shook her hand once more. "Thanks so much for coming in, Mrs....uh, Dotie. We should be making a decision in the next few days. We'll call you."

"Uh-huh. Oh, Lordy!" Dotie jumped aside

to avoid being run over by a pot-bellied pig that had long since stopped being miniature. Without another word she fled across the parking lot and climbed into an immaculate electric blue pickup truck.

Clean truck. Another point in Dotie's favor. But two was not nearly enough. She shut the door on Dotie, turned and caught Emma's eye as she checked in the pig. Emma shook her head slightly and whispered, "As if."

"So it's still just us," Barbara said. "Pray the next one is exactly the person we want. We have to have some help or we're going to implode."

"Stephen will help."

Barbara turned away and whispered, "That's all I need. More Stephen."

CHAPTER TEN

BARBARA WALKED OUT of one of the examining rooms as Stephen walked in carrying a deli bag. Except for checking on Orville, he had not come to the clinic for several days.

"Thanks, Doc," said the small man who followed Barbara with an animal carrier. The animal inside whimpered. "This dang dog is going to get hisself runned over for good instead of knocked out of the way if he don't stop running out the back door ahead of me."

"He was lucky you stopped in time, Abe. He'll be sore, but the cuts and bruises are superficial and will heal on their own with the antibiotic ointment. If he shows any sign of infection, bring him back."

She turned and saw Stephen.

He gave her what he hoped was a dazzling smile. The one she gave him back certainly qualified. His heart lifted. He'd always considered that one of those idiotic and unscientific clichés, but he felt as though the organ physically moved in his chest, lifting his spirits, as well.

"I figured to surprise you and Emma with lunch," he said." I realized I didn't know what kind of sandwiches you might want, so I have ham-and-cheese and turkey-and-cheese, along with pickles, chips and sodas. Will that do?"

"Compared to the canned soup we generally have, it's a feast," Barbara told him. "To what do we owe the pleasure?"

"I didn't want to eat alone, so I took a chance you were both sticking close to the clinic." He gave her a small grin. "Plus it got me away from the computer and out of the house."

"Emma and I generally stay in for lunch, although we lock the door and put the Closed sign on it for an hour. We occasionally drive into Williamston to have lunch at the café, but it's too long to drive every day when there are people waiting. Does Emma know you're here?"

"Nope."

"Come on, it's time to close. We have to make it fast. I have someone coming in an hour and a half about the assistant job. I just interviewed one lady, but she didn't fit."

"You got that right," Emma called from behind the reception desk. "Stephen, you mind coming in here and hanging the sign on the door while I haul my hippo self out of this chair?"

He did, and she did.

"The job description for what I do—or did before I got too big—is dogsbody or gofer," Emma said. "Mostly it's 'other duties as assigned.' Did you come back to visit Orville?"

"No, I'm here to wine you and dine you. I have vintage sodas and Michelin three-star sandwiches."

"No bananas Foster on fire?" She picked up napkins from the counter that held the coffee urn and several paper plates from the shelf underneath. "Any lower down and you'd have to reach them. I don't bend any longer. Here you go."

"Don't people get upset when they come in the middle of the day and find you're closed?"

"We have them well-trained, unless it's a genuine emergency," Barbara said.

"Then we miss lunch," Emma added. "Sit down. We can eat on our laps unless you want to go formal and pull up one of the side tables."

"Lap is fine. I don't do formal. Who wants what?"

They parceled out the food and drink and ate in companionable silence. Emma looked on the verge of exhaustion. He knew she didn't want to let down Barbara, but he intended to speak to her in private and let her know that if she needed more time off and Barbara couldn't replace her, he would take her place. He could do his research from here on his laptop just as easily as he could from home. He'd always been able to concentrate in the center of the whirlwind.

"Is the notice about closing Friday week in the Marquette paper?" Barbara asked Emma.

"Scheduled the next two weeks. I asked for space next to the half-page ad for the fair, but they never promise position unless you pay a lot more money. Tom at the radio station is going to announce it every day next week on the community announcements."

"Including that Dr. Kirksey will be handling emergencies?"

"Yes, Barbara," Emma said with weary patience.

"You're closing?" Stephen asked. "Going out of town?"

"No. Tuesday through Saturday week is the Williamston County Fair."

"Barnum and Bailey it is not," Emma said and rolled her eyes.

"It's one of those traveling carnivals. They come every year with all the usual midway rides and stuff, plus there's livestock judging, cooking, quilting…" Barbara added.

"Making sorghum for your biscuits," Emma said and wiggled her nose. "Not my thing, but some people love it. Interesting to watch them cook it, but these days I'll probably smell it and barf."

"No you will not, Miss Emma," said Barbara. "You give this year a miss just for me, all right? You have no business being jostled and breathing in other people's germs. You stay home with your feet up, read a book. Since we have to close the office, get some rest."

"Why exactly, do you have to close the office?" he asked.

"The local vets share the chores at the fair every year," Barbara said. "That Friday is down as my day. I have to get to the fairgrounds south of Williamston by seven in the morning to check the animals that are being shown in the breed classes. After that I deal with problems on an *ad hog* basis."

He rolled his eyes. "I will ignore that, thank you. Like what?" Stephen asked.

"Usually cuts and scrapes, lameness, sows getting stressed and trying to eat their piglets… Don't look like that. Hogs are very sensitive. Mostly I get to hang out, eat myself sick on greasy food that is guaranteed to put five pounds on me overnight and ride the rides."

"You what?"

"Well, some of the rides. The Ferris wheel terrifies me. When I was in high school, the boy I went to the fair with conned me into riding the Ferris wheel with him. We got stuck at the top."

"And he, being a teenaged boy in a confined space beside a teenaged girl, trapped between heaven and earth…"

"Right, he rocked the gondola. Hard."

"I'm sure he had some dumb idea that you would scream and cling so he could snatch a kiss or two." Stephen chortled. "What did you actually do?"

"Oh, I screamed and clung all right, until we got down and out onto the boardwalk, then I slugged him and begged a ride home from my best friend. I gave the boy a black eye. He never told anyone how he got it and neither did I. I haven't ridden on a Ferris wheel since and don't intend to ride one again in this lifetime. Now, the roller coaster I love."

"You are insane. Roller coasters, even the small ones, horrify me. My youngest daughter, Anne, who rides large horses over tall fences, has never seen a roller coaster that she didn't want to bring home with her and set up in the backyard. When Nina and I took the girls to the fair every year, Nina had to go with Anne on the roller coaster until her patience or my cash ran out. My elder girl, Elaine, stayed on the ground with me. What do you do when you are not vetting, eating, or riding the roller coaster?"

"See the fair. Check out the livestock, watch the animal judging. Talk to people. There's harness racing in the afternoon. No betting—well, not overt—but no harness-racing enthusiast could miss having a little flier with his buddies. The police generally turn a blind eye. I listen to the high-school band and maybe watch the sunset. Then I drive home carefully, since I'm usually so tired by that point I'm cross-eyed. Once home I make certain the animals have been fed and watered and that the place is locked up."

"Who looks after them while you're not here? Not Emma, surely."

"Since that's the day all the kids are out of school for their fair day, the girl who comes in the afternoon does it. Although I thought I'd surely have a full-time replacement for Emma by this time."

"Sounds like an awfully responsible job for a youngster," Stephen said.

Emma ran her hands over her shoulders and eased her neck. "What she's not telling you is that Seth and Earl will drive by a couple of times to be sure there aren't any problems." She glanced over at Barbara. "So will I." She held her hands in front of her. "Don't look at me like that, Barbara. I promise I won't spend the day here, but I will stop by a couple of times, and I'll have the clinic phone switched over to my house. Heather has done the after-noon feeding and watering several times. She knows when to panic."

"We won't do any nonemergency surgery that day," Barbara said. "Dr. Kirksey has a full-time vet tech, so if he has to go out to do an emergency delivery or something on Fri-day, he can go in my place." She stood, col-lected the detritus from lunch, balled it up and stuffed it into the sack Stephen had brought it in.

"I wouldn't have thought Williamston was a large enough town to have an annual fair," Stephen said.

"Complete with a midway," Barbara said. She leaned back and closed her eyes.

"It's been going strong since just after the First World War," said Emma. "The blue ribbons for the biggest hog or the most colorful quilt are prized and argued over all year by everyone in town. Nearly all the churches have food tents that sell pure cholesterol and sugar."

Stephen gave Emma an arm to hold onto as she struggled to stand.

"I'm off to the bathroom for the fortieth time. Thanks for lunch, Stephen."

They watched her toddle off. Stephen asked Barbara, "Does your fair have fried custard?"

Barbara lifted her eyebrows and tossed the trash bag into the wastebasket beside Emma's desk. "So you know about that, do you? We can beat that. We have fried butter!"

"You're joking."

"Am not. They take a whole stick of butter, roll it in bread crumbs and fry it."

"That is right up there with dining on chocolate-covered crickets. What happens when you bite into it?"

"What do you think? It's supposed to be fried so fast that the butter doesn't melt, like chicken Kiev. Most of the time, however, the minute you bite it goes *sploosh* and squirts out all over everything."

"I thought fried custard was bad. What else?"

"Tamales and foot-long hot dogs, corn dogs and corn on the cob, cotton candy, fried catfish, barbecue, turkey legs and—"

"Stop!" He held up his hands. "I give up. Do the EMTs run a mobile trauma unit to revive the gourmands who keel over with heart attacks on the fairgrounds?"

"No idea. I'm only concerned with the animals. I hate having to close, even though I start reminding the clients about the date weeks before the day I'm at the fair. Dr. Kirksey and I coordinate our answering services. He has a much larger operation than I do, but as a general rule, he does small animals only. With luck, by next year this time I'll have another vet working with me and someone on the front desk full-time. Keep your fingers crossed."

"Are you interviewing anyone for the veterinarian's spot?" he asked.

Barbara looked over at the restroom door. Emma had not yet reappeared.

"I've written to two—one woman, one man—both new graduates who have passed their boards and are ready to get their feet wet in the real world of veterinary medicine. Another full-time vet will mean that we'll all be able to work decent schedules. Ideally, one vet will work in the office handling clinic calls, and one will be on the road dealing with large animals and emergencies. A full-time clerk will manage the office part, then I need a full-time trained vet tech to assist the vets."

"So you'll have more free time?" He could hear the eagerness in his voice. You'll be able to leave the clinic? Actually go out to dinner, maybe a movie occasionally? Possibly even the theater in Memphis when they have something good on?"

Emma froze. "More likely, I will go to bed early and not fall asleep at lunch. I'm used to being alone and making my own decisions. That won't change, but another vet should mean more clients. I still won't be able to go gallivanting off if I feel like it."

"So you're trying to reach critical mass all over again with more staff?"

"Not immediately. This is a professional decision, Stephen. In no way is it for my personal convenience. Or yours."

"Uh-huh." He grinned at her.

"I may still be looking to hire this time next year."

"Surely not," he said. "So, who are these newly minted vets? What schools did they attend?"

"It is none of your business."

"I'm curious, is all."

BUTTING IN, WAS ALL, Barbara thought. "The woman is from the University of Alabama. The man is from Mississippi State. They both have significant experience with both large and small animals, but the woman has some wild-animal experience with their local rehabilitators. It's not a deal breaker, but it would help if the person I hire can deal with skunks and raccoons and foxes. We don't have badgers or black-footed ferrets this far east, but you'd be amazed at what some people will buy for pets. I don't approve of keeping exotic pets, but I intend to see it's well taken care of once it's acquired. Then we occasionally are asked to treat a really wild animal. We have cougars—what the local farmers call painters—moving up from the south toward eastern Kentucky. Possibly because of global warming and lack of habitat. And we have black bears from time to time. I've never had to deal with one, but my colleagues around the Carolina border have. In the spring when they're hungry and have cubs, they are very dangerous."

She was suddenly struck by the fact that she had no other frame of reference but the animals she served.

Stephen talked about going out to dinner or even going to Memphis to the theater. She and John used to drive to Memphis to see plays, but she hadn't seen live theater since he'd died. She hated even going to the movies alone. She might as well have walled herself up.

Intellect withered in isolation. So did emotion. She funneled all hers into the animals she served. Had she totally lost the ability to connect with people about anything other than their dogs and cats and their cattle and goats? She realized she had not heard what he was saying. She couldn't even listen to human speech properly.

"Bears are not a problem I have to deal with in my classes," Stephen said. "Although there are times when a bear might be preferable to my students."

He hadn't noticed her lack of attention, so she asked, "Do you have any pets at the moment?" Again with the pets.

"I grew up with hounds and house cats," Stephen said. "Then, after Nina and I married, we got a Labrador. He died several years ago, and when Nina was sick, the doctor said it was inadvisable for her to have another dog. If I had it to do over, I'd have found her a small, cuddly dog to stay beside her. After she died, getting a dog became the least of my worries. Maybe it's time to start looking at the shelters."

"I'll be happy to help," Barbara said.

"The most exotic animal I ever owned was a chameleon I bought at the fair when I was ten."

"Did it survive?"

"Oddly enough, it lived very well for a couple of years. Orville is the only creature I ever helped rescue. Probably why I am so invested in his health."

"Nothing I've found feeds the ego like rescuing an endangered animal. When I was growing up we raised pigs and goats and sheep and cattle—not very successfully, I'm afraid," Barbara said. "We did most of our own vet care because we couldn't afford to hire it done. Our cats lived in the barn and kept the rats down. Our dogs protected the critters. No real house pets. But I brought home abandoned raccoons and possums, and even bats. If it's hurt or abandoned, I'm going to try to fix it."

Emma opened the restroom door and walked out. Barbara let out the breath she had been holding.

"Send her home," Stephen whispered. "I'll stay."

Barbara stared at him. "You can't…"

"Of course I can. I don't want a salary, however. Have dinner with me tonight. In town at the café or anywhere else you choose. Nonnegotiable. My treat."

"You're going to pay for working?"

"What else do I have to spend money on? Emma told me that up here all sorts of things would seem more interesting than the work I was supposed to do—in my case write a textbook.

"I'd also like to help you out at the fair. I thought I had iron discipline, but spending the day at the fair with you seems much more appealing than staring at my computer screen or checking references from the Library of Congress."

She sat up straight and frowned at him. "You definitely want to come with me?"

"If you'll have me."

"You'd be bored out of your mind."

"With you? Hardly. I'll make you a deal. If you will ride the Ferris wheel, I'll ride the roller coaster."

Barbara longed to say that she did not need him and did not want him. That was only half a lie. Maybe this would be an opportunity to boss him around and get him to back off from intruding on her life. "If you come, remember—me, veterinarian, you, gofer."

He held up his hands. "Gofer, it is."

"Stephen," Emma said as she sat down with a sigh. "Turn the sign to Open, please."

"No."

"I beg your pardon."

"Not until you leave. Go home, Emma. I'm your substitute."

"But you…"

"Don't know the system or how to operate the computer? I'm sure I can figure it out. All right with you, Barbara?"

"He's right, Emma. He's crazy, but he's right. Go home, put your feet up and read a book."

Emma closed her eyes. "Thank you, Stephen. I admit my ankles are swollen. But call me if there are any problems."

"Scout's honor."

Emma got up with greater ease than she'd

sat down, picked up her purse and turned the sign on the front door to Open.

As she left, a broad woman carrying a cardboard box that made puppy noises passed her in the doorway.

"Ophelia," Barbara said, "how many did you wind up with?"

"Four. Suzy can't figure out how she wound up with four extra Chihuahuas, but she's a good mother."

"Come on back with me, Ophelia, so we can check everybody out. Sit down, Stephen. Take notes until I get back out here to check you out on the computer system," Barbara whispered. "Emma may be healthy as a horse, but she's *not* a horse."

If he couldn't figure out the computer, he and Barbara could check his notes and transfer them to the computer after the office closed. Possibly after dinner. A pleasant way to spend what would have been a lonely evening.

Stephen was thankful the afternoon was unusually slow. He actually figured out the computer program the clinic used for appointments on his own.

Barbara would be pleased. Why should that give him a pleasant glow? He enjoyed her company as he had no other woman's since

Nina died. He wanted more of it. He had to convince her that his company could be worth her leaving her comfort zone, as well.

CHAPTER ELEVEN

WAITING TO INTERVIEW the woman who might want the clinic job, Barbara realized why she was conflicted about Stephen. He seemed to be trying to take over her life. First, he started helping out at the clinic. Now, they were going to spend the entire day together at the fair. Why hadn't she said she didn't want him? Because a secret part of her thought that having him there might be fun.

She remembered fun, didn't she? Somewhere in the past? She and John had always had fun. And for once, Stephen or no Stephen, she planned to have some more.

Tall and thin, her interviewee had arms with muscles like heavy ropes. Whether she liked hard labor and was a self-starter was a question the interview should answer.

When she'd come into the waiting room and seen the animals, she'd said, "Oooh," and grinned. She'd checked in with Stephen at the front desk, introduced herself as Mary Frances Reilly, then bent to pick up a rough-coated

Dachshund puppy that had escaped from his owner and was dragging his leash. He'd licked her face enthusiastically and sent Mary Frances off into giggles.

"I am so sorry. Rusty just has to go call on everybody he meets," said his owner. She took the puppy from Mary Frances and set him down on the floor, where he immediately let forth a stream of urine. "Rusty, you bad boy!"

Without asking, Mary Frances took several sheets from the extra-large roll of paper towels on the counter, cleaned up the wet spot, squirted it with the spray bottle of animal urine descenter from the counter, then tossed the towels into a metal garbage can that was a quarter full. "He's just a baby and he's excited. He's a good boy." She scratched behind his ears and received a loopy dog grin in response. She turned to Stephen. "Sir, is there someplace I can wash my hands?"

He pointed to the door to the left marked Restrooms with both male and female silhouettes on it. As soon as the door closed behind the woman, he buzzed Barbara and whispered, "This one looks promising."

"From your mouth to God's ear. Be right there."

Mary Frances's cleanup had won over Stephen.

THE INTERVIEW WON Barbara over.

"Me 'n' Herb just moved up here from Jackson to be close to his folks," she said. "They're getting older and his mama's not in real good health. We don't have kids, so I can work pretty much whenever you need somebody. I worked for a cleaning company before, and sometimes they wanted folks' offices cleaned before seven in the morning, and my daddy raised cows until he got arthritis in his knees. I'm used to gettin' up early."

"Do you know anything about computers?"

"I did the billing for the cleaning company on their computer sometimes, but you'd have to teach me your system." She glanced toward the hall door. The reception area was now empty. "Are y'all real busy?"

"This afternoon is unusual. Does being busy bother you? Most of the time it's crazy around here, and we are very short-staffed. That's why we're looking to hire somebody like you."

"Busy don't bother me. I like to keep going, but when it's quiet I got time to do the extras, like cleaning out cabinets and such like."

"You do know we keep drugs in our cabinets? We keep them locked and log out drugs when we use them. The government requires we keep a log."

"Me 'n' Herb don't even have a beer on a Saturday night, ma'am, but I understand if you want me to take a drug test.

"We'll want you to at some point. Just a formality…"

"That's fine, ma'am. Herb had to take one when he went to work down to the feed store."

That meant her husband worked for Mayor Sonny Prather. If he'd hired the man, he must be trustworthy. Barbara would call him later to check. Mary Frances had already given her a letter of recommendation from her previous employer.

"Does your husband mind your working late when we have an emergency?"

"He's so busy at his job and watchin' out for his folks, he doesn't have much time to worry about me. I've always loved animals. I used to drive my folks crazy bringing home every stray in the neighborhood and finding homes for 'em. I would'a liked to be a vet like you, but we didn't have the money, and I don't have the sense."

"Ever thought of studying to be a licensed veterinary technician? The community college has classes. And here you could learn to run some of the equipment if you liked."

"Could I? Blood and such don't bother me, ma'am. I'll learn anything you want to teach me."

"The staff here are all on a first-name basis."

"Even you, ma'am?"

Barbara smiled. "Even me. We're more formal with our clients. What do you like to be called?"

"Just plain old Mary Frances, ma'am."

"Not ma'am. Just Barbara or Doc."

Barbara spent another twenty minutes with Mary Frances explaining salary, hours, insurance and the requirements for the job. She talked about Emma's pregnancy and the need for someone full-time to take over most of her duties soon. Finally, she said, "Would you like to give the job a shot?"

The woman's face lit up. Barbara thought she was actually very pretty, despite the slightly bucked teeth and the mousy hair that needed a trim. She had probably been a beauty in her teens. Her jeans were washed and pressed, and her plaid shirt, although a veteran of many washes, was ironed and fresh.

While Mary Frances talked to Stephen, Barbara managed to get Sonny Prather. He knew her family and vouched for them. That was good enough for Barbara.

When, eventually, Barbara went back into the waiting room, she gave Stephen an eyebrow lift and a thumbs-up. "Mary Frances is going to be joining us. She has some time this afternoon, so I thought you might like to start showing her our system on the computer."

"I've just about figured it out myself."

Barbara looked at the empty waiting room. "Let's get to it while we have a break in traffic. She starts full-time at eight tomorrow morning, five and a half days a week."

When Heather came in at four to clean up and met the new hire, she was ecstatic. Barbara realized that everything had slipped further and further behind in the past few months.

Now, if she could only hire another vet before Thanksgiving, life would *really* be fine on the clinic front. Thanksgiving meant a small celebration with her children—possibly the new vet and his family, assuming she hired one with a family—lots of good food, everyone on their best behavior. What could possibly go wrong?

More help in the clinic meant more free time for Barbara. She had plenty to keep her busy if Stephen didn't hover around expecting her to go on actual dates. Good grief, she was acting like a child.

What was she so afraid of?

Having him around messed with her attention span. She had plenty of casual male friends. Plenty of attractive male clients, too, some of whom had hit on her after John died. She'd had no problem keeping her objectivity and her distance with *them*. Stephen was different. She felt like a high-school girl who swears she hates a boy but still hangs out after school to catch a glimpse of him.

She did not have time for anything—anyone—else in her life, and definitely not somebody like Stephen MacDonald.

ON HIS DRIVE back to his cottage from the clinic, Stephen called Seth.

"I took off early to pick up some groceries for Emma," Seth said. "She said you were filling in for her at the clinic. Thanks for that. How'd it go?"

"Why don't you come over for a beer?"

He heard Seth's voice grow tight. "What's up?"

"If you could use the beer, I could use the company."

Ten minutes later, sitting in the cool autumn evening on the front porch, Seth asked, "Was Emma feeling bad? She'd never tell me, but I know she came home early."

"She's fine, or as fine as a heavily pregnant woman can be. Thing is, it's time she stopped working for Barbara, except maybe a half day a week to keep from going nuts." He held up a hand. "Barbara hired a full-time office assistant this afternoon. She has some minor computer skills and she seems bright enough and wants to learn." He took a deep breath. "I intended to work out a schedule with Barbara to sit in for Emma until she comes back after the baby is born, assuming she wants to. Now that Barbara's hired this new lady, I may be off the hook. We'll see." Actually, he hoped he'd still be needed at the clinic. It was an excuse to see Barbara.

"I'm looking in on Orville. He doesn't enjoy my company any more than he did when I brought him in, but I keep talking to him and encouraging him, for what that's worth. I do understand that he's not a parrot, capable of speech, but if ever there was a creature with a 'speaking countenance,' Orville is that creature." He grinned. "I guess he has more of a 'cussing countenance.' Probably a good thing he can't talk.

"I've offered to teach the new girl how to use the computer more fully, by the way, but who knows how much time that will take."

"What about your book?"

"Orville and the clinic have become much more important. Certainly much more interesting than real-estate transfers after the great plague or rampant inflation after the First World War. Frankly, now that I see first hand how busy it is, I cannot figure out how Emma and Barbara and one part-time teenager have managed the clinic as well as they have."

"Barbara had a full-time person until a few months before Emma started helping her out, but you're right. I don't know how Barbara will be able to keep going at her present level, if she doesn't get another vet in with her soon to help out."

"She says winter is her slack time."

"As opposed to what? Total chaos? So how do we keep my wife at home baking cookies?"

Stephen chortled. "Unless she's changed, Emma can't bake. She and my Anne tried to make cookies for Christmas one year. I could have reroofed the house with them. Speaking of roofing, it looks from the outside as if you're down to the wire on your construction. Are you ready for the baby?"

"The contractors are working on the punch list. Construction slows down in the winter, so Earl and I are trying to find these guys some jobs to tide them over after our job is finished. So far we're not finding much."

"How small a job would they consider?" Stephen asked.

"If it comes with a paycheck, I think they'd at least consider it. Why, what do you have in mind?"

Stephen took a deep breath. "Your pasture."

"I beg your pardon?"

Stephen held up his hands. "Just listen to me before you tell me I am nuts. It's not that far from when Orville will be ready to learn to fly again."

"Is that what Barbara thinks?"

"I haven't asked her. I can feel it, see it in the way he moves around his cage."

"You better ask her before you go making plans for Orville. And what's that got to do with my pasture? Emma's pasture, actually. She inherited it, not me."

"You are husband and wife."

"Right."

"I took a look at it… Before you get excited, I did not cross the barbed-wire fence, as you requested. But since the leaves are thinner now, I could see most of it including the remains of the barn." He decided this was not the time to cloud the issue with Guy Fawkes and his possible bonfire. "The barn looks as though it needs to be cleaned out to the walls and reroofed. The walls are sound, am I correct?"

"Yeah, dirty, but there's a heck of a lot of old wood and rusted metal roofing and heaven knows what all in there."

"Before one can assess how much work would be needed to refit the barn, one would have to begin by bushhogging the acreage, cleaning up the edges of the pond, and, uh, getting rid of the debris."

"One heck of a job. Cost a bundle. You planning on putting the flight cage—see, I haven't forgotten—actually inside the barn?"

"Possibly. Or attached to it. It would be an excellent setup for the local rehabilitators group."

"Seems to me you need Barbara's input on this. Do you have a spare government grant in your pocket to pay for all this?" Seth sounded irritated.

"Possibly we could get one eventually, but

like all government grants, it would take time. I want to plan it all out, then surprise Barbara."

"I don't think that's a good idea. Barbara likes to make her own decisions."

Stephen leaned forward and dropped his forearms between his knees. "Of course, I want Barbara's input. If I present her with plans, however, she's much more likely to actually do something. Or let me."

"Barbara and her group are always doing fund-raisers to make enough money to pay for the little they are able to do. They don't have that kind of money."

"I'll buy it." Stephen sat back, flabbergasted at the words that had just come out of his mouth. Anne always said he needed to engage his brain before he engaged his mouth.

"Buy what? The pasture? Stephen, what the heck do you need with ten acres, a turtle-infested pond and a derelict barn with no roof on it? Did you hurt your head when you ran into that eagle?"

Barbara might well hate the idea and be furious at him for planning something this big behind her back. In place of a wonderful surprise, she might view the entire idea as an intrusion into her business.

He'd be safer courting her with a dozen

roses. Still, a little planning couldn't hurt before he broached the subject with her.

"I will unleash the Bush Hog on your pasture this Saturday morning after I return from my walk," Stephen said. "With your tractor, which you will teach me to use. Saturday afternoon, we will see where we are with the barn. Then, we will talk to your construction crew about clearing out the barn and building a flight cage either in or outside the barn, whichever Barbara feels is better."

"I don't know what to charge for that pasture, even if we did want to sell it."

"Then find out. A long-term lease might work just as well. Ask Sonny Prather. Didn't Emma say he owns half the rental property in the area? I will call my banker and find out if I can afford it."

"Farmland around here isn't cheap," Seth said.

"Neither of us has an idea what that means in terms of dollars and cents. Please, don't mention this—"

"The term you are searching for is 'harebrained scheme,'" Seth said drily. "I wouldn't dream of mentioning this to Emma."

"Aside from the minor problems, Seth, what do you think?"

"Oh, I think it's downright brilliant, if nutty. But I also think it is a pipedream." He set his beer on the table beside him. "First, you don't know what Barbara would think. Second, it's a totally separate venue from her clinic and two miles away. Third, it would be expensive and labor-intensive. Fourth, you do not need or want a pasture, a dilapidated barn and a turtle-infested pond. Then here's the biggie—you're supposed to be writing a book." He glanced at his watch and stood up abruptly. "Shoot, I've left Emma alone too long."

"I'm supposed to be picking up Barbara for dinner at the café in fifteen minutes." Stephen also rose.

"You seem to be doing that a lot lately." Seth raised his eyebrows.

"As often as she'll let me. Sometimes one or the other of us cooks or gets take out, but since we're both alone, it makes a pleasant end to the day."

"Yeah, I bet." Seth stuck out his hand. "If you're serious, talk to Barbara before you go any further. I'll teach you Tractor Driving 101 on Saturday morning, but if you bring down the barn on your head or get devoured by a snapping turtle, don't blame me. I'm on call, so I may not be around to pick up the pieces."

Stephen watched Seth run back across the road to his house, which looked welcoming with the lights on and a warm wife inside.

He couldn't possibly have conceived this folly simply to impress Barbara, could he? Was it all for a bird who needed a place to fly? Maybe he did deserve to be locked up.

He had no idea what this craziness would cost. Seemed, however, like something worthwhile to spend his money on. He needed Orville to be able to fly again, to go back to the life he'd had, the life he deserved. He couldn't stand the thought of the fierce creature being stuck in a cage the rest of his life. How would Stephen have felt if he'd been stuck in the rehab facility the rest of his days? Plus, after Orville flew away—and he would—the flight cage would be available for other rescued birds that needed a place to practice.

Elaine would have a conniption at a major expenditure for something she would think was not his job.

He wouldn't tell her, or Anne, or anyone else but Seth, who could tell Emma. He should definitely discuss the plan with Barbara before he actually spent money on the project, but he'd wait until he had something concrete to present to her. That seemed rational, didn't it?

When was the last time he had really wanted to do something different? The last time he'd had an idea that galvanized him? Made him want to pump his fist in the air?

He picked up the empties and took them with him into the house. Something told him Barbara would rain on his parade hard and from a great height. He'd just have to find a way to win her over.

CHAPTER TWELVE

"How come you're so cheerful tonight?" Barbara asked Stephen over her steak at the café. "I figured you'd be exhausted after the crazy afternoon we had. I was certain you wouldn't stick it out this long, but it's almost Halloween, and you're still coming in. You're grinning like you know where all the Christmas presents are hidden."

Stephen tried to sober his expression. "It's Friday. End of my particular work week. Seth wants to persuade Emma to stay home entirely until after the baby is born. She's down to just over a month before she's due. But she still wants to come in at least one morning a week."

"Was he meaning to discuss it with me? Or with her? Or me? Seems as though some one should discuss it with me."

"He and I share a beer after work sometimes and…"

"The big strong men decided for the poor little pregnant woman and her boss?"

"Of course not, but you have mentioned it."

"It may be the right thing to do. After her last appointment, she told me her doctor is a trifle concerned about her ankles, although her blood pressure is fine."

"After we finish dessert tonight we will schedule the hours I will fill in until you hire a new vet," Stephen said.

"Oh, we will, will we?"

"Absolutely. And before you accuse me of being a dilettante, I have scrubbed floors and cleaned up bodily fluids. When Nina and I started out, we were both in graduate school, and after that I was a lowly teaching assistant. We were lucky to have peanut-butter-and-jelly sandwiches. Housemaids and nannies did not fit into the budget. Between Mary Frances, Heather and me, we have the office running relatively smoothly.

"You're avoiding the other issue, Stephen. You promised to finish your book."

He waved a hand. "I have until Easter. Most of the research is done, I simply have to write the dratted thing. You let me worry about the book."

"Well, somebody has to." She laid her knife

and fork along the side of her plate. "If you are serious about filling in for Emma full-time at some point, then as long as we are in the clinic, it's my house, my rules. Can you live with that?"

"Of course. The way Mary Frances is working out, you may not need me at all shortly."

"I don't think she wants to be a full-time caregiver for Herb's parents," Barbara said and laid down her knife and fork. "Herb's mother has a reputation for being difficult."

"That's one of the reasons I wanted to move up here," Stephen said. "My daughter Anne is not the caregiver type, except in the case of horses, but she would have given it a heroic effort if she was convinced I needed looking after."

"What about your other daughter?"

He opened up the menu to check on desserts and hid behind it. "Elaine figures she was born to rule the world. She likes giving orders. Besides, she's busy being the wife of a corporate lawyer. She would try to oversee every step I took, blame *me* if she wasn't there to check on me, feel guilty, resent that she did and make us both miserable. Or in my case, murderous."

Barbara had started to snicker at the begin-

ning of his speech and was laughing by the
end of it.

"Mark and Caitlyn, my two, figure I can
look after myself."

"Neither is married?"

"Not yet. If I am lucky, they'll come to me
for Thanksgiving, but I won't feel bad if they
don't. Invariably somebody's horse colics or
somebody's goat breaks a leg while I'm carv-
ing the turkey. My usual Thanksgiving dinner is leftovers at my breakfast bar after they
are long gone."

"Not this year. I'm already making plans.
If we can arrange schedules, we'll have you,
Anne, Elaine, her husband, your two, Emma,
Seth and Seth's mother, Laila, whom I met at
their wedding. I don't have that much space
in my dining room, but I can make it work."

Barbara leaned both forearms on the table
and stared at him. "Was there an invitation in
there someplace, or did I miss it?"

"My treat. The café has agreed to cater."

"Catered? That will cost a fortune! I can
cook the food. Thanksgiving is easy."

He shook his head. "And have the turkey
half done because you abandoned it in favor
of a blocked gut? My invitation, my rules."

"My two will probably go off somewhere with their friends."

"That's even more reason for me to host the dinner. Consider this a command performance. Unless Emma goes into labor. Then all bets are off."

"You said Elaine was the bossy one. I can see where she gets it." She didn't smile when she said it.

Velma came up, topped off their iced tea and asked, "Y'all gonna split some apple cobbler with ice cream on top and have some coffee?"

Stephen met Barbara's eyes.

"You mean I get to choose?" she asked. "Why not? I've had enough calories tonight to carry me up to Christmas as it is. I could use some comfort food."

After Velma left to get the cobbler, Stephen asked, "How come neither of your children went into veterinary medicine?"

"They grew up knowing that if both John and I were doing something we couldn't stop, they might have to leave soccer practice and stay at a friend's house until we could pick them up. They were as good as gone when they left for college. They both wanted a cleaner life that made more money and left time for actually living. We get along, but we're very different people."

"Don't you miss them?"

"We talk on our cells and email. They were closer to John, I guess. He was the perfect father. I was never the perfect mother. I couldn't leave off suturing a gaping wound to get to Mark's T-ball game."

"But your husband could?"

"He managed more often than I did. Then suddenly he was gone. That left me a single parent to make a living for us. Don't guilt-trip me. I do enough of that by myself."

"I'm sure you are a great mother."

She blushed and dropped her eyes. "Thank you."

She didn't invite him in when they got back to her apartment.

She had office hours in the morning; he had tractor-driving class with Seth. Since she would be occupied at the clinic, she might not find out about his clearing the land. He told himself not to push it.

Who was he kidding? Someone would tell her. Nobody could keep a secret in this town. The menu for their dinner at the café would probably be discussed over Williamston's breakfast tables. He gave her a friendly good-night kiss, turned away, turned back, wrapped his arms around her and planted one on her.

Her response was all he could have hoped for. His heart hammered to the rhythm of hers. Her head fell back and she leaned against him with a sigh of pleasure.

He didn't want to let her go. "May I come in?" he whispered.

She pulled away. "Go home, Stephen. Thank you for a lovely dinner." She escaped inside, shutting the door of her apartment before he could muster a cogent reason to stay.

He turned away in frustration.

Since he'd met Barbara, his vision had narrowed. She was the only woman he thought about.

Why was Barbara different?

Simple chemistry? What was he, fourteen all over again?

He walked through the darkened barn, where the security lights gave only a dim glow that didn't bother the animals. As he passed their stalls, most stirred at being awakened. One of the horses continued to snore. One stomped an annoyed hoof. The fawns wriggled deeper into their hay and snuffled.

He wanted to check on Orville, but the big

bird no doubt sleeping. He'd come visit tomorrow after he finished mowing Emma's pasture.

Orville's love life, when he had one, seemed much less complicated than Stephen's.

He'd give Orville a chance to find his mate again. At least one of them wouldn't be alone.

The fancy leather seats in his equally fancy new truck had grown cold in the time he'd taken to escort Barbara to her door. He envied the fawns curled against one another warm in the hay.

Seth and Emma's house was dark. When he pulled into his driveway, he felt as though every other creature in the world had a partner to cuddle up with except him.

He and Orville were cold and alone. Neither of them deserved it. He was working hard to return Orville to his family, assuming he still had one.

He wasn't interested in cuddling with anyone but Barbara. He needed to see whether she was interested back.

BARBARA LEANED AGAINST her front door and listened to Stephen's footsteps in the barn aisle. He wasn't the first man who had tried to romance her since John died. He was, however, the only man she'd wanted to say yes to.

She really didn't know him at all. What could he possibly see in her when he put her up against the beautiful, sophisticated women he knew in Memphis. She didn't think he was the sort of man for whom a woman was merely a convenience. But her heart had already taken one huge loss, been wounded to the quick. How could she risk what was left of her heart on someone who might get bored with her and the novelty of country life and run back to his real life in Memphis? She couldn't take another chance on love. Just when you trusted it, it jumped up and took the one you loved away from you. Once was enough. Never love again, never lose again. Sound advice.

Besides, there simply was no room in her life for one more person or one more feeling. Her date book was full and bursting at the seams.

Then the whole Thanksgiving thing! Obviously he was trying to be thoughtful, but the word she would use was pushy. Stephen didn't even know Mark and Caitlyn. Heck, she didn't know herself whether they were planning on coming home for Thanksgiving. Stephen was turning a quiet family affair into a big party. Did he bother to ask whether that was what she wanted? What her own plans were? Her children wouldn't be pleased to be lumped in with a bunch of strangers.

She sank onto her bed and dropped her head in her hands. Drat the man! His heart might be in the right place, but he was beginning to get on her last nerve.

CHAPTER THIRTEEN

SATURDAY MORNING DAWNED cold and foggy
with rime frost covering the grass and the
roofs. Stephen decided he would count the
bushhogging as a substitute for his walk. His
upper body needed exercise, too, didn't it?

His leg was stiffer than usual. Probably the
weather.

He was finishing his toast and coffee when
Seth called. "You still game to drive the tractor?" he asked.

"Of course."

"Anytime you're ready. Emma's not up yet,
but I'm betting she'll be glad to have me out
of the house."

Stephen rinsed out his coffee cup, stowed it
in the dishwasher, slipped on his Wellies and
his windbreaker and walked over to meet Seth.
The air was still with patchy fog in the low-
lying areas. The temperature sat in the fifties.
Usually fall lasted until the second week in
November, then, invariably, a cold front with

high winds would blast through and rip the remaining leaves off the trees. That would be the start of true winter. Today was one of those soft, cloudy, tender days that felt cool on the skin, but not cold.

"This is a prime day for hunting," Seth told him. "The deer love to wander in this sort of weather. Not too cold, not too damp, not too sunny. That means I have to check you out on the tractor, then make the rounds in my official vehicle to head off the badasses who want more than their fair share of deer meat. I'll be on call. Emma is at home. Keep out of trouble. Emma would be upset if you got yourself killed."

"Thank you from the bottom of my heart for your deep concern. Now, let's have some tractor tutelage."

Stephen had driven a riding lawn mower once or twice, but never a big agricultural job complete with front loader as well as bush hog. He went over all the gears, the brakes, the steering, acceleration, the different foot pedals, levers, and took to heart Seth's warnings about how easily the entire apparatus could get away from him.

With Seth standing beside him coaching, he practiced with the gears and levers until he felt he knew the principles and the placement. He wasn't certain he'd remember it all in a crunch. Better not have any crunches. "Shouldn't be too difficult," he said and hoped he wasn't lying.

"Don't get cocky," Seth said. "Remember you have separate brakes that control each side, so when you turn, you slow each wheel, make the turn and release the brake to start off again. You have gears to raise and lower the front loader and other gears to tilt the bucket up or down. Leave them alone. Don't mess with the front-loader bucket at all. You shouldn't have to. It is well out of your way.

"Those levers raise and lower the Bush Hog, and this gear engages it." The two men worked through the mechanics until they both felt comfortable.

"Whatever you do," Seth advised, "keep your turns slow and even. These critters turn over if they get ticked off at you. And don't fall out."

"How can I fall out? The cab is enclosed."

"Doors come open. Tractors tip on uneven ground and spring the locks. Brakes lock up. Front loaders dig into the dirt and try to stand you on your head…"

"You, Seth, are a perfect little ray of sun-

shine. I will be slow, careful, and if I kill myself I won't sue you."

"Yeah, but you'll upset Emma. Time to head
out across the road. I've already clipped the
barbed wire from the road frontage so you can
drive straight in."

Stephen felt the charge that he enjoyed when
driving powerful vehicles. This one might not
be a mighty mite like his poor wounded Triumph, but it made up for its lack of speed with
size and complexity.

He calmed himself down, checked for cars
before he crossed the road, drove into the overgrown pasture and stopped.

Seth said, "Run through your checklist
again."

Stephen did with gestures.

"Don't forget you have to pull out the choke
to shut off the engine. Otherwise it keeps running. If you don't disengage the gears, it's
happy to run right over you."

"Yes, sir."

"Now, before you engage the Bush Hog and
start cutting, I am backing off and so you can't
run over *me*."

"You have no faith!" Stephen said with a
grin.

Stephen inhaled a deep breath, lowered the

Bush Hog, checked that the front loader was safely off the ground, checked and rechecked, and finally moved the accelerator lever forward.

It worked.

Now this was living!

It actually functioned precisely the way Seth had explained it would. He began to cut. The grinding noise was terrific, but not as loud as he'd feared.

He glanced back over his shoulder. Seth was relaxing by the road with his hands in his pockets.

Thud! Bump! Stephen felt a jolt. *What was that?* His heart gave an answering lurch. He barely touched the right brake pedal, but the monster pivoted to the right.

He looked down to see a fallen sapling hidden below the level of the grass, invisible to anyone not almost on top of it.

"Damn!" he whispered, pulled back on the accelerator, took his foot off the brake, came to a halt and sat a moment to get his pulse under control. It hit him that he was all alone in the cab of a giant, complex machine that cost a fortune and could land him in a heap of trouble in a millisecond.

"It's okay, Seth," he called and gave a

thumbs-up sign. Seth smiled and returned it, but did not come to his aid.

He expelled his anxious breath, squared his shoulders and started again.

This time he bumped easily across the sapling.

This was nothing but a big lawn mower after all. He could handle it. He increased his speed as he became more comfortable. Ten acres hadn't seemed like a lot. Now, seen from the cab of the tractor, it stretched away like the Great Plains—with a pond in the middle full of lily pads and no discernible boundaries between muddy marsh and dry land. The water was still and silver in the foggy morning.

"Whatever you do, do *not* drive into the pond." He repeated Seth's words. "Don't even get close." He glanced behind him. He'd created a neat, clipped swath.

Apparently satisfied that he was safe—well, safe-ish—at the controls, Seth no longer watched him but had gone back up his driveway.

Stephen began to whistle tunelessly. Time to check out the barn.

He drove carefully and kept the brush pile between himself and the pond. On closer view, the barn didn't seem to be in such bad shape.

The back third of the metal roof had fallen inside and hung precariously from one side of the rafters to the concrete floor. The remainder looked rusty but sound. It would all have to be pulled out and replaced.

None of the rafters had fallen. They might be rotten, but they, too, could be easily replaced.

Everything outside and inside was filthy, festooned with love vine and poison ivy and hung with spiderwebs. Easy to clean out. With a large enough crew, most of the work could be done in a couple of days. If a power washer could be hooked up to draw water from the pond, cleaning the walls and concrete floor would be relatively simple. Sonny Prather could sell him a generator to use until the county electrical authority ran lines from his house to provide power.

He had no idea about the state of the plumbing, assuming there was or had ever been any plumbing at all. As a city man, he had never concerned himself with septic tanks or wells. The Hovel had both. The well water in his house came from the aquifer that served the area and was soft, clean and sweet. Did the barn have a well? Or did it just pump water from the pond suitable for livestock but not for human consumption?

And how did one set up a new septic tank? Surely Seth could educate him.

He had been cutting the pasture on automatic pilot. Behind him the area he had finished wasn't as smooth or as weed-free as a golf course, but reseeded and fertilized in the spring, it would make fine grazing. He could hardly wait to show Barbara what he had accomplished.

There must be plans for the barn somewhere. Emma might know where they were located. If not, then surely there were such creatures as county planners and trustees who kept plans. He was a researcher. If they existed—and they must—he would locate them.

There were no windows set into the solid barn walls, and no doors across either end, although the hardware to hang them was there. It would probably have to be replaced as well. There seemed to be sufficient height to build a flight cage inside the building. Barbara would have to call the shots on the rest of the interior, depending on what she decided should be done with it. If she wanted it for her rehabilitators, or to bring in more animal foundlings, or as a large animal adjunct to her clinic, that would be her choice. If she didn't want to keep the place after Orville no longer strengthened his wings there, then he could rent it out as Emma and Seth had planned to do.

What if Emma didn't want to sell? Or if he couldn't afford it? She might not even want to lease it to him.

She had to. He was counting on it.

He wanted to give Barbara her flight cage for Christmas.

No, Orville needed it sooner. How soon should Orville start trying to fly? When could he be released? If they couldn't work out a proper place to build his strength and teach him to catch his prey on the wing again, Barbara would be forced either to send him to the Memphis zoo, or to the facility in Kentucky. Orville would be essentially gone for good, whatever happened to him. He must convince her that keeping Orville under their control until they released him was doable.

He turned away from barn and lake and set the Bush Hog to cut again.

He'd have to work out the details with Barbara. If this wasn't feasible, he'd do something else. Plan B was to enlarge Emma's cage at

The Hovel. Surely Orville wouldn't need all that room for his initial attempts at flight.

He cut his way past the barn to the back of the acres farthest from the road and soon settled into a routine. He would not have been able to cut the overgrown back acreage if Seth had not already cut it once. The heavy brush and most of the downed saplings had already been piled up, which would be perfect for the Guy Fawkes bonfire that he hoped to have. He had less than ten days to find out about permits and hire the volunteer fire brigade to keep the fire under control.

Today, he hoped merely to avoid bouncing over more obstacles.

He had not accurately calculated the length of time the cutting required, or how quickly driving the tractor exhausted him. He'd imagined he would feel no more tension than he would driving a car. His Triumph was a simple animal compared to this. He felt as though he was guiding the first lunar rover over the unknown surface on the moon.

His head and neck ached, his back muscles pulled. His bum leg felt hot and sore.

No matter. He'd finish the job, even if he wound up back in the hospital when it was done. He couldn't wait to show Barbara.

By the time he finished all but the area around the pond, a weak sun attempted to burn through the clouds. He slipped off his jacket and hung it over the back of the tractor seat. He was feeling confident. Who said farmers were born, not made? Simply a matter of embracing new skills. Old dogs—well, middle-aged dogs—could certainly learn new tricks. He felt as though he was really getting the hang of this country life.

He checked his watch. He'd been at this since about eight o'clock. Now it was close to noon. Seth had said he wouldn't be coming home from checking deer stands for a while, so he'd finish up, rinse the dirt off the tractor, park it back in its carport, knock on Emma's door and convince her to go down to the café for lunch with him.

Barbara closed the clinic at noon on Saturdays, perhaps she'd come along. Then he could drive her by the pasture and brag about his skill with a tractor.

He drove circumspectly alongside the pond by the edge of the lily pads, where the ground was dry enough to hold the tractor. He was creating an actual divide between water and land.

He remembered reading someplace that lilies were frequently planted in polluted water. The plants sucked up the pollution into their roots and recycled them. Cities planted water lilies in their septic lagoons to clean them. The water he could see in the center of the pond looked crystal clear. Probably an illusion, but it must be potable for livestock and wildlife. He watched as a giant snapping turtle surfaced and slid back under the water the moment it glimpsed him. It looked big enough to eat the Bush Hog in one gulp. A holdover from the dinosaurs. At least there were no alligators... none that Seth had mentioned anyway.

He remembered Emma telling him about the deer that took refuge in the old barn. On this cloudy day, they would no doubt be out foraging and would be invisible to all but the trained eye. Seth could spot them among the trees, but Stephen doubted he could. So far he had not even seen a squirrel. Hardly surprising given the noise he made. Plenty of time for raccoons and rabbits to race out of his way.

Slurp.

In an instant the whole equipage slid sideways.

He jammed on both brakes and locked up all four tires.

That stopped the forward momentum, but

the large rear tires continued their sideways slide, burying themselves in the mud along the edge of the pond.

The Bush Hog was lighter than the tractor. It didn't slide, and kept the tractor nearly upright. It had twisted on its hitch, however, and now stood at an acute angle to both tractor and water.

Stephen looked behind him. How could he back the tractor up without jackknifing the Bush Hog farther and tearing it off its hitch?

The obvious solution was to pull forward. The Bush Hog would straighten up and follow the tractor back to straight and level ground. Dry ground.

He leaned out the open door on the left side and peered down to see if forward movement was possible. Then he remembered Seth's comment about falling out. Doors came open. Or fools opened them and hung out of them. Precisely what Seth warned him not to do.

Nothing for it. He had to climb out and see firsthand. Before he got down, however, he had to shut down the tractor and engage all his brakes—however many there were. He thought he remembered. Wouldn't do to leave even one brake disengaged while he was playing in the mud.

And mud it would be. He pulled his folding hiking stick from the pocket of his windbreaker. Not enough room in the cab to fully extend the stick, so he slipped the loop over his wrist so he couldn't drop it in the mud or have it sucked out of his grip, held it outside the door and flicked it open.

He carefully stuck the tip down into the mud outside his door.

Oh, great. Just great. The good news was that the ferrule struck what felt like solid ground only a foot down in the mud. The bad news was that he was sitting in the cab of a giant tractor with its wheels stuck in a foot of mud. One foot between him and freedom.

Nothing for it but to climb down and leave the tractor unoccupied and driverless, while he floundered in the mud and tried not to slide under either the tractor or the Bush Hog and carve himself into small, bloody pieces on the blades.

Never mind getting it out of the mud. That came later. One of his professors used to say, "First, assess. Second, confess." He'd have to confess.

He would have to call Seth to rescue him. He would have preferred to be beaten with whips and chains.

He must not call Emma. She would run across the road, or what passed for running at her stage of pregnancy, and attempt to help.

He swung out of the cab, stood for a second on the step, shoved his stick as deep as he could, closed his eyes, took a deep breath and stepped down.

For an instant the tractor shuddered and seemed to settle closer toward him.

Strictly an illusion. Wasn't it?

He hated mud. Always had. When other children had made mud pies, he'd built sand castles. He told himself sand gave greater scope for architectural creativity in castles and forts than mud. Actually, he hated the way it squeezed between his fingers, and that it frequently stank. He was fully aware of both of those things now.

The rear tires—the big ones—were the only ones actually stuck in the mud, and only the left tire was sunk so deep that the hole it made had seeped full of water. The smaller front tires had been lifted clear like the front paws of a dog ready to jump on his master.

He held on to the front loader and sloshed his way around to the right side. At each step the mud tried unsuccessfully to pull his boot off his foot. By halfway around, he had worked out a method. First, plunge his stick into the mud. Second, pull his boot free of the mud. Third, step down into the mud and get stuck all over again. Stick, pull, repeat.

Breathe, if possible.

Though the right rear tire was not buried as deeply as the left, the moment he tried to rock it until it moved forward, it would bury itself hubcap-deep. He'd be on an even keel all right. He'd be stuck on both sides, not just one.

If he had a shovel and enough stamina, he might be able to dig himself out. Or if he could move some of those saplings to put under the tires, he might be able to use them as a kind of ramp.

Who was he kidding? They'd find him dead of a heart attack. He might be able to do it with Seth's help but not alone.

He sat on the tractor's step and pulled his cell phone out of his pocket.

CHAPTER FOURTEEN

"You did what?" Barbara asked.

"I was cutting Emma's pasture and got the tractor stuck in the mud. You have no idea how much damage making this phone call has done to my ego. I intend to go climb into a hole and not come out for the foreseeable future. Hey! Don't you dare laugh!"

"I'm not laughing. Really." She snickered. "All right, a tiny bit."

"Oh, heck, go right ahead and dissolve in spasms of glee! I deserve it. How do I get it out?"

"Have you called Seth or Emma?"

"No! I do not dare call Emma. Seth is out on patrol heaven knows where. The only good thing is that so far Emma has not come out on her porch and noticed there is a problem. I pray she won't."

"Describe the situation."

He gave her what he hoped were simple, cogent facts that did not adversely impact his manhood or make him look like a bigger idiot than he felt.

"Okay. I'm giving first shots to a Westie puppy, then we close for the weekend. I'll be there in twenty minutes."

"To do what?"

"Get you out, doofus."

BARBARA'S TRUCK PULLED into the pasture only ten minutes later.

"Don't you get stuck, too," Stephen said as he held her door open.

"This truck is equipped with four-wheel drive, heavy-duty transmission and winches front and back. There's fifty feet of heavy chain in reserve back in the truck bed. I have to haul trailers and drive through muck all the time." She reached up and touched his cheek with her index finger, then wiped it on his shirt front. "You have a long streak of mud down the side of your face. Not certain how you managed that, but it's there. You have some on your shirt, too, so there's no sense in getting myself dirty when you're already a mess." She sauntered over to the tractor.

Stephen noted that her rubber boots came higher than her knees, almost like fishing waders.

She frowned at the tractor, circled it, both Bush Hog and front loader, much more easily than Stephen had. When she came back to him, she said, "Didn't Seth warn you about the pond?"

"He did. I assumed—incorrectly, as it turned out—that so long as I stayed on the bank above the lily pads I was on safe ground." He knew he sounded pompous as he tried to snatch some iota of dignity.

"Ask *Emma* about where the mud ends," Barbara said. "When she came out here to explore, she only stuck her foot in the mud, not the whole tractor. Actually, this isn't too bad. I may not even need the chain. Have you tried driving it out?"

"Of course. While I waited for you. I stopped when I saw I was making it worse."

"Right. Let's get started. Go sit in my truck out of the way."

"But..."

"When was the last time you hauled a tractor out of the mud?"

"Never."

"I have never taught a college history class, either. How about we play to our strengths. If I need you, I'll holler."

"Be careful."

"Always."

He trudged over and perched sideways on the front seat of Barbara's truck with his feet in the mud. He watched her climb into the cab, leaving the left-hand door open as he had, and start the engine. She was going to try to rock it out of the mud. He'd tried. It didn't work.

What if *she* fell out and was pulled under the wheels or the Bush Hog? What if the tractor turned over? Why had he called *her* and not Seth? If he got her hurt, he might as well let that Bush Hog roll right over him, too. He'd lost one love. He couldn't bear to lose another. He ignored his choice of words.

He watched as the arms of the front loader lifted and stretched forward until the bucket between them moved up six or seven feet in the air. At its apex, she rotated the bucket until it faced straight down, curled over like a paw. She lowered it until its back rim dug into the mud.

Slowly she began to extend the arms forward like a child shoving away from the dining-room table. Against that much power, the tractor inched back.

Behind it, the Bush Hog continued to pivot. Barbara followed it as it turned.

She had to reposition the arms of the front

loader three times as it continued to inch the tractor back.

Then with a pop, the wheels rolled free of the mud onto relatively dry ground.

Brakes squealed. The tractor halted. The Bush Hog was now attached at an acute angle, narrowly avoiding jackknifing against the rear of the tractor. She raised the bucket once more so that it was out of the mud, then put the tractor in gear, steered it to the right of the rut in which it had been stuck and drove tractor and Bush Hog smoothly out of the mud and up the small incline onto solid ground.

She turned off the engine, climbed down from the cab and sauntered over to her truck where Stephen stood waiting. "Next problem?"

He grabbed her around the waist, swung her, then kissed her long and hard. She wrapped her arms around his neck and kissed him back just as hard.

When he finally released her, he said, "That's what I get for trying to impress you. My ego will never recover. By rights I ought to kill you and bury you in that old barn, so you can't snitch to anyone about your having to rescue me. I am usually the rescuer in my family."

She laughed up at him. "I'd come back to haunt you."

"That was fantastic. Thank you."

"Not my first rodeo, cowboy. I won't even give you a ballpark figure on how many pieces of equipment I've gotten stuck in the mud. After a while, you know what to do. You were right not to call Emma. Are you through cutting?"

"Except around the lake. I am not about to try that again today."

"Then drive on back across the road. I closed the clinic before I came, so you owe me lunch."

"Unlike you, I'm covered with mud. I can't take you to the café. Except for those pirate boots, you're still clean. I don't know how you managed it."

"I whacked off the tops of John's old fishing waders, so my boots come higher than yours. He had very small feet."

"I'll drive the tractor back under Seth's carport and give it a quick rinse. I could do with some lunch, as well, but not before a long hot shower and some clean clothes. Can you wait?"

"Just about. While you clean up, I'll go visit Emma. Maybe she'll join us for lunch." She held up her hands. "I promise I won't tell her about your getting stuck. You tell her. It's too good a story to keep to yourself."

Stephen parked the tractor, rinsed it off with Seth's garden hose, carried his jacket and his hiking cane, and called from the back steps to Emma's new kitchen. "Emma? Barbara? I'm too dirty to come in."

Emma opened the door. She had on bunny slippers and a maroon maternity warm-up suit stretched tight across her belly. "In this house, we're used to mud."

"Not like this. This is glue mixed with plaster of paris. How about a late lunch in town at the café? I'm driving and buying."

"You take Barbara. Seth should be home soon to watch football. I want a good long nap."

Barbara appeared behind her shoulder. "Are you sure?"

"A shower and clean dry clothes," he said, "and I'll be good to go." His leg was killing him. He needed to soak it and probably wrap his knee.

"I'll walk back over here when I'm ready. Okay?" He looked at Emma uneasily to see whether she had any inkling about his debacle. Her expression didn't give anything away.

He turned and concentrated on walking back across to his front porch without limping. Hurt like hell, but he managed.

After a long hot shower, he sank onto his sofa and stretched his leg in front of him. Stomping around in the mud was tough on muscles and bones. He'd take five minutes rest before we went back to Emma's.

He hoped they would not gossip about what he'd done.

Both Emma and Barbara seemed completely innocent, but with women you never knew. If Barbara kept his secret, she was even more remarkable than he already considered her.

This was the second time he'd gotten himself involved with an amazing woman. Barbara seemed so different from Nina but both were warm, honorable, caring.

Also hard-headed, opinionated, stubborn, independent to a fault. Barbara was probably also capable of driving him as nuts as Nina could when he pushed her too hard in the direction he felt was best. Nina had never let him get away with that. Pretty good bet Barbara wouldn't, either.

He'd fallen in love with Nina quickly, although he hadn't realized at the time that's what was happening. Surely, he couldn't be falling in love with Barbara.

CHAPTER FIFTEEN

Since Emma didn't want to join them for lunch, Barbara and Stephen drove to the café in Stephen's truck. The remaining diners turned to stare when the two of them walked in together and took a table at the back of the restaurant. Stephen probably thought it was because of his cane. Barbara knew better. It was because Stephen was a relative stranger and with her.

"Hey, y'all," Velma said. "We got turnip greens today and purple hull peas and pot roast."

"Works for me," Stephen said.

Barbara nodded. Outside, the wind had shifted to the northwest to bring gray clouds and a threat of rain. As much as Barbara appreciated rain, it meant mud in all the pastures and the barnyards. It could have turned the pond into such a quagmire that even she couldn't have maneuvered Seth's tractor away from it. *Poor Stephen*, she thought. *He would have hated explaining that to Seth.*

"I'm driving to Memphis for a meeting with my dean in the next couple of weeks," Stephen said and squeezed lemon into his sweet iced tea. "He wants a progress report on my new textbook."

"He could get that over the telephone."

"He also wants to see for himself that my physical condition is improving. Which it is. I hardly use my cane at all any longer."

"You had your stick today. ESP?"

"More like experience. My leg has fooled me before. I am considering lying like a rug about the progress of the book. Unfortunately, the dean knows me too well. I'll reassure him, after which I'm having lunch with my daughters. I am not looking forward to it."

"Why not? You haven't seen them since you moved up here."

"Anne and I talk on the phone most nights, and she reports to Elaine. Better for all of us. You'll like my Anne. She works at one of the local horse barns outside of Memphis."

Barbara suspected he hadn't mentioned anything about her liking Elaine because he doubted she would.

As a shadow fell across their table, Barbara looked up to see Seth and his partner, Earl, by their table.

"Hey, folks. May we join you? Stephen, I don't think you've met my partner, Earl Maxwell." The men shook hands and sat in the other two seats at the table.

Velma made iced tea magically appear at both their places as she asked, "Special?" Both men nodded and off she went.

"How'd the cutting go?" Seth asked Stephen. Barbara caught his eye and raised her eyebrows in an up-to-you expression. Stephen took a hefty swig of iced tea, squared his shoulders and launched into the story of the stuck tractor. "Thanks to Barbara, I didn't cause any damage that couldn't be remedied with the garden hose."

By the time he finished, both men were chuckling. "Both of us have been stuck out there at least once," Earl said. "The pond bank moves depending on whether we're talking hot, dry weather in the summer or cold, damp weather in the rest of the year. The lily pads grow and shrink with the bank. What'd you think about the barn?"

"Doable. The more I think about it, the more I think fresh trusses in the ceiling and fresh metal on the roof, plus a good cleaning should be all that's needed initially."

"I spoke to the construction guys that did

the work on our house," Seth said. "They're interested in rehabbing the space at a reasonable cost." He pulled a card from his shirt pocket and handed it to Stephen. "That's the foreman's cell-phone number. I don't think they have a landline. They move around a lot. I asked Emma about the land. She doesn't want to sell, even though she doesn't want to use it herself at the moment. I think she might be open to a long-term lease, deducting the money you spend in rehabbing the place from the rent."

"Win-win. Call me this evening when and if Emma feels like discussing it. I'll walk over."

BARBARA LEANED OUT of the way as Velma set their plates in front of them. The three men were avoiding one another's eyes. Like little boys, they were up to something. She had a suspicion that whatever it was, she wouldn't like it. She also suspected that Stephen was the ringleader of whatever scheme they were hatching. "What are we talking about here?" She caught another conspiratorial glance among the three men. "Okay, Stephen, give."

"Never you mind," he said. "I'll tell you later after I've spoken to Emma."

She narrowed her eyes. "Just so you know, I hate secrets."

"How do you deal with Christmas?"

"I was one of those children who hunted for gifts ahead of time. I never found them. My mother took them all to her best friend's house and kept me away from there until Christmas morning. All the same…"

"We'll talk tomorrow."

"Yes, we will." Barbara glanced at her watch. "Oh, I forgot to tell you. I've got those vets I mentioned coming this afternoon to discuss joining the practice. You mind driving me back to the clinic? I figured it would be easier to have them drive in on the weekend after we close."

"Since it's either that or make you walk ten miles, I suppose I'd better."

"I knew I should have brought my own truck," she said. She reached for her check, but Stephen put his hand over hers. "I invited you, remember? My treat."

"DR. PETERSON, WELCOME. I'm Barbara Carew." *Right on time*, Barbara thought. She'd barely beaten him to the clinic.

"Vincent Peterson, ma'am, but everybody

calls me Vince." The young man brushed a wayward shock of light brown hair off his forehead. "I'm still not used to being called Doctor. I shouldn't admit that."

"I felt the same way. Still do, some days."

He wasn't handsome exactly. When he smiled the left side of his mouth quirked as though at some point the nerves might have been damaged. It gave him an almost piratical aspect, as though he might shout, "Ha-a-ar, me hearties," at any moment. He was not quite as tall as Stephen, but with muscles that revealed the excellent upper-body strength of a young man who worked hard and worked out, as well. He could probably flip a heifer without much assistance from the farmer. His eyes were hazel and already crinkled at the corners from spending hours in the sun.

Barbara could feel the tingle of neighboring feminine antennae tuning into him. His application said he was single and would be twenty-eight on his next birthday. She could think of several young ladies who would be interested in finding out whether he was good husband material. Of course, there might already be a love interest waiting in the wings for him to pass his tests and get a job.

First impression? She liked him. "Tell me about yourself," she said.

"My family's been farmers outside Mc-Comb, Mississippi, long as I can remember. Naturally, I went to Mississippi State. It's hard to get a place at their vet school in Starkville, but I had the grades and the letters of recommendation. I've always known I wanted to be a veterinarian. I guess I like animals better than people. Humans spend a lot of time screwing up animals' lives. I like unscrewing them when I can." He took a breath, as though he had delivered a short form of his résumé.

"So, at some point you might go home and take over the farm?"

He laughed. "My two older brothers got that locked up. No'm, I want a place to make a career and settle down where my family's not breathing down my neck and second-guessing me about trimming a goat's hooves. Down home, I'll always be the Peterson boys' little brother."

Barbara nodded. Good. She did not need to train a young vet who would rush off to become a gentleman farmer when Daddy crooked his little finger. "You do know I am looking for somebody who can eventually become a partner?"

"Yes, ma'am. That's what I'm looking for, too."

"Mississippi State has a great vet school."

"Really good with large animals."

"Is that what you prefer?"

"If it needs treatment and it's anything other than human, I want to help."

Talks a good game, but we'll see. "You know this is a mixed practice. When the clinic is open, we have mostly dogs and cats in the office, but not necessarily.

"We're open on Saturday mornings. Mostly for emergencies. You missed the alpaca that came in first thing this morning with an abscessed tooth I had to pull and the young stallion that had to be castrated. One thing about this practice—you're never bored."

"That sounds great, long as I can read up on animals I'm not familiar with."

"We do a good deal of wild-animal rehabilitation. That is not actually part of the job description, but I don't know a single vet that won't help the rehabilitators when needed. Our group has raised everything from skunks to turkey buzzards to Burmese pythons. Those we relocate to zoos or reptile conservation places. We never release them."

"Yeah. I know about pythons."

"At first, I'll try to keep you mostly here in the office until you learn the ropes, unless I need you in the field with me. You look as if you can pull a calf stuck in the birth canal."

"Yes, ma'am, and I am real good at putting back prolapsed uteruses." He brushed his hair off his forehead again.

"How's your surgery?"

"I guess you read my letters of recommendation. Best in my class. Not as good as you, I'm sure, but..."

Barbara rescued him. "I've got a few years experience on you, right? I'll try to go easy on you at first, but I know you interns at Mississippi State get a bunch of hands-on experience."

"I've been helping one of our local vets since I was in high school, and I spent some time breaking horses on a ranch up in Wyoming. Wrangled cattle, too. I don't mind being on my own, though I'd like to be able to call you for help or ask your advice if I need it."

She nodded. "When I'm here, I am always available. Initially, I'll try to take you with me to meet the clients and give me a hand. But that depends on how much time we can snitch together out of the office. It's hard to tell right now. Things slow down for Thanksgiving and Christmas—except when they don't. You okay with that?"

"Yes, ma'am."

"We're all on first-name basis here. Call me Barbara."

"Yes, ma—uh, Barbara."

"This has been a one-vet clinic for quite a while. For every quiet day, we have a dozen that are flat-out crazy. You'll go home worn out, and just when you get comfortable, you'll get a call out on the other side of the county."

Barbara's intercom buzzed. "Excuse me." She stepped out in the hall to listen. When she came back in, she said, "You're about to show me how great you are with a prolapsed uterus. You game?"

"Yes, ma'am!"

"Then mount up, cowboy, and let's go do it."

Her cell rang as she led Vince down the hall to the back door. Mary Frances had left her a voice message. Nuts. Probably another emergency. She picked up to hear Mary Frances's message.

"That lady vet called to cancel her appointment this afternoon. Said she took a job with a dog and cat practice."

Then let's hope this one works out.

BARBARA SETTLED THE animals at the clinic for the night, evaded a half-hearted attack by Mabel the goose, delivered two thawed mice to Orville, who screamed his displeasure when they didn't run from him. She fed and hayed the animals in the barn before she walked back to her apartment.

She poured herself a glass of white wine, carved a slice of extra sharp cheddar cheese to nibble with the wine, and sank onto the couch and called Stephen.

"Guess what?" she said a little breathlessly. "I hired another vet this afternoon."

"Just like that?"

She sipped her wine, then took a hefty swig. She deserved it. "The woman I was supposed to interview didn't come. She took a dog-and-cat job in south Mississippi."

"You check out his credentials?"

"Yes, Stephen." She sighed, exasperated. "I did that a week ago. The other one obviously didn't want to be attached to a mixed practice out in the boonies. The new hire is from Mississippi. Farm background. After the way he pushed a uterus back into a cow this afternoon, I am definitely hoping he'll stick around. Cute, too."

"Then send him packing! I refuse to worry about your messing about with a young, cute vet who is a dab hand with uteruses, even bovine oncs."

She laughed. "He's definitely cute. At this point it's a provisional appointment, but he is definitely hired unless he screws up big time."

"Is he staying with you?"

"Of course not. I was going to put him up at Sonny's B and B in Williamston, but he chose to drive home to Mississippi tonight."

"Long drive."

"He's young. He can handle it. He's due back a week from Monday. He has things to finish at home. That means he won't be available at the clinic on Friday when I'm at the fair, but it can't be helped. Plus, I'd already planned to close. After you dropped me off, did you get your walking in for the day?"

She heard his hesitation.

"I do have a book to write."

"So you're saying you worked on your book?"

"In a manner of speaking. Actually, I went back and walked the pasture to review my handiwork and look at the mess I made at the pond. Not too bad, actually. Something needs to be done about it, however, before something or someone rolls into the pond and drowns. Gravel or sand around the edges, perhaps."

"Anything you spread will just slide off the bank and under the water. The only thing that might help is to carve the edges with the front loader from Seth's tractor."

"Someone else can do that, thank you."

"What are you and Seth not telling me?"

"How would you like your very own flight cage for Orville?"

"What? Where?'

"Inside Seth's old barn. Seth's construction foreman met me there late this afternoon while you were messing about with the rear end of a cow. He says he and his crew can be finished before Thanksgiving."

"Orville needs to try his wings in the next few weeks chasing live prey. When he can handle that, we can release him. Stephen, I can't afford the cost of building a flight cage, even if I wanted one two miles from the clinic. This is the first bird I've ever had that needed this sort of rehabbing. Not cost-effective when there are other alternatives, even if I'm not fond of them."

"My bird, my barn, my cage, my money. Seriously, Barbara, the area has to be cleaned out anyway. These guys are out of a job for the moment, so they are giving me a good price. I hoped to have it done by November fifth, but the foreman says that's too little time."

"Why November fifth?"

"That's when I am burning the brush pile. Didn't I mention that?"

Half an hour later, Seth came in to Stephen's living room. He brought back a couple of beers from Stephen's refrigerator with casual familiarity. He handed one to Stephen, sat in one of the wing chairs in front of Stephen's open fire, popped the top off his bottle of beer and let his shoulders relax. He propped his stocking feet on the footstool in front of the chair and drank deeply. "This is turning into a tradition—my coming over after work for a beer."

"I enjoy your company. Do you have any updates on my November-the-fifth bonfire permit?"

"Made a couple of calls this afternoon after the game. I have good news and bad news. You can have your burn permit, but only if you burn during daylight hours."

Stephen sat up straight. "That's ridiculous. What difference does it make? Even if I light it at noon, there's enough wood there to keep it smoldering after dark."

"Mostly ashes by then. Less possibility that it could get out of control."

Stephen shoved his hand through his hair in exasperation. "A Guy Fawkes bonfire is traditionally held at night. I was planning to invite you, Emma and Barbara over for steaks while we watch. I'm sorry, Seth, that makes no sense at all."

"Don't shoot the messenger. The fire departments are becoming sticklers about any sort of open fire after the last couple of summers we've had. Frankly, if I were you, I'd forget the whole thing, bring in a construction Dumpster and let the crew you hire to clear the barn clear the brush, as well."

"This is frustrating," Stephen said. "I wanted to burn the brush piles to clear some land to build Barbara a flight cage. Orville needs room to exercise his wings before we release him. I don't want to have to move him someplace else that has the right cage."

Seth leaned back and finished his beer. "Don't forget there is already a good-size cage right outside The Hovel. Adding on to Emma's existing structure is a better option. Then you'd be able to watch Orville strengthen his wings from your living room window. Think about it, Stephen—you and Barbara could watch him together."

"I assumed Emma would prefer to have such a large cage built away from The Hovel. It is, after all, rental property."

"Which you are renting. Do you care if the flight cage is built beside your house?"

"Not at all."

Seth raised his hands. "Then go for it. Get your crew to extend Emma's cage. They can do it in a day. It'll be cheaper, faster and let you watch Orville's progress."

Stephen hated to admit it, but Seth made sense. "I'll call your contractor and see if he can do it right away at a reasonable price." He tried to keep the disappointment out of his voice. He'd had visions of what the old barn might look like not only with the flight cage, but also as space for the rehabilitators. Seth was right. He was thinking of it as a gift from Stephen to Barbara. He kept trying to impress her and falling flat.

So, no Guy Fawkes bonfire. At least not this year. To a history professor, Guy Fawkes was an excuse for a party. Every time Stephen thought he had this country life figured out, he ran into another way in which things were radically different. College professor meets Southern bureaucracy. Bureaucracy almost always won.

If he did extend Emma's cage, he and Barbara could move Orville down from the clinic soon. Barbara could join him after work to check his progress. Together they'd watch Orville toughen up, prove that he was ready to be released. Sooner or later he would fly.

Having Orville with him meant Barbara would visit often. A definite positive.

CHAPTER SIXTEEN

"This is a barbaric time of day to be up and about on a Friday morning," Stephen grumbled as he climbed into Barbara's van. The sun was inching above the horizon as if it wanted a few more minutes before it had to climb out of bed. "Here. Milk and two sweeteners, right?" He handed her a tall insulated plastic mug.

"Stephen, you angel," Barbara said, then blew through the hole in the lid of the mug and sipped cautiously. "You can always go back to bed, you know. You *volunteered* to go to the fair with me this week. I warned you I need to be there by seven."

"I get to spend the day with you. That's worth getting up at the crack of dawn."

"And a beautiful morning it looks to be. Cool enough for comfort. Last year it was close to a hundred and rainy most of the week."

"More mud. After the tractor incident, I am

off mud for the duration. So, what happens once we get to the fairgrounds?"

"I check in at the office in the big stock barn, pick up any requests for my services, take care of whatever animal problems have arisen since yesterday evening when my colleague left, then we can see the fair. Unless I am called about another animal in distress. The office has loudspeakers in all the barns to make announcements, so I'll be able to hear a page even if we're on the midway. Somewhere along the way, we have breakfast. As thoughtful as this coffee is, it won't hold us until lunch."

"What do I do while you are doctoring? I doubt I'll be much help."

"You may be surprised. Check out the animals, watch the livestock judging in the arena, talk to the farmers and the 4-H kids who are showing. I am especially fond of pigs and the people who raise them."

"Wake me when we get there," Stephen said, then crossed his arms and promptly fell asleep. Barbara glanced over at him. She had already grown fond of him, more than fond. Ridiculous. She hadn't been interested in a man since John died. She'd tried dating a couple of times, but the encounters had always ended in disaster or boredom. They were always annoyed when they tried to kiss her good-night and she turned away.

She felt differently about Stephen's kisses. They made her long for more.

She wanted to feel his arms around her, to be held until she fell asleep with her head on his shoulder and wake up to his smile.

How long would he be content to spend time with her? Take things slow? He was used to a very different sort of people. She suspected his social group were casual about relationships. She couldn't ever be casual when it came to her heart. That's why she was still alone. Maybe that's why he was, too.

They were both used to being in charge.

Stephen kept making choices that he expected her to applaud. Barbara couldn't have cared less that they were good choices that she might have made herself—given the opportunity. He was desperately trying to be helpful. She had not yet come out and told him to "back off." He didn't deserve to have his feelings hurt because he was trying to be kind. She already cared about him too much to want to hurt him.

She'd been on her own, built her own business, raised two children, paid her bills, kept up with her medical knowledge and skills. She'd been making her own decisions and doing a good job of it. Suggestions she could tolerate from him and even appreciate. Directions—no. She might be oversensitive, but that was tough.

Meanwhile I may wreck the van because I am not paying attention to my driving.

What on earth was she thinking? It was seven fifteen on Friday morning and they were on their way to a giant stock barn chock-full of cows and hogs and sheep and goats and rabbits and guinea pigs...

She glanced over at him. His head was resting against the seat back. His arms were still folded neatly across his chest. He didn't snore and his mouth stayed closed. That was a plus. His dark lashes—longer than any man deserved—curled on his cheek. The wrinkles at the corners of his eyes gave his face character—not that it needed any more.

Her mother had told her years ago that the only human beings who looked attractive while they slept were under six years old. Stephen proved her wrong. He wasn't conventionally handsome, with his slightly sharp nose and too strong chin, but it was a good face. She smiled over at him. Slightly too strong was an understatement. She'd bet his students tried to keep on his good side. He'd be a champion glarer when provoked by a lazy student.

Not a morning person, obviously, but he'd gotten up early enough to brew coffee and fix hers the way she liked it. He'd actually taken the time to discover how she drank it. Grumpy but thoughtful. Not a bad combination at 7:00 a.m.

They drove through Williamston and across the bridge over the Tennessee River tributary that divided the small town. To the north perched the town itself, with its courthouse in the square surrounded on four sides by shops built circa 1900. She considered stopping in at the café to pick up doughnuts but didn't want to disturb Stephen. Plenty of pickings at the fairgrounds that would be much more appetizing and damaging to her waistline.

South of the bridge and through what passed for suburbia in Williamston was the park where the fair set up for ten days each fall. The rest of the year it was home to soccer fields and playgrounds for children, cattle auctions, antique bazaars, car and boat shows—whatever could fit the grounds or the permanent buildings beside the traveling midway set up for the fair. Past those barns sat a large greenhouse attached to one small exhibit hall where quilts, pickles and jams, and prize plants were exhibited for ribbons and bragging rights.

The midway brought with it rides like the Tilt-A-Whirl and the bumper cars, as well as games like ring toss and the shooting alley. There was even a tunnel of love on an elevated platform filled with water from a nearby hose.

At the very back of the midway stood the roller coaster and the Ferris wheel. Because they traveled with the carnival and were set up and taken down at each new location, both were grand old classics. The coaster didn't turn itself inside out and upside down out like those at the permanent amusement parks. The Ferris wheel did not have a second wheel on top that fell precipitously as it swapped places with its twin.

Not yet open for business, the two rides looked as formidable as dozing T. rexes hungering for prey. Bad analogy, Barbara thought. She closed her eyes for a second and wondered why she had agreed to swap a ride on the wheel for Stephen's ride on the coaster. She really wanted to take a turn on the lovingly restored Parker carousel, which was housed in its own permanent building in the park. She'd fallen in love with horses when her grandfather had held her on a white horse with a pink saddle at the antique carousel in Memphis when she was no more than three. Maybe she could convince Stephen to avoid both wheel and coaster in favor of the gentler wooden equines.

She rolled up to the front gate of the fairgrounds, where a man in a green uniform with Midway Security on the pocket held up a hand to stop her, then came over to the window of her vet van.

"Morning, Dr. Carew. You on call today?"

She smiled and nodded. "Friday is always my day, Bobby Joe."

"Who's Sleeping Beauty?" he whispered as Stephen opened his eyes, yawned and stretched.

"My vet tech."

"Okay. Here's some passes. Y'all can ride all day for free."

"Why, thank you." She felt her stomach lurch. That's all she needed. Ride all day for free. Yikes.

"County don't pay none of you vets for this, ma'am. Passes is all we can do. Put this sign on your dashboard, so's you don't get a ticket. We saved all you vets the best parking place on the grounds down back of the stock barn, where the office is. We been chasing folks off that space all week." He pointed to his right. "Go down yonder and drive all the way around on the gravel drive past the rides and the midway."

"Same as usual."

"Oh, you know where you're going, ma'am. We gave you two parking spaces in case you brought a trailer with you. Tacked a sign up says Reserved, DVM."

"You think most people know what a DVM is?"

"Everybody down that end owns stock. They know." He looked past her shoulder. "Uh-oh, we've got us a little traffic jam behind you. Have a nice day, Doc." He waved her through.

The road led around the perimeter of the midway, the food tents and the rides. The music of a dozen competing sound systems pumped out songs. The barkers limbered up their voices to entice the early arrivals. Through the open windows of Barbara's van, she smelled beignets, doughnuts and hot grease.

"Here we go," Barbara said and pulled into her parking spot, mercifully not yet purloined by a stockman looking to unload his cattle close to the judging arena.

"Ah, the heady smell of manure in the morning," Stephen said as he joined her beside the arena. The stands were already filling with parents ready to cheer on their children and the animals they had raised, while farmers and ranchers checked out their competition.

"I'll run into the office to see if I've had any calls," Barbara said.

WHILE HE WAITED for Barbara, Stephen checked out the spectators. Both sexes and all ages wore much the same costume. Faded jeans, cowboy shirts that always closed with snaps instead of buttons so that they could be ripped open fast in the event of an accident, dusty boots and battered, sweat-darkened Stetson hats. If Stephen had learned anything from his years as a horse-show father, it was that new, expensive and too neat spelled amateur.

Barbara tapped him on the shoulder. "I've got a quarter-horse mare with a capped hock down there in the end stall, and an Angora goat in the next barn over that lost an altercation with a concrete pillar and tore a horn. Then we're free to go find breakfast."

"Good. I'm starving."

But his hopes of eating soon dimmed. Stephen watched Barbara calm the lanky teenage girl who sobbed as she clung to the neck of her bulky quarter-horse mare.

"We're supposed to be in the barrel-racing at two this afternoon," the girl wailed. "Ladybug and me've been training all year. I'm up for the state championship."

"What happened?"

"She must've bumped the side of the trailer on the way over here. She was fine when we left home."

"If we can help it, I don't want to give her any drugs that will disqualify her. Can't promise anything, Jean Anne, but here's what you do. Take Ladybug down to the wash rack and run the hose on that hock for at least thirty minutes, rub in some liniment, give her some rest, then in a couple of hours do it again. Walk her between. She's not a bit lame, and there's no heat. With luck the swelling will be down by noon. Give me a call and let me know. She ought to be okay to race unless she does go lame or the hock swells up more."

"Oh, thank you, Dr. Barbara!" Jean Anne flung her arms around Barbara's neck.

Stephen followed Barbara to the next barn, where a long-haired and beautifully groomed

Angora goat dripped blood from the base of his left horn. His owner met Barbara at his stall.

"I know I can't show him today with this, but I don't want to dehorn him right now, either."

"Horn's not torn completely. I can stop the bleeding, wrap it, give him antibiotics. He should be good to go until you get home to your own vet."

"Do it."

She did.

She slipped her hand under Stephen's arm. "Breakfast?"

"You got it." They meandered down the aisle toward the open side facing the parking lot and the midway.

As they strolled toward the exits, someone shouted from one aisle over. A moment later came a bawl that sounded more like a scream.

"That's a cow!" Barbara said. "What's happening back there?"

"It sounds more like a cavalry charge," Stephen shouted over the increasing din.

A dozen people, male and female, erupted around the corner and ran toward them. An older man shouted, "Out of the way! He's loose!"

Air horns blared from the rafters. "Loose animal! Loose animal!" a voice yelled from the loudspeakers.

"Not cavalry," Stephen whispered. "Pamplona! Barbara, come on!" He wrapped his arms around her and yanked her into an empty stall as a black bull galloped down the aisle toward them, eyes rolling, veering from side to side, bumping into stalls, slipping on the dirt footing. Stephen held the stall door shut as the bull thundered by.

"Let me go!" Barbara reached for the door. "He's terrified."

"You can't stop him. He'll kill you."

"If he gets loose on the midway, they'll shoot him." She yanked the stall gate open.

Stephen attempted to drag her back, but she shook her arm free.

Some brave soul pulled his dually truck across the end of the aisle to block it so the bull couldn't escape that way. At the other end another truck slid into place to block that route as well. The bull was effectively trapped in the aisle unless he decided to jump over a truck that was marginally larger than he was. He must have decided he'd never make it. He lowered his head, snorted, pawed and shook his heavy shoulders in frustration.

A short, burly man climbed out of the truck's passenger seat and sauntered around to face the bull with nothing in his hands but a rope.

"Get back in here, Barbara," Stephen snapped.

"It's okay. That's Joe Nightingale. It's his bull. He knows what he's doing."

People peeked out from the stalls and from behind the hay bales, where they had taken cover. Suddenly, the barn went quiet.

"Now, Montague, old son, I know you're scared. Ain't nobody gonna hurt you." Nightingale looked over the bull's shoulder and spotted Barbara. "Ain't that right, Doc? Why this ol' boy don't want nothing but his own pasture and his own ladies. You got any tranquilizer, Doc? Ketamine, maybe?" Same quiet, conversational tone.

Montague watched Nightingale avidly, but he no longer snorted or pawed.

"How much does he weigh?"

"More'n a ton, Doc."

"Ketamine takes too long. Give me a minute. I have some new stuff. Won't knock him out but should calm him down fast. Have to be IM, in the muscle. I am not about to try to find a vein."

"Understood."

BARBARA STEPPED BACK into the stall and tried not to be distracted by Stephen's presence. She opened her case, hunted among her medicine vials, found the one she wanted, filled a syringe and smiled up at Stephen. "I am not planning to get hurt, Stephen. There's an open stall right beside the bull's rump. I'll duck in there after I inject him."

"What if he runs in after you? I have seen bullfights, Barbara. You are no torero." He held out a hand. "I'll do it."

"Where's your cape, matador? I know where to jab and how hard. They don't call it cowhide for nothing. I don't have a death wish, I promise."

"I could stop you." He stepped in front of the open stall door.

"Don't even try it. It is my job, Stephen, and I will do it without interference, well meant though it may be. Just wish me luck. This will be fine. I've treated Montague before. He's generally a sweetie. He's het up because he's away from home. I wonder how he got loose. Maybe there's a cow in season he can smell."

"Doc?"

"Coming, Joe."

"I got a rope through his nose ring. I can't hang on to him if he freaks out, but it'll keep his attention some. He'll try to pull back, not stomp me."

"Won't that ring in his nose hurt?" said a woman from a safe vantage point at the corner.

"No more than piercing your earlobes," Barbara said, pointing to the giant hoops that stretched the lobes of the woman's ears.

"Gets his attention is all," said Joe.

"I'm going to saunter down behind his rump," Barbara said. "Little afternoon stroll."

Several of the spectators tittered.

"After I pop him, he may go nuts, or he may just stand there and doze. Never know with a bull."

"Barbara, you must not do this," Stephen said.

"No choice." She touched his cheek. "It's why they pay me the big bucks."

As with so many possible disasters, this one was a nonevent.

When Barbara shot the syringe of tranquilizer through the ridge of muscle beside Montague's tail, he snorted as though he'd been bitten by a greenfly, swung his head far enough to feel the tug of the rope, then watched Barbara slide back into the safety of the stall where Stephen waited. The bull stood quietly in the aisle, a little bemused, but no longer freaking out.

"I'm gonna walk him back down to his stall," Joe said. "Doc, I'll be right back soon as he's secure. Don't want him to fall asleep in the aisle. That'd be a real hazard to navigation."

The crowd ducked smartly out of Montague's way as he walked by with Joe on the end of a slack rope.

Barbara waved to Joe. A moment later her legs gave way. Stephen caught her and sat her down on a bale of hay in the aisle outside the stall.

"Oh, boy, I don't ever want to do that again," she said.

"Don't worry. You won't get the chance. If you ever try, I swear I'll chain you to the wall. Woman, what were you thinking?"

"That I had a job to do! It was not a time for a committee meeting with you or anybody else!" She took a deep breath and tried to calm down. "It wasn't that dangerous, Stephen. I know Montague. He's a pussycat generally. He got scared, and bulls don't have much impulse control."

"Oh, really. I hadn't noticed. Much good I was."

"It was not your decision or your job." She touched his cheek. "You were here ready to snatch me away from the dragon."

"You're the one with the shining armor. Seems you get to do all the rescuing, first with the tractor…"

"Stephen, you are in *my* world at the moment. You think I could stand up in a lecture hall and stare down fifty bored students?"

"Not even the worst of my students has ever tried to drive a horn through my heart. Ah, here's your friend Mr. Nightingale."

"Hey, Joe," Barbara said. She didn't try to stand. "How on earth did he get loose?"

"Got a new groom don't know how to tie a decent knot. Montague was tethered on the line when some fool popped one of those cherry bombs under his belly. If I find out who did it, I'm gonna feed him to Montague for supper. Thought it was funny." He grimaced. "He better be long gone. I'll funny *him* if I catch him. Montague yanked on his rope, the knot came loose and off he went. He was just trying to get away from the noise, but bulls don't generally stop once they get going."

"Could have been bad if he'd gotten out of the barn—bull versus midway."

"My groom did have sense enough to pull

my truck across the exit, so maybe I won't fire his ass." He sat on the hay bale beside Barbara. "What I ought to do is exile him to the Boy Scouts 'til he learns to tie a knot. Got to tell you, Doc, I have not been that scared since Afghanistan, and I *know* that bull's not mean. I don't know what you're gonna charge me, Doc, but it darned well ain't enough." He sauntered back in the direction of his stalls.

Barbara held out a hand to Stephen. He pulled her up and into his arms, where she rested her head against his shoulder. She whispered, "I'm tired. I'm hungry. And after this, riding the Ferris wheel will be a piece of cake."

Barbara managed to endure the Ferris wheel, as Stephen carefully steadied the gondola, even when they stopped at the top of the arc. She kept her hand under his elbow and clung to his side at first, but once she felt more comfortable, and trusted him not to play any stupid tricks, she opened her eyes and looked around. "It really is beautiful from up here."

"Why do you think most people ride Ferris wheels? Not simply to scare their girlfriends, although that's a considerable part of the appeal."

"I'll still be glad to get down someplace that doesn't go up and down in circles."

"Want to ride it again?"

"No! I've paid off my bet, now you have to pay off yours. Look, Stephen, there's the carousel down there. Can we ride the carousel? I know it's not part of the bet."

"You ride as much as you like after the roller coaster. Unless, you'd rather swap? The carousel in place of the roller coaster?"

"Good try, Stephen. Pay up."

The roller coaster proved more problematic. As the car slid into the landing at the end of the ride, Barbara saw that Stephen had turned an interesting shade of puce. "Are you going to throw up?" she whispered as he clambered out of the car.

"I need a soda to settle my stomach or I might. Why did I let you talk me into that?"

"Because you are a brave soul, and you promised. Let's do something quiet. How about the bumper cars?"

"That's your idea of quiet?"

"Oh, I didn't think—your leg, I mean."

"Do I get flashbacks? No. Actually, I would enjoy a ride where I can kick your beautiful rear end."

"Them's fightin' words! Come on." She grabbed his hand and hurried him to the bumper car box office.

HE HAD BROUGHT his aluminum cane with him in case, then left it in Barbara's van, the length of the midway away from the rides. Purely for emergencies. His leg would ache tonight, but he was determined to go without the cane in public. Now, he realized that he wasn't limping. Not the world's smoothest walk, but balanced. He had been determined to keep up with Barbara all day, even if it killed him.

It wasn't killing him. Maybe his body didn't need the cane as much as his head did. She was having such a good time that he discovered he was having fun watching her.

He did kick her beautiful rear end on the bumpers. If there was one thing he could do, it was to drive a car, even a small electric one specifically designed to bash the competition.

As they went down the stairs after the ride, Stephen said, "Okay, let's ride the carousel. Then, isn't it time for some fried butter?"

He watched Barbara clamber onto a white carousel horse and ride with as much joy as if it was a real, live unicorn. He couldn't remember when he had experienced joy. It had slipped away at the funeral home or in the operating room or rehab. Now he'd found it again in Barbara's laughter. He wasn't about to lose it. He knew how easy it was to lose someone you loved without warning.

Since neither could actually stomach the idea of fried butter, they munched their way through fried chicken, corn on the cob and funnel cakes at one of the picnic tables under the trees.

"I hope you are driving us home," Stephen said. "I might fall asleep at the wheel. I could use a nap."

"Me, too."

After lunch, they spread their windbreakers on the cool autumn grass, and Stephen stretched out with his head in Barbara's lap.

"Glad you came?" Barbara sked.

"I would go to the Arctic Circle with you."

"No, you wouldn't. I wouldn't be there."

He slipped his hand behind her head and pulled her down so that he could kiss her.

"Stephen, people will see."

"Who cares?"

"True." She bent to return his kiss, and a very nice kiss it was, too. But chaste. Well, relatively chaste. She had a reputation to maintain in Williamston, even if he didn't.

"Everyone in town must know by now that you and I are an item."

"We are? Nobody told me." She stared

around to see if they were being watched. "You certainly didn't mention it. I'm not thrilled to be stared at and snickered over."

He sat up and swung around to face her. "Who cares what they think? Come on. If I don't move, I'll wake up next Tuesday. I am going to win you a teddy bear."

"Those games are rigged." She stalked away from him. "Don't waste your money."

"Watch and see."

Thirty minutes later they staggered to Barbara's SUV carrying a giant stuffed panda, a giant stuffed grizzly and a giant stuffed raccoon.

They shoehorned the toys into the back seat. Stephen said, "Told ya."

"Kicks will enjoy them once he or she is bigger than they are. Where did you learn to shoot like that?"

"On Granddad's farm. Same place I learned to drive a car. Not, unfortunately, a mammoth tractor."

Barbara had two minor calls during the afternoon while the two of them strolled through the stock barns and the craft exhibits, but nothing as spectacular as the escaped bull. The swollen capped hock resolved itself, as Barbara had said it would. The quarter horse came in second in the barrel-racing and made her owner very proud.

They watched the harness horses race around the temporary track that had been laid down for them. Barbara refused to bet. "Bad politics," she said. "If I lose, it's because I don't know anything about harness horses. If I win, it's because I either know something the rest of the spectators don't, or I am busy shooting dope into either the winners or the losers, depending who's telling the tale and whether he won or lost."

When Barbara finally went off duty at five thirty, it was nearly dark.

As they walked down the row of tents, they bought more fast food to take home.

"Once a year, we can clog our arteries," Barbara said.

"Keep telling yourself that while the EMTs are prepping us both for quintuple-bypass surgery."

Barbara knew he hadn't realized what he'd said. He was only making a smart-aleck remark, but he had reminded her how easily a heart could be stopped, a life ended. A marriage ended. She didn't call him on it. He'd have been horrified at what he'd said so casually.

She refused to allow one silly remark to blunt the fun they'd had together, the joy she felt in his company. Losing John had nearly destroyed her. Did she have the guts to risk loving and possibly losing again?

"What on earth?" she said as they drove around the curve before reaching Stephen's house. "Your outdoor lights are on. Something's happened. Look at all those trucks."

A half dozen were parked under the trees. She could hear men's voices punctuated with Latin music.

"Are you being robbed?" Barbara whispered. "Should you call the sheriff?"

"Not necessary. *Hola*, Rudy!"

A burly, squarish man in overalls detached himself from the group. "You caught us, Doctor. We planned to be finished and out of here before you came home."

"Stephen, what is this?" Barbara asked.

"Your early Christmas present. It's a flight cage for Orville."

CHAPTER SEVENTEEN

"WHAT ARE YOU talking about, Stephen? Who are those men? What flight cage? Aren't those the men who updated Emma's kitchen and built the addition on their house?"

He handed her a bag from the fair and picked up another to carry inside. "Let's go eat some of that evil food we brought home with us," Stephen said. "Let me go speak to Rudy while you dish up, okay?"

"You better come back and tell me what you're talking about."

While Stephen was outside, Barbara pulled plates and glasses from the cabinets and assembled servings of barbecued ribs, baked beans, slaw and potato logs. She was pouring iced tea when he came back in the front door with a suspiciously satisfied grin on his face.

"They've basically finished, just straightening up. Let's eat. After the lunch we had I didn't think I'd ever eat again, but I smelled that barbecue and suddenly I'm starving."

"Oh, no, you don't. Not one bite until you tell me what's going on."

Stephen. found napkins and utensils in the kitchen drawers. "I so seldom eat anything here except takeout or frozen dinners, I haven't really explored. You seem to know more about this kitchen than I do."

"I spent plenty of time here before Emma married Seth and moved out. Now, what's all this about a flight cage. They showed up after we left this morning? You'd planned this? How? When?"

"Seth gave me Rudy's name and said he and his men were looking for construction jobs since they finished Emma's addition. So I went and talked to them. Orville needed a flight cage. I didn't want to move Orville anywhere that had one, and Emma's just needed to be enlarged."

"You did this on your own without mentioning it to me?" Barbara asked. She poured sauce on her barbecue. "Do you even know the proper dimensions? What is required to train the bird?" She didn't like surprises like this. It must have cost a bundle, certainly with a crew that size completing it in a day—just to give her an early Christmas present? Just one more burden to add to her others—and what a terrible way to think of Thanksgiving and Christmas, as burdens.

"Orville needs it now, doesn't he?" Stephen said. "Or at least before Thanksgiving. And I haven't forgotten our plans for Thanksgiving dinner. Now we can include your new vet— what's his name? Vince Peterson?"

"Have you actually invited people?"

"And received acceptances from everyone."

"I'm not certain this is a good idea. Neither you nor I have room enough for a sit-down party for this many people."

"All taken care of."

"How?"

"It's a surprise."

"Stephen, I hate surprises. I'm not kidding." Though, maybe with Stephen doing the planning, she'd actually get through an entire meal without being called out to an emergency. If she was, she'd either take Vince with her or send him on his own.

She was annoyed at the way he was arranging her personal and professional life, making plans without asking her first.

If he could waltz in and take over, he could as easily waltz right out again if he got bored. Or had another accident, or a heart attack.

She'd barely kept going after John died. She couldn't face a loss like that again.

After their dinner, she rinsed and stacked the dishes in the small dishwasher, added soap and turned it on. "There."

She felt rather than saw Stephen walk into the small galley kitchen behind her. He wrapped his arms around her shoulders and nestled his cheek against her hair.

"Stay," he whispered.

She leaned back into the warmth of his body, but she kept her tone light. "I have barely enough stamina to drive home without falling asleep. I have animals to feed at the crack of dawn."

"We need to move Orville down here to try out his new cage."

"No, *I* need to check it out. I am not an amateur. I have built and used flight cages before. You have not. I will not be comfortable moving him unless I am certain what you had built is appropriate for Orville. I don't want obstacles that can hurt him."

"I agree that we need to check it out first. I did talk to Seth about the dimensions. If it's not all right, I'll bring the guys back in to change whatever you say needs fixing. After we check it out, I will help you feed the animals, then I'll make you pancakes for breakfast."

She twisted away from him. "I thought we were going to eat sensibly after today. Pancakes are not sensible."

"I will fix you lawn clippings if they will entice you to stay."

Everything in her psyche was screaming "Stay!"

She changed the subject. That's what she always did when the subject was uncomfortable or she was annoyed. It usually worked. "How did you extend the flight cage so fast without anyone's finding out you were having it done?"

He took a disappointed breath and a step back. "It's in place of the bonfire the powers that be won't allow me to have."

When he told her the story of the daylight restrictions, she rolled her eyes and shook her head. "Everybody wants you to jump through more hoops. I'm surprised you didn't have to pull a construction permit for the flight cage."

"It doesn't count as a permanent structure. Why don't you stay here tonight? I can sleep on the couch," Stephen offered. "You admit you're tired. We'll move Orville tomorrow after the clinic closes."

"Stephen, you and I have fun together. Let's enjoy that and not push it, please. We haven't known each other that long."

His cell phone buzzed. He gave it an annoyed glance, said, "Oh, damn," and answered it. "Good evening, Dean. Late for you to be calling, isn't it?" He looked at his watch. "I had no idea it was this early. I have had a long day."

He listened, blinked. "You're not playing golf on Sunday?" He rolled his eyes, said, "Yes, of course I'll be there. May I bring someone with me?" He said goodbye and hung up. "Now what is that all about?"

"Trouble?"

"He didn't sound as if there was trouble. I intended to drive down one day next week, but he says his golf game fell through, so he wanted to move up the meeting to check on the progress of the book."

Barbara laughed. "Progress? What progress? Are you going to tell him the truth?"

"Probably not." He turned her to face him. "Come with me. The clinic is closed on Sunday. I'll have a short meeting, calm the dean's fears, then we can have a leisurely brunch and drive home. The weather is supposed to be glorious. I went to the fair with you—for all the good my being there did—so now you come with me. I was planning to abscond with you for a long drive anyway. What do you say? *Yes* would be good."

This was a way out. "I'd love to ride to Memphis with you and have a wonderful lunch. I will not, however, stay here tonight."

He opened his mouth to protest, so she kissed him, grabbed her purse and started out before he could protest. "Oh, and Stephen… after the clinic closes tomorrow, you and I can move Orville to your fancy new flight cage and see what he does. Good night."

THE NEXT MORNING, Barbara fed the animals, checked her answering service, gave thanks that there had been no emergency calls, fixed coffee and orange juice and sweet rolls. Tired as she was, she had stayed awake and had been so antsy she'd had to unwrap the covers from around herself at four in the morning and start to settle down all over again.

While she finished her chores, she had time to think. Unfortunately.

She had fallen for this guy. She didn't want it to end, didn't want him to take the blasted textbook he was supposed to be writing, run back to Memphis and all the beautiful women who would be overjoyed.

Oh, for pity's sake, I have lost my mind.

No, just my heart.

It was mid afternoon by the time she finished assembling the equipment she needed for Orville, including a half-dozen thawed mice. Stephen pulled in beside her SUV with his red truck.

"You're getting to be a real countryman," she said. "Your truck has mud on it."

"I painted it on especially as camouflage to confuse the natives."

He set the mug on his hood, then held out his arms. She stepped into both his arms and his kiss.

Orville broke up their embrace with an importune shriek, which they could hear from outside the building.

They both laughed. "I swear he knows something's up," Barbara said.

"Now who's anthropomorphizing? Let's go check on the suitability of your new toy."

It passed with flying colors. The next step after they got back to the clinic was to entice Orville into his travel cage.

Stephen offered to help, but Barbara waved him off. "I'm the one with the heavy gloves.

Come here, Orville. And stop trying to poke my eyes out."

After they finally managed to shut Orville into his cage, they loaded the cage in Stephen's truck, along with the rest of the supplies Barbara had assembled, and drove to The Hovel, pulling as close to the enlarged cage as possible.

He managed to evade Barbara when she tried to catch him to release him in the flight cage. He couldn't get out of the travel cage and he couldn't fly, but he could hop. He was bigger, heavier and meaner than Mabel. Barbara finally managed to snare him in a blanket.

She spread half a dozen thawed mice along the two-by-four that served as a perch across the middle of the cage. Then she set Orville on the perch beside the mice. Would he see them? Recognize them as edible? Would he turn his back and sulk?

He chose to sulk.

He jumped off his perch and landed on the floor of the cage.

"You can't walk home, dummy," Barbara said. Another chase, another capture, another positioning on the beam.

"Stephen, hand me that spool of thread from my jacket pocket. I'm going to fix it so that the thread slides off when he grabs the mouse. I don't want him to swallow it or get his feet tangled, but if I wriggle it along just right, I may con him into thinking it's alive."

She carefully tied a thread around a mouse, laid it on the two-by-four and pulled it along.

Orville regarded it over his shoulder, then turned his back on it.

"Oh, c'mon, bird," Barbara snapped. "You've been eating these all along. See? Live mouse."

Orville turned angry eyes on her as if to say, "The heck it is."

It was like a battle between an exasperated parent and a picky eater. After an hour the score was a million to one in favor of the picky eater.

Orville was now easier to catch. He was tired. Stephen took over putting him back on his perch. The big bird quit trying to fly down and simply settled on the two-by-four more like a vulture than an eagle. He glared.

"If you were a vulture, you would love thawed mice, dumb bird," Barbara said.

"He's not a vulture, Barbara, my love, but a noble eagle."

"Noble my foot. He's a dumb bird that I am ready to allow to starve—or at least to miss a meal or two." She laid a different mouse on the beam and wiggled it. At least Orville didn't turn his back on this one. He began to scooch sideways on the beam. Barbara and Stephen held their respective breaths.

He grabbed the mouse and stuffed it into his mouth. A moment later he turned his back on them again.

"Yeah!" Barbara whispered. "Stephen, put a couple more up there. Don't bother with the thread. Let's see what he does."

He fussed and clicked his beak at them, but he ate. Barbara sat down on the dead log that Emma's skunks had played on. "Put one on the ground," Barbara said. "Let's see what he does."

Orville ignored the mouse, so Barbara fixed it up with the thread and pulled it along like a toy.

At first, he acted as though this was a trick. Or maybe he wasn't hungry any longer.

Then, without warning, he launched himself off his perch and flapped his wings—both of them. He landed beside the mouse and scarfed it up.

"Yes!" Barbara jumped off her log and launched *herself* at Stephen.

Highly offended, Orville hopped and

flapped to the other end of the cage, where he could eat his mouse in peace.

"It works! It's weak, but the wing works!" Stephen swirled Barbara around in his arms, then kissed her. "Shall we leave him here?"

"Absolutely. Beer anyone?"

"It should be champagne. We have to celebrate." He put her down. "We get to watch his progress, and you get to teach him the way you want to do it, and not the way a zoo vet sixty miles away wants to do it."

"You still should have told me before you enlarged the cage."

She slipped her arm through his and leaned against him. "I admit you did good. I'm glad he's here and not in some strange cage sixty miles away."

CHAPTER EIGHTEEN

SUNDAY MORNING DID indeed promise to be one of the last glorious Indian summer days before the chill of late autumn set in and started the downhill slide toward winter.

Barbara had done her best to look as though she belonged on a college campus and at a decent restaurant and not in a barn, but she worried that she hadn't done a very good job of it.

Stephen used their trip to explore the abilities of his new truck. He sped. "I am a mild-mannered professor, until I am behind the wheel of any sort of vehicle. Then the tiger rises. You should have learned that after my adventure with the tractor."

"Your accident didn't change your feelings about fast cars?"

"I was unconscious through most of it."

"How *is* your precious sports car, by the way?"

"My mechanic is still scouring the continent for a new grille to replace the one Orville destroyed. Last time I spoke to him, he said he might have found one in Saskatchewan."

She gave him a sad little smile. "Maybe it's time to let it go, Stephen."

"Ah, yes, now that I have a shiny new mistress."

Barbara blinked up at him. Mistress? Shiny? He patted his dashboard. Talk about being put in her place.

"I want to let my old relic go on my terms, however. It's a paradox. If my mechanic can restore it, I'll want to keep it. If he can't, then I have abandoned it in its hour of need."

"It's just a car."

"I know, I know. I forgot to tell you. I asked Elaine and Anne to join us for lunch.

"You did what?"

"I wanted you to meet them."

So they can assess me, more like, Barbara thought. *Why, oh, why, didn't I take the time to get my hair cut? Plus a good dye job or some streaks, a decent manicure, and a starvation diet to help me drop thirty pounds in two days. Not telling her they were coming was downright rude.*

She glanced down at her hands. Not a pretty sight. Frequent alcohol scrubs were not a beauty treatment, no matter how much hand lotion she rubbed in afterward. "You should have warned me that I'd be meeting your children. Do they know I'm coming or are you going to spring me on them?"

"Dearest Barbara, you are not being introduced to the Archbishop of Canterbury. Jerry is a scruffy academic who forgets where he parks his car unless his secretary reminds him."

"I wasn't talking about the dean, but afterward. Lunch at some fancy restaurant with your daughters."

He threw up his hands. "My girls will adore you. Say 'horse' to Anne and she'll follow you like a puppy."

"That's not the point. You must stop springing things on me. I warned you I don't do surprises well. What do I say to Elaine?"

"Smile and say 'how interesting' from time to time. She never listens to anyone else. You'll be forced to endure stories of how brilliant Roger is and how he's the youngest lawyer in his firm to make partner."

"Is she really an ogre?"

"Junior Ogress. Have to be precise about these things, Barbara. Nina kept her in check, but I've never had the knack. I tend to look the other way. Elaine is smart, beautiful and incredibly insecure. Roger is older than she is. Most of her girlfriends have careers as well as families. She will be jealous of what you've accomplished."

"I feel sorry for her."

"Me, too. Thank God she married Roger, who would love her if she sat around the house with baggy stockings rolled down to her knees and a Cuban cigar between her lips. She is a gourmet cook, keeps an immaculate house that Andrea, Emma's stepmother, helped her decorate, and Andrea has corralled her into volunteering for a couple of charity boards. Still, no avalanche of 'atta girls' is enough. Don't let her get to you. It's envy, not malice."

Barbara smiled. *Oh, lovely. One horse person who will talk to me about horse diseases, blood and pus, over lunch, while one ogress will try to prove that having a career is superfluous for a female because she doesn't have one yet. Hooray! Aren't I glad I'm going with Stephen? He didn't tell me until we were on the road. I'll get him for that.*

"My dear Dr. Carew, I am delighted to meet the reason Stephen has been avoiding my calls. I am no competition for a beautiful woman."

Barbara blushed. "Dean, I'm afraid your

real competition weighs twenty-two pounds. He screams like fingernails down a blackboard."

"Ah, yes, he's told me about Orville the eagle. Lucky they weren't both killed. How's the leg, Stephen?"

"Improving daily. I carry the cane as protection against the neighborhood dogs now rather than to keep from tripping."

"Good, good, glad to hear it." The dean cleared his throat. "And how's the new book coming?"

Barbara caught Stephen's eye.

"Slowly, but it's coming."

"So is Easter. You promised…"

"My dear Jerry, it is not Christmas yet. Have a little faith."

Barbara extended her hand. "I know you two have things to discuss, so I'm going to wander the campus. Stephen, call me on my cell when you're ready to go."

Both men waited until the door closed behind her, then the dean dropped into the oversize leather wing chair behind his desk. Stephen took its smaller cousin on the other side.

The dean templed his hands against his lips. "Are you planning to stop by your office before you return to the wilds of the Tennessee River Valley?"

"The department secretary sends me a packet of mail every three days, and I answer what should be answered on paper. The rest is email. Nothing earthshaking, I promise you. The book is indeed coming slowly, my leg is indeed stronger and I am more and more exploring the idea of switching to adjunct status in the spring and doing my lectures over the internet. What would be the ramifications of that sort of arrangement?"

The dean fell back in his chair. His white eyebrows nearly met his receding hairline. "My, my. What has caused the change of heart?"

"The truth? You just met her. I'm coming alive again, Jerry. I love teaching, I love writing, and I think I am good at both..."

"You are. But?"

"I don't want to be limited to either one any longer."

"I know I have been rather a jackass pushing you the way I have..."

"You want an infusion of younger blood, I know."

"Nothing of the sort. I am older than you by more than ten years—never you mind how *much* more—and I feel as though I'm just getting started. But every beautiful afternoon in the spring when the crappie are biting on the lake, I wish I could throw it all off and move to Wyoming. What you seem to be suggesting is hedging your bets. You teach a couple of upper-level courses each semester over the internet from this place you are living. You write your books. You drive down here for important stuff like faculty meetings…"

"Important?"

"Don't be nasty. Theoretically important meetings as needed."

"Like this one?"

"Touché. I am actually using you to avoid my wife's aunt and uncle, who are staying with us and driving me up the wall. I'm a dean, I get to misbehave like that from time to time. From the presence of your beautiful companion, I would say I did not cause you too much *agita*."

"Okay."

"You could continue to direct your graduate assistants as you have been and take on more as those graduate. The rest of the time you would be free to court the lovely doctor, do some traveling, continue to be paid as an adjunct professor, not as a retiree. Your pension would continue to grow. What about your house? Would you sell it?"

"No idea. This is early days. You've obviously given the idea some thought already."

"It was the obvious solution if I wanted to keep you working. I am aware that you have not been happy as things were. But if the lovely doctor breaks your heart, there may not be a place here for you to return to."

"I'm no dog in the manger. Jerry, I haven't been a fully active member of staff since the accident. You've already had people taking my classes…"

Jerry brushed off the words. "Graduate assistants. Teaching largely from your notes and your books. Not bad, but when I walk past one of your erstwhile classes these days, I hear neither laughter nor voices raised in argument. I miss that. The students miss it. They miss *you*. Could you maintain that relationship if you were a talking head seventy miles away?"

"Honestly, I don't know. If the classes were interactive, then maybe."

"When would you want to start this long-distance teaching? Spring semester?"

"Spring? Yes, as a test. Let's see if it works. If I can do it. If the technical people can set me up and teach me how to run the equipment."

"Let me talk to some of the trustees," Jerry said. "Personally, I think it's a marvelous idea. Win-win, as they say, but who knows what those old fogies will think."

Stephen stood. A moment later, so did the dean. The two men shook hands.

"Write it all down for me, would you, Stephen? So I have something tangible to present to the board? Say, before Christmas break?"

"Will do. Thanks, Jerry. I should have done this before now. I've been thinking about it seriously, but I wasn't ready to talk about it to you."

"Ah, but the lovely doctor was not on your horizon before."

"Come on, Jerry, it's not serious."

Of course *he* was serious, but he didn't plan to discuss his depth of feeling for Barbara with his dean or anyone else. Not even Barbara. Too much risk to his fragile heart.

The dean burst out laughing. "The devil it isn't. I saw the way you two look at each other. Go for it. You deserve it. For all I know, so does she."

IN THE FIRST moment after meeting Elaine, Barbara knew she shouldn't have come. Both women, Anne and Elaine, had inherited Stephen's height, bone structure and fast metabolism, but their mother had contributed real physical beauty. Anne might take hers for granted. Elaine didn't.

Anne wore an oversize rust-colored turtleneck sweater over skin-tight beige riding britches and dusty tall boots. "Sorry," she said, "I've been out at the barn since breakfast."

Her straight, chin-length brown hair shone but needed a trim every bit as much as Barbara thought hers did. When she shook Barbara's hand, Anne's felt as calloused as Barbara's.

Elaine, on the other hand, wore a pair of strappy fuschia shoes with heels that must have topped five inches and screamed Choo or Manolo. Her handbag had cost some reptile his life before he'd been ignominiously dyed to match the shoes. Her makeup was perfect. Her hair might be as straight and brown as Anne's in its natural state, but it had probably not faced the world unlayered and unhighlighted since she'd reached puberty.

In those shoes, Elaine was as tall as Stephen. Which meant she came close to dwarfing both Anne and Barbara, both of whom were above average height.

Dressed to kill, Barbara thought. *Works, too. I'm scared to death.*

Elaine's simple black wool sheath fitted so perfectly that constructing it must have required a course in calculus.

Oh, wow! She's wearing fuchsia stockings and fuchsia fingernail polish!

Barbara guessed the double string of pearls at her throat was real. Not quite as big as golf balls, but she could shoot marbles with them.

Anne was effusive about Barbara's job and immediately peppered Barbara with esoteric questions about new treatments and new medications. Thankfully, Barbara knew the answers and had applied most of the treatments on her clients' horses.

Elaine sat back, smiled with perfect teeth and let her sister keep the conversation going.

Barbara refused wine in favor of unsweet tea and ignored the hot popovers the server sat on the table, although she was so hungry she could have devoured the whole basket before their order was taken, with a half pound of butter.

Anne and Stephen ate. Elaine nibbled.

Over the Coquilles St. Jacques, a specialty of the restaurant, Elaine launched into stories of her life. The others were too busy eating to chat.

Stephen had been right. The occasional

"how interesting," and Elaine was happy to babble on. Anne tried to draw Barbara into a discussion of new treatments for ringbone and sidebone, diseases that lamed older and heavier horses, but Elaine talked over her.

Eventually, the party—or whatever it was—broke up. The girls hugged their father, shook hands with Barbara and marched off to different cars. Anne drove an older, dirty Land Rover with muddy tires. Elaine drove a shining black Lexus that was probably waxed every night.

Both women had laughed over Stephen's new red truck. "Are you finally going to send the sports car to what amounts to the elephants' graveyard for cars?" Elaine had said. "It is not only an embarrassment, it is obviously dangerous."

"Don't go there," Anne had whispered. "Come on. I'm due at the barn in forty minutes."

The minute Barbara settled into the seat beside Stephen, she felt the tension in her shoulders loosen. Whatever Anne thought, Elaine didn't like her. Her father deserved better... class? Money? Whatever, she'd made it quite clear that Barbara did not fit in.

Stephen laid his hand on her thigh as he

pulled out of the parking lot. "That wasn't so bad, now, was it?"

As compared to a month in an iron maiden or being tossed into the arena with the lions?

She gave him what she hoped was a fulsome and forthright smile and shook her head. "Anne is a sweetie. She sounds like a conscientious trainer."

"She is. Elaine was on her best behavior. I think she likes you."

Barbara turned in her seat to gape at him. How, then, did she treat people she hated?

"Would you mind if I ran by my house before we drive back to Williamston?" Stephen asked. "Anne is living there and swears everything is fine, but since we're so close, I should probably at least stick my head in the door." He turned to see the effect his words had on her. "Anne won't be there, by the way."

She managed to keep her face composed. But would Elaine? "Of course. As long as we're home in time to feed the animals, I'm fine."

She didn't know what she expected, but Stephen's house was an early twentieth-century Tudor-style mansion in the Garden District. Stephen pulled into the long driveway and cut the engine.

"If you're just going to check on things, Stephen, I'll be happy to wait right here."

She was surprised when he merely nodded as though he understood. He strode to the front door, unlocked it and disappeared inside.

She did not want to go inside the house that Stephen had shared with his wife. Her presence would be an intrusion into his past.

She had changed very little in the apartment she had shared with John. She'd replaced the broken dishwasher and added sit-arounds her children had given her, but little else. She hadn't created a shrine, but after the craziness at the clinic, her apartment was a refuge.

Ten minutes later, Stephen came out onto the stoop, pulled the massive door closed behind him, ran down the steps with barely a limp and climbed into the truck.

He leaned over and kissed her. "I didn't mean to abandon you."

"Everything okay?" she asked.

He started the truck and backed out onto the road. "Fine. Anne's not there long enough to mess things up, and I have a lady who comes in once a week to get rid of the dust kittens. So, any errands you need to do in town, or can we get on the road for home?"

"Home, please." She was worn out from

sheer tension. She watched his profile, the practiced ease with which he drove.

Whatever she tried to tell herself, she had to admit he was more than a friend.

He pushed her, irritated her, dragged her away from her safe life and scared her with feelings she thought she'd outgrown, yet, somehow, she'd fallen in love with him.

And she didn't want any part of it.

CHAPTER NINETEEN

THE SUNDAY BEFORE Thanksgiving Barbara and
Stephen drove Orville to Reelfoot Lake. Each
afternoon after office hours they had flown
Orville in the flight cage. Each afternoon he'd
grown stronger and more difficult to handle.

At last they agreed it was time. Barbara
checked with her ranger friend for directions
to the place he recommended for the release.
Neither of them could manage to eat any
breakfast, nor did they feed Orville.

"Better he looks for prey as soon as possible," Barbara said.

The closer they came to the lake, the more
fog they encountered. "Is there something
called lake-effect fog, like lake-effect snow
on the Great Lakes?" Barbara asked.

"Looking at the way the fog is drifting from
the direction of the lake, I would assume so. It
should dissipate with sunshine and breeze. Not
supposed to be any rain. Just dreary."

Barbara shivered. Orville's cage filled

the whole back seat of Stephen's truck, but they had agreed that he would be chilled in the truck bed. Barbara had covered the cage with a blanket to keep him quiet. So far it had worked. Driving three hours to the lake would have been unendurable if Orville had decided to give them a shriek-fest on the way.

Barbara kept an eye peeled for the side road that led to the spot recommended as a release point for Orville. She was shaking and was afraid she was going to throw up. If Orville flew free, then Stephen could drop his emotional and physical baggage and see himself as a whole man again.

If Orville failed...

She'd have to convince Stephen that failure was a temporary setback. She'd say that his wing was not yet strong enough.

In the flight cage, he had managed to steer and snatch his prey. He ought to be ready for release.

If he wasn't, she refused to allow Stephen to despair. She hadn't interfered in Stephen's physical growth because he seemed to be doing fine on his own. If Orville didn't fly, then both he and Stephen might need an intervention. She'd find the time to walk with Stephen and train Orville more frequently. She'd make Stephen realize that Orville's success or failure did not translate into *Stephen's* success or failure. He'd never discussed how important a symbol Orville had become to him, but she'd seen the way he watched Orville, glowed with every success, worried with every failure.

And if he did fly? Would Stephen fade out of her life? What else did they have to hold them together? She knew how important he had become to her, but was she really more than the latest woman in his life?

"WHAT IF HE DOESN'T FLY?" Stephen whispered. The closer Orville came to being released, the more personally invested Stephen became in his success. He should never have equated his own recovery with Orville's, but he had, and he was stuck with it.

"He's *been* flying in his cage, Stephen. According to the X-rays, his wing is completely healed. We've both watched him fly from one end of the flight cage to the other. He's picking up his meals off his perches. He's stronger every day. It is time." She laid a hand on his thigh. "I warned you. It's what we do. It's like children—if you do your job right, they leave you."

"The children come back occasionally to

visit." He craned around to look into the grill at the front of Orville's cage. "He won't." The bird was hunkered down under the blanket they had thrown over his cage and seemed to be asleep. "Is he strong enough for long flights over water? If he crashes into the lake, we can't rescue him. Once he's out of his cage, he's not about to come back. He's not a puppy. He won't come if we clap our hands and whistle."

"He's going home. All we can do is let him go. What happens to him after that is out of our hands. That's the way it always is for rehabilitators. The creatures we help are not members of our species. They have their own regulations, their own etiquette, lives very different from ours. If we do our job properly, they leave and we never see them again."

"So you keep telling me."

"There's a gravel road up there to the left. I think that's the one leading to the field where we're going to toss Orville." She reached into the satchel between her feet and pulled out a pair of heavy leather gauntlets long enough to cover her arms to the elbow. "Pull in. It's one of the work roads the rangers use that leads to the edge of the lake, so we shouldn't be disturbed."

"I've never been up here. Always wanted to come, but there never seemed to be time."

"It's a beautiful place, but it's also eerie. The eagles don't generally come back en masse until December and January, although some of them stay all year round. They occasionally wander off the way Orville did. We're a little early for the largest number of them."

"Should we take Orville back to his flight cage? Come back here after Christmas?"

"Chill, Stephen. Look, the fog's blowing away. I love this place, but it makes me nervous. I keep expecting to see ghosts. Come on, let's do this."

They parked on the grass a quarter of a mile from the leafless cypress trees that squatted on their fat knees in the water. Between the fog and the cold, the lake was still and totally quiet. Barbara shivered in her parka.

Stephen hauled Orville's cage out of the back seat, removed the blanket and handed it to Barbara, then set down the carrier with the door facing the lake.

She pulled on her heavy gauntlets.

As if he recognized the place, Orville shrieked.

From far across the water came an answering call.

Both of them jumped.

"Welcome home, my friend," Stephen whispered. "How do we do this exactly?"

"You stand back beside the cage, unhook the door, open it and get out of the way. I reach in, grab Orville in the blanket, move away from the cage, dump the blanket and launch him."

"Launch him?"

"Throw him up in the air as high as I can. If we've done everything right, he'll lift off and keep going."

"What if he falls into the water?"

She shrugged. "It's his lookout. Have faith, Stephen."

Stephen stopped breathing. He felt as though his chest was paralyzed. Barbara nodded. He unhooked the door of the cage. Barbara swung it open and reached in with both hands.

Orville shrank toward the back of the cage and regarded her with his mad eyes.

She did not plan to get her face anywhere within talon or beak range. "Good boy," she whispered. "Come to Mama." She wrapped her hands around his body in one smooth motion and walked him toward her.

"Orville, you're fat!" She turned with him

held between her gloves, took two steps toward the lake and tossed him up and away.

He dropped. One moment he was in the air, the next he was flailing around on the ground.

"Fly, dammit!" Stephen shouted. At the sound, Orville twisted his white head to look back over his shoulder. For a moment, Stephen thought he might slip back into his sanctuary. He took one hop forward, then another, like an airplane getting up speed to take off. He was coming dangerously close to the edge of the water.

He gave one final leap, wings beating. He was up! Too close to the surface of the water to suit Stephen, but flying.

He seemed to realize that he was free. He gained altitude, banked left, used his tail as a perfect rudder, gained more altitude and soared.

His screams now sounded like exultation.

"Look, Stephen," Barbara whispered. From the leafless trees across the lake another bird flew toward him. "It's a female."

"Don't tell me it's his mate."

"Of course not. That would be ridiculous. Anyway, if it was, we'd never know. Oooh!"

Orville folded his wings and plummeted toward the water.

"Stephen!" she gasped.

"Barbara, he's stooping."

A moment later his talons swept the surface of the water, then he rose clutching a good-sized fish in his talons.

"Better than frozen mice, huh, buddy?" Stephen shouted to him.

Together they watched him until he disappeared in the fog that still hung over the far end of the lake.

"Barbara, my love, are you crying?"

"Darned straight I'm crying! Now do you see why I work with the rehabilitators?"

"I always did." He turned her to face him. "Barbara, will you marry me?"

"What? Where did that come from? Of course I won't marry you. Don't be ridiculous."

"I swore that if Orville could fly, so could I. Marry me. Mate for life. Soar with me…"

"Eat live fish and frozen mice with you?"

"I'm serious.

"You can't be."

"Just listen to me. Hear me out."

"I HEAR YOU, but I don't *heed* you. You can't be serious. Why would I marry you?"

"Because you're in love with me."

"Who says?"

"I says. Also because I am in love with you."

"Stephen, don't joke."

"Who's joking? Can you deny that you are in love with me?"

"Stop this right now! How can I be in love with you? I've only known you a few months. It's not even Thanksgiving. Why on earth would you want to marry *me*? I'm a hard-working woman with calluses on my palms and two children. I live in a barn seventy miles from where your job and your house and your children and your friends are. I don't own a pair of designer jeans. Half the time I am covered with dirt and mud, the other half I'm covered in blood and worse. I do not fit in at your faculty club. We don't match up. Marriage is about property and children. It is not about love."

"Who says? Swear you don't love me."

She turned away. "I'll do no such thing."

He clapped. "Hah! You do love me. Your earlobes are bright red. I can see the pulse in your throat throb, and I suspect your blood pressure just went up. I am in love, and if you've got the gumption to admit it, so are you. You can't deny what we feel."

"I managed fine before I met you. I was content with my life…"

He grabbed both her hands. "No, you weren't. Neither was I before I knew you. There's living, and then there's what you and I were doing. Not the same thing."

"What on earth has that to do with *marriage*? Be sensible. You came up here to write a book and rehab your leg. Then you're going back to your real home and your real life. For you, this is *time out*. For me, this is the only life I have. I like it. I want it to continue just the way it is. If you hadn't hit Orville, we might never have met, except over a glass of wine at Emma and Seth's. Maybe not even then."

"I never thought of Orville as Cupid, but he qualifies. The point is, we did meet. And however it happened, we did fall in love."

"We'll get over it. Why are you so hot about marriage? I thought you didn't want to push things, that we were taking our time, getting to know one another…"

"I want to introduce you as my wife, not my friend."

"When you introduced me to the dean, you called me your friend. What's wrong with that? The dean was very pleasant, but then

I suppose he's nice to anyone he thinks has money to leave or a child to enroll. I could see that he wondered how on earth you'd gotten mixed up with me."

"That's not true. He liked you. He told me so. He also told me he could tell we were— I don't think he used the words *in love*, but he implied it.

"I want a ring on your finger and one on mine. Bell, book and candle. I want to endow you with all my worldly goods, such as they are. I want to be with you at the rising of the moon and the setting of the sun."

She started back toward the truck. "How about what *I* want?"

He called after her. "At least listen to me. I never thought it could happen twice in a lifetime. I figured I had lost my only chance at love. I told myself I was okay with that. But it *has* happened twice, and I don't intend to lose out. Marry me and I'll do everything in my power to make you happy."

She stopped but didn't turn around to look at him. She squared her shoulders and took a deep breath. "You marched into my life, my satisfying, successful life alone. Sometimes it was chaos, but it was chaos that I felt competent to handle. I did things my way, and my way generally worked. I slept well. I made my own decisions right or wrong."

"Were you happy?" he asked.

"I thought I was. Then you butted in, questioned my decisions, woke up a bunch of feelings I had gotten along without. Like you, I had one love. I lost him. Why take the chance on loving again, perhaps losing again? You have more guts than I do, Stephen. I'm scared. You're not."

"The hell I'm not. But I'm even more scared of letting you go. Together our lives could be so much better. Can you admit you want me?"

"I am a woman, Stephen, not some anchorite living walled up in a nunnery."

"I noticed."

"But one of us has to be practical. We don't fit. You have a life, a career, a house, children, friends, responsibilities."

"So do you."

"That's my point. I do—miles away from your life. From your sort of people, your sort of life. I spend *my* life up to my shoulders in gore. You spend yours neat, clean, surrounded by other people who work with their minds, not their hands. I can't leave my practice, Stephen. I won't."

"I would never ask you to. I can, however,

leave *my* life, this career you think I am so in-vested in. Maybe I was once, when I thought that was all I had. If you agree to marry me, I'll put my house up for sale this afternoon and send the dean my resignation tomorrow."

"Stephen, no! You don't mean that."

"I do if that's what it takes to convince you to marry me. I'm working on a compromise, but I'm not ready to talk about it yet."

"If you retire, you'll regret it, and sooner or later you'll blame me for the decision. What would you do instead? What sort of compro-mise? More secrets? Don't keep doing that."

"You say we need to be practical—I'm try-ing. Just give me a little time to work out the details. Elaine and Roger are planning to have kids. I'll sell the house in Memphis to them."

"Can they afford it?"

"They can if I hold the mortgage."

"What would you do if you didn't teach? Move here permanently? To The Hovel? You really would go crazy and drive me right along with you. Doesn't matter whether *I* need you or not. Your students need you. You said your Nina saw that you truly had something to give your students. That hasn't changed. You'd have to teach during the week, not to mention main-taining office hours for your students and going to a million meetings. You'd be on the road more often than you're home. You may think you enjoy driving now, but that would be like turning into an over-the-road trucker. You would hate it. *I* would hate it."

She turned away again, as though she could only talk to him when she didn't see his face, when she could avoid those blue eyes that seemed to pierce her soul.

"I said I'm working on that." He moved toward her. "Trust me."

She backed away again. She was only safe from his words at a distance. "There is no viable solution—not one that I am ready to live with."

"Very well. Here's the thing. Come spring I will likely be doing my classes via satellite from Williamston."

This time she did turn to stare at him. "What? How?"

"The dean and I are working out the details." He pointed a half mile or so down the lake. "Come on, walk with me. Who knows, we might even catch a glimpse of Orville.

"It's not a new idea. We have adjuncts all over the state doing the same thing. I'd still be commuting to the campus perhaps once a week for office hours and meetings, but the rest of the time I can work from home. Seth and Emma can always find a new tenant for The Hovel. Maybe Vince Peterson, your new hire."

She stared at him, then raised her hands, palms out, as though to ward off an attacker. "Oh, no. You can't move in with me. There's not enough room, I'm a lousy housekeeper and I have to have somewhere to get away from the animals and all the people or I'll implode. I'm being honest, Stephen. After John died, I got used to being alone. Where would you entertain? You do entertain, don't you? Friends, students, other faculty members. I'll bet your wife was brilliant at it, wasn't she? Inventive cook? I'll bet she arranged flowers for centerpieces. You would not be able to entertain in my apartment behind a barn filled with sick and wounded animals. No matter how clean it is, it smells."

He slipped his hand under her arm and walked off.

She was forced to come along.

"Then I'll keep my socks at The Hovel, but spend my time with you. I'll even take some veterinary technician courses if that gives us more time together."

"You really have this planned out without

even mentioning it to me, much less discussing it, the way you did with the flight cage. I can't live with a man who pats me on the head as though I was a slightly loopy dog and presents me with the solution to my problems, whether I like it or not. You hit me with this marriage thing when my defenses were down. Well, they are back up."

"I'll keep asking you until you agree. We belong together."

"You barely know me."

"I fell for you over pimento cheese sandwiches the night we rescued Orville. Can you seriously say you didn't feel something?"

Looking back on that night, she knew she had. Maybe not love at first sight, but a pull between them that had grown deeper every day.

"Marriage is not only about property and children, Barbara, and you know it. I agree that the logistics of two families, two households, jobs, finances can be mind-boggling, but we can work things out as long as we are together. We've both learned tomorrow is not a guarantee. I don't want to waste even one of my tomorrows without you."

"Why now? Because Orville can fly?" She

flung herself away from him and stalked to the edge of the water.

"Oh, no, you don't." He followed her, stopping short of the edge of the lake. "You say I don't discuss with you. You wanted practical. Here's practical. With the money from selling my house, plus my retirement income, my textbook royalties and visiting lecturer gigs, money wouldn't be an issue. We can add on to the clinic. We can build a house with room for each of us to get away from the other when we like. You have plenty of room on your land, or I really can buy Emma's pasture. Vince could live on site in the barn apartment. We could travel. I want to show you Florence and Paris and London." He started to go down on one knee, then stopped. "I probably can't get up if I do that, so take the word for the deed. Dr. Barbara Carew, will you marry me?"

"You tell me what I should do, then you tell me what you *intend* to do. Notice the difference? Are you planning on scheduling my root canal, too, or can I make the appointment all by myself?"

"Whenever you like, so long as I can tell the world that you are my fiancée in the meantime."

"Don't you dare. We have children who may be horrified that we're more than friends."

"I'm sure they'll be happy for us."

"Don't count on it." She rubbed her palm across her eyes. When she lifted her face, tears showed in her eyes and spilled out down her cheeks. "You should be declared certifiably nuts. You belong in a padded cell." She hugged her arms across her chest. "I do love you, but I won't be pushed into marrying you. Not now, not ever."

CHAPTER TWENTY

"YOU'RE DOING IT AGAIN," Barbara said.

"What?" Stephen asked. He looked up from the copy of the *Marquette News* that had just been delivered at the foot of his driveway. He had brought it with him when he came up to Barbara's apartment to join her for breakfast.

"Going on with your catered Thanksgiving dinner for all those people. Caitlyn emailed me and told me. When you stopped talking about it, I figured you'd dropped the idea along with Guy Fawkes. I should have known better. Stephen, it will cost a fortune."

"It's simply a way to get our families and friends together for Thanksgiving. This way nobody has to cook. No pressure."

She fell back in her chair. "No *pressure*? You haven't even met my children. I've only met Elaine and Anne once at that peculiar lunch in Memphis. Emma's going to be a week away from giving birth. We'll have to invite Seth's mother, Laila, and Vince if he doesn't plan to be in McComb. Neither your house nor mine is big enough for that."

He folded the paper and laid it beside his sweet roll. "That's all right. We're having dinner at the café."

She blew out a breath. "Stephen, honey, the café is never open on Thanksgiving."

He grinned at her. "They are now. I reserved it for us along with the catering. Simple. So far everyone has agreed to come." He closed his eyes and sighed. "It's going to be fine."

She simply stared at him. "You really are insane. How did you even get Caitlyn and Mark's telephone numbers?"

"Checked your online address book on the clinic computer. They were a bit surprised at the invitation, but they're planning to come."

"You went into my address book?"

"You were spaying a cat. I checked the clinic computer."

"They were both coming home anyway, but I planned to cook. Turkey is easy. Mark will probably stay for the weekend, but I doubt Caitlyn will."

"It's the perfect time to announce our engagement," Stephen said.

"Do *what*?" Barbara spilled half her cup

of coffee on the counter. "Stephen, I haven't said yes."

"All but the words. I want our families to share the happiness."

"You can't bring a roomful of strangers together and hit them with something this momentous." Her cell phone rang. "Oh, bother!" She answered, covered the receiver with her palm and whispered to Stephen, "We'll talk later."

Removing her palm, she said into the phone, "This is Dr. Carew. Oh, Mr. Baines, what's up?" She listened and nodded. "Sounds like choke all right. I'll be right there." She hung up the phone and turned to Stephen. "The animals are fed and watered already. Can you tell Mary Frances I'm on a call and to open the clinic, then warn Vince he's holding the fort? Baines has a Belgian draft gelding with a case of choke." She slid off her bar stool. "With luck, I'll be back in an hour or so." She grabbed her parka off the hook by her back door, slid into her Wellington boots, leaned over to kiss his cheek in passing and stopped on the threshold. "While I'm gone, I may consider murdering you instead of marrying you."

Before he could reply she was out the door and gone.

"Goodbye to you, too! And have a nice day," he called after her. He rinsed both coffee cups and put them in the dishwasher. "They will be happy for us. Once they get used to the idea. They have to be. Then Barbara will be."

AFTER VELMA AND the waitstaff finished clearing the Thanksgiving dinner and serving the coffee, Stephen touched Barbara's hand under the table, stood and clinked his knife against his wineglass. "Everyone, listen up."

It took a few seconds for the conversations to dwindle away to silence and heads to turn to listen to what he had to say.

He set his half-full glass of Chardonnay beside his dessert plate. His hand didn't shake, nor did he spill any of the wine, but inside he was shaking.

Good grief, he was afraid of his children! He was even more afraid of Barbara's.

He and Barbara were adults—they had changed diapers, attended parent-teacher conferences and waited up every time a child was late coming home. And all the other adult jobs parents did.

Now they were considering the one thing parents must never, ever do. All right, the second thing—the first was dying and thrusting said children into the world of adulthood without backup.

The second unacceptable action was to change. Overthrow the status quo. If you couldn't rely on your parents to stay the same while you were allowed to change around them, what good were they?

He'd had to promise Barbara he wouldn't mention marriage. A great deal rested on the outcome of this dinner.

Reserving the café for the two families was enough to give the dinner a cachet it wouldn't have had otherwise, even at Thanksgiving.

The children were not stupid. His family plus her family sure looked like an attempt to create "our family." So far everyone was on their best behavior, but that could change quickly.

"Thank you all for coming to this holiday dinner. I hope it will be the first of many."

Smiles and lifted glasses. Except Elaine on one side of the table and Caitlyn on the other. Stephen glanced down at Barbara. She was watching for any adverse reaction. Elaine was staring at her with mounting suspicion.

Stephen swallowed a gulp of ice water, because his throat was so dry he didn't think he could get another word out without croaking. "We're both making major changes in our lives in the coming months." This was not the engagement announcement he had originally thought to make, but until Barbara relented— and she would—it was the best he could do.

"Barbara has finally hired another vet to come in with her, as well as some office help. She'll no longer be on call twenty-four/seven. In the same vein, I am continuing to stay in Seth and Emma's rental house for the foreseeable future. I will be teaching in the spring semester as an adjunct professor, largely over the net."

Everyone began talking at once.

"Who said the only constant is change?" he said and sat down.

"What about Mother's house in Memphis?" Elaine asked. "It's home. You can't sell it and move away. Can you afford to cut back teaching full-time at school?"

"Sixty miles is not Antarctica, Elaine, and my finances are not your concern."

"I'm glad you'll have some help, Mom," Mark said. "Is there enough business for two vets?"

"As Stephen said, Mark, darling, don't you worry about that. I haven't had a vacation in years. John and I kept planning to travel, but there never seemed to be time or money enough. Maybe there will finally be both."

Anne whispered to Elaine, "Alone or with a roommate?"

Elaine glared at her.

Barbara lifted her arms in a who-knows? gesture. "I might even build myself a house on the property and let the new vet move into my old apartment. I'm comfortable enough in my apartment, but a real house would be wonderful."

"What about all Daddy's stuff?" Caitlyn asked.

"You can help get ready for the garage sale."

"No way. You can't."

Elaine turned to her father. "You've only been here a few months, and you're upending your whole life for *her*?"

"Come on, Elaine, don't be rude," Anne said.

"Think of all the attractive women in Memphis crazy about you. I knew we should never have allowed you to come up here all alone. You're just lonely. You can't give up your job and move to…what does Emma call it, The Hovel? And sell *our* house? My father must not live in a a barn. What would people think? The two of you are completely incompatible."

"We are not incompatible. I promise you."

"And you know this how? Don't answer that!"

"I hadn't planned to."

"I can certainly see why she would want you. I do not see, however, why on earth you respond. You have nothing in common. It's because you're so isolated up here. Come back to town. I guarantee you in a month you'll be back in your old groove." With each sentence, Elaine's voice rose a few decibels—whispers had reached a conversational level, but with an edge.

"Don't bet on that," Stephen said. He vacillated between anger at his bossy child and amusement that she thought all she had to do was wave her hand to break up his romance. Bad fairy or bossy witch? Didn't matter. Wouldn't work. "You mean well, but stop trying to make my decisions for me, and try to remain civil." He caught his breath and turned to stare at Barbara with his mouth open.

Wasn't that precisely what he had been doing to Barbara? *His* heart was in the right place, too. He was trying to help, impress, present her with ready-made solutions. No wonder he annoyed her.

"Hey, Daddy, you're a catch," Anne said.

"Otherwise how come half the widows in Memphis brought you casseroles after Mother died? You're reasonably attractive, with a fantastic job, a respected position in the community and a fair amount of money. You're not supporting ex-wives or minor children—"

"I beg your pardon?" Stephen said.

"Sorry if that upsets you, Daddy, but you're not. You're not an alcoholic. You don't smoke or do drugs. Except for your leg, you're healthy. You are a catch."

"Yes, he is," Elaine said bitterly. "If you were to marry her, God forbid, she can quit work tomorrow. Who wouldn't want to settle down to a life of leisure after doing what she does? All that blood and dirt." Elaine actually shivered. "The chances are that you'll die first, so she'll inherit at least half of your estate, assuming you leave the trust funds you and Mother set up for us children in place."

"If you keep on like this, I will make the ASPCA the beneficiary of your trust funds. I am legally entitled to do that, aren't I, Roger?"

"You don't mean that, Daddy," Anne said.

"What about any grandchildren you might have?" Elaine said. "Would you cut them off? You see, Daddy? This thing is driving a wedge between us. She'll destroy us as a family."

"You're the one who's doing all the wedge-driving that I can see," Stephen said. He was growing angry. What kind of greedy vipers had he reared? They didn't care what happiness he and Barbara would gain. All that mattered to them was the portion of his estate they might lose if he took a wife, any wife. "You might remember that your mother was younger than I but did not outlive me."

"That's another issue," Anne said. Her eyes held tears that threatened to spill over onto her cheeks. "It's a slap in the face to Mother. To go from one of the sweetest, gentlest and most elegant ladies to a veterinarian."

"I thought you loved veterinarians."

"I do. They're marvelous people, but you don't marry them. You employ them to look after your animals. How can you betray your marriage to Mother?"

"Your mother wanted me to find someone else, Anne. I was the one who felt certain I'd never have another chance. Yes, Barbara and I have grown close, and, yes, she is very different from Nina except in ways that truly matter. What she and I have, and I hope will continue to have, is different from the feelings Nina and I shared. But it is just as valid and, I hope, just as long-lasting."

CHAPTER TWENTY-ONE

BARBARA WOULD HAVE killed for a glass of iced tea. She had expected some flak. Kids did not like change in their parents' lives no matter how grown-up they were. "Velma?" she called. Velma stuck her head out of the kitchen.

"Could we have that table in the back room for a few minutes?"

"Sure. Nobody's here except y'all."

"Come on, gang," she said. "Stephen, we're moving to the table in the back where you can discuss things with a bit more privacy." She cut her eyes at Stephen and caught his slight nod. This was deteriorating into a nasty scene. She and Stephen had not planned on this, but as things stood it was obviously better to separate the combatant groups. So far her children had pretty much kept their mouths shut, but she could tell Caitlyn was close to the boiling point.

Five minutes later after the two families

were settled at their separate tables Caitlyn asked her mother, "How can you even consider getting rid of any of Daddy's things? You and Daddy *worked* together. What has this guy got to offer you except a lot more work? He doesn't understand that you're dedicated to your animals, not to waiting on him."

"Who says he'll want to be waited on?" Barbara asked. "Maybe he wants to wait on me."

Caitlyn huffed. "A college professor? Trust me, he's used to being waited on. He walks with a limp!"

"Hey, not fair. He's in great shape. Better than I am," Mark said, glancing down at the beginning of a paunch below his belt. "Mom's spent her life working, and a chunk of it alone. This guy's solvent—he can take care of Mom. They can travel, take cruises, do that rehabilitator stuff Mom's into."

"Mark, don't you dare take her side!"

"It's not her *side*, sister dear, it's her *life*. It is not yours or mine or even Stephen's. It is Mom's. She's entitled to live it the way she wants."

Caitlyn wailed, "Everything will change. We'll be stuck staring at these people across the table at Thanksgiving and Christmas and birthdays. We'll never be a family again with all these strangers in our lives every time we turn around. Making polite conversation."

"You call this being polite?" Barbara asked. "I'd love to run out of space at the dining room table, and maybe having eventually to set up a children's table like they used to have when I was growing up. We had a great time. I've always missed that for you two, since neither your father nor I had any close relatives. Nobody we kept in touch with, anyway. I'm trying to make you understand, Caitlyn. We didn't bring you up here to ask your permission to see each other, but to let you know we're seeing one another seriously and exclusively."

Barbara watched Caitlyn try to get her blood pressure down to a reasonable level.

"Mother, you've known each other a few months. Much too short a time to make any sort of commitment."

"You're betting our relationship won't last."

"That's exactly what I'm saying. Face it, you're available, period. Sooner or later he'll go home and pick up with his other lady friends.

"We might make things permanent." She realized as she said the words that they weren't merely to annoy Caitlyn. She meant them.

Caitlyn actually snorted. "Right. Like that's going to happen. How's this for a deal? If you don't hate each other at the end of a year and should decide to get married, we could start planning a private, quiet wedding in the county courthouse with the mayor officiating."

Barbara rolled her eyes. "Actually, I've always thought that if by any chance I should get married again, it should be in St Mary's Cathedral in Memphis with a dozen bridesmaids and a wedding dress with a humongous hoop skirt and a train."

"Mother!"

Barbara caught Mark's eyes, and they both dissolved in giggles. "I could, you know. John and I never had a fancy wedding, just a justice of the peace in Birmingham the day we graduated from vet school. I could have white roses and a veil and look very silly. But if I should ever consider remarrying—and I haven't— it might be nice to marry in a church with a priest presiding."

"I cannot believe I am hearing this." Caitlyn slumped down in her chair. "You can't wear white unless you're a virgin. Just promise me you won't do anything final before talking about it with us."

"You're the ones talking about marriage,"

Barbara said. "Neither Stephen nor I has mentioned it to you."

"You don't have this kind of gathering to announce you are 'seeing each other,'" Caitlyn said. "I don't even want to think what that means."

"Caitlyn," Mark said, "knock it off."

"You're trying to introduce the idea, so we'll get used to it, then you'll spring it on us."

"Oh, for Pete's sake," Mark said. "Just shut up about it."

"Do not consider this insane thing. If you do, I won't attend."

Barbara took a deep breath. "Then, dear, we would miss you."

Caitlyn gawked at her mother, pulled herself out of her chair and stalked off down the hall. A moment later the door to the ladies' room slammed.

"Hey, Mom, don't cry." Mark dropped his arm around her shoulder and hugged her. "If you do marry Stephen, I'll be there, I promise. I like Stephen. You two seem good together. I know you've been lonely out here all by yourself. Besides, I live in Nashville. I'm out of the firing line. Caitlyn and I do not run in the same circles. We seldom see one another."

Barbara snickered. Then both of them exploded into laughter. Barbara was still crying through her tears when Caitlyn slammed the door to the restroom and strode back to them. She picked up her coat from the chair where'd she'd left it when she arrived, and said, "I am driving home. Call me when you've come to your senses and dumped this guy."

She strode out and slammed the front door behind her. The glass rattled alarmingly but remained intact. A moment later a car revved its engine and peeled out.

"I thought this discussion was hypothetical," Mark said. "When did it go from don't marry him to dump him? My sister can be a pain."

"I hope Stephen is having an easier time than this. This was supposed to be a pleasant family meet-and-greet, not a Wagnerian tragedy."

"In this family, Mom? We're used to you being alone and available. Most of the time, anyway. Now instead of Mom, singular, unless you split up, we have to think in terms of Mom and Stephen."

"Is that the way you feel as well, Mark?"

"Sure, but I know it's a fantasy that parents will stay the same forever. So does Caitlyn. She just refuses to admit it, even to herself.

Neither Caitlyn nor I had to endure having divorced parents like a bunch of our friends."

"Your father *died*."

"Losing Dad so suddenly makes you mistrust life. If Dad, the patriarch, the fount of all strength and all wisdom could die—"

"He was far from that."

"But he was to us, me and Caitlyn. If he could just up and die on us, then what in this life *can* we count on? Better to stay still and not take any more chances. Isn't that what you've done, Mom, up to now? You could lose this guy the same way."

"I've come to realize that everybody loses people they love, Mark. I assume one day you'll lose me. So, do you stop loving me in the meantime? Of course not. I should have spent more time with you…"

"You were trying to keep a roof over our heads. You were always there when we really needed you."

"If John hadn't set up those trust funds for your college, I would never have been able to send you. He left life insurance, too, but it's never enough. I had to make a go of the clinic, You lived in a barn, Mark. You didn't mind, but Caitlyn did. She loathed having dates pick her up in a barn. She went off to college and never really came home again."

"I come home whenever I run out of money."

"Which hasn't been often. You always have some sort of job. I worried about you doing drugs."

"Never my thing. I don't even smoke cigarettes. I saw too much of what drugs can do. When you're working as closely as I do with electricity, drugs can get you fried."

"Are you always going to do the set-up thing?"

"I'm not a full time roadie. I work for an audio-visual company, not a band. Next step, floor manager for television news if I'm lucky. May take a while, but I have some feelers out. When things are slow, I can get in some traveling. It's all good."

"I'm so glad you didn't go on trying to be a musician."

"The people that know say talent tells. My talent says I don't have any."

Her cell phone rang. She cussed it but picked it up. "Dr. Carew." She listened, said "uh-huh" a couple of times, then added, "Sure, be right out." She hung up and turned to Mark. "Gotta go."

"Now?" He shook his head. "Why am I

not surprised? I don't think we've ever had a holiday dinner where you were around after dessert. What about this fancy new doc you hired?"

"He'll probably be on call next year."

"Do you really have to go? Can't it wait?"

"Sorry, baby. A mare's having trouble foaling."

"So you gotta get there fast, right?" He shrugged and sighed. "Don't speed too much, okay? See you at home later? I'm spending the night. That is, if you're going to be alone…"

"Yes, Mark. There are clean sheets on your bed. I'll tell everybody where I'm going and say goodbye. With luck, Stephen will come with me. He'll be happy to get away."

"I guess Caitlyn drove home like she said."

"Who knows? If she would rather drive home and pout, let her go." Barbara pulled on her coat and gloves. As always, her work gear and her boots were in the back of her van. She and Stephen had come separately, not only to cover this sort of emergency, but also to avoid showing off their relationship. "You have your key to the apartment. If you get hungry later, there's plenty to eat in the fridge, and Velma's boxing up some leftovers. Please take them with you. I'll say goodbye to the others and leave. See you later."

"Yes, ma'am."

When she apologized to the others and explained that she was going to a mare having trouble foaling, Stephen went to get his coat. "I'll ride along with you."

"But, Daddy," Elaine said. "We haven't finished talking."

"We've talked too much. Now the rest of you talk. Come on, love, let's go foal a mare."

As the café door closed behind them, Barbara said, "I feel like Adam and Eve being chased out of the Garden of Eden."

"They were naked. We've at least got our coats."

"It's a toss up who I'd cast as the snake. Come on, leave them to it. It's going to be all right."

"And if it's not?"

"I THINK IF I hadn't gotten the call about the mare I might have invented it," Barbara said as she pulled into the parking lot in front of the barn where the mare was trying to have her baby. "The dinner started out freaky. Everybody was too polite. Best behavior and then some. But when you made your announcement?"

"Once Seth and Emma and Laila left, we had everyone together, well fed and mellow. Theoretically."

"Stephen, I can't face fracturing two families."

"We've worried the problem enough tonight. We have a mare to foal."

Since she was dressed for the party, Barbara pulled on overalls over her slacks and changed her dress shoes for her Wellies.

"Come on," Stephen said, "let's go see if you can help."

The mare was miserable; even Stephen could tell that. She paced around her stall in small circles and kicked at her belly every fourth or fifth step. Stephen had seen his own two children born—not his choice to be there, but Nina had insisted. He had not found it the rich, emotional experience his colleagues had told him about. He would have preferred the old-fashioned custom of walking the floor in the waiting room. He'd hated seeing Nina in pain. Later, when she'd been so sick, watching her suffer had been worse than the pain he'd felt after his accident.

At least he had no vested interest in the birth

of the foal, but he did feel concern. Barbara had explained on their way that mares foaled quickly as a rule. If they didn't, then both foal and mare could die. "This is very late in the year to have a mare foaling. Especially a race-horse. You want a racehorse born as soon after New Year's Day as you can manage. They turn one year old on New Year's. This baby will be six or eight months younger than her contemporaries. Hey, Ben. Still no foal?"

The owner of the mare and his wife leaned against the stall door outside of the stall where the mare paced. "It's been too long," he said. "I can't feel but one foot."

Barbara pulled on her shoulder-length obstetrical gloves and squeezed gel on them. "Grab her halter, Ben. I need to see what's going on inside." She reached in, said, "Ugh, here's the problem," and shoved against the mare's hindquarters. A moment later the mare sank onto her chest in the hay, and it seemed to Stephen no more than another second until two hooves slid out, followed quickly by a nose and then the rest of the foal. It was already fighting to get the birth membrane off its face.

"Doc, you're a miracle worker," said Ben.

"Your filly—that's what she is, a filly—was

trying to be born with one foot back under her. I just popped it loose. Now, let's do some cleanup, and we can all go home to bed."

TWENTY MINUTES LATER Stephen drove Barbara's van out of the farmer's paddock. As he had done on their way to the fair, Barbara slept in the other seat. She made soft snuffling noises. He prayed there would be no more emergencies and wished that Vince was here to take them. He vowed that next year Vince would be on call instead of her. The way their families were behaving, he and Barbara might fly to the Seychelles for Thanksgiving. Or lock them out of the house. Better to be alone than with a house full of bad vibes.

Time to get this marriage thing under way. He needed to persuade her to go ahead and marry him. He longed to show her off as his very own wife.

He began to make mental notes of the logistics involved in marrying her.

Once it was a done deal, the children would come around.

Uh-oh. He was trying to push what he wanted onto Barbara again. He ought to have learned by now he simply annoyed her and put her back up when he tried.

CHAPTER TWENTY-TWO

"YOU'VE HARDLY EATEN anything, Emma," Barbara said. "At least have a bite of apple crumble. The fruit'll be good for you. Granny Smith apples—can't beat that."

"I'm not hungry, really, although I love your homemade vegetable soup. Thank you so much for inviting Seth and me to Sunday night dinner."

"I'm sorry Seth is too late to join us. The new vet, Vince Peterson, hoped to come, too, but he called to say he won't be back in town until very late because of the ice. I saved Seth a plate." Barbara blew out a breath. "Actually, I wanted to rehash that debacle at Thanksgiving dinner with you. What are we going to do with our children?"

"Let 'em stew," Stephen said. "They are acting like knotheads—all except for Mark. Give them a chance to come to terms with the change in the status quo."

"That's why we only announced we were seeing one another seriously," Stephen said.

Emma kept checking the front window for the lights on Seth's SUV. "I wish Seth would come. We need to get home before the roads glaze over any more than they have already."

"I brought you. I'll take you home," Stephen said.

"Oh, no, you don't," Barbara said. "Emma has no business being at home alone. If this sleet keeps up, the phone'll go out and maybe the lights." She glanced at Emma, then she *frowned* at Emma. "You all right?"

Emma wriggled in her chair. "Some more of those pesky Braxton-Hicks contractions my doctor warned me about. I'm not due for another week. Everybody tells me first babies are usually late. I hope this one is on time."

"These twinges—do you have them often?" Barbara asked.

"A couple of days ago Seth actually drove me to the hospital because I was complaining. We were sure this was it, but it wasn't. They kept me sitting in the waiting room for an hour before they checked me and sent me home. I'm apparently not sufficiently effaced or dilated or something."

"That can happen fast."

"Let's hope. I was so tired I didn't pay attention. I fell into bed once we got home."

Emma's phone rang. She clicked it on speaker. "Seth? Where on earth are you? You missed dinner."

"Sorry, hon. I'm going to miss more than dinner. The ice is building up faster than predicted. I was following one of the salt trucks back to you, but we just ran up on a tree across the road. Have to wait for one of the big road graders to shove it out of the way. In the meantime, Earl and I are helping the Staties get folks that have spun out back on the road. My supply of cat litter is almost used up."

"Should I get Stephen to take me home?"

"No!" He came as close to shouting as Seth ever did. "You're warm, you're safe, you've got company. Ask Barbara if you can spend the night."

"I was planning on it," Barbara called over Emma's shoulder. She pointed at Stephen and mouthed, *You, too.* Then at the couch.

"How bad is it?" Stephen asked.

"Right now it's nasty. The weather guys say the wind should switch to the southwest by morning and turn this junk to rain. In the meantime, it's a skating rink. Barbara? You there?"

"Yes, Seth."

"Your generator in working order?"

"Of course. I have plenty of diesel, plenty of wood for the fireplace. We should be good to go."

"Please keep checking in." Emma sounded plaintive. "I'll worry myself sick until you show up."

"As long as we have phone service, I'll keep calling, but don't worry about me. The tires on this SUV are made for this stuff. I love you. Look after Kicks for me."

"I love you, too." She sounded weepy.

Barbara caught Stephen's eye. "Emma, you still having those fake contractions?"

"Don't fuss. I'm going to the bathroom."

The minute the bathroom door shut behind Emma, Barbara said, "Call me an alarmist, but I am not sure she's having fake contractions."

"She's having real contractions? My God, call an ambulance."

"With a tree across the road? Besides, I'm probably wrong."

"Barbara, can you come here please?" Emma called from the bathroom.

Barbara went.

"I'm afraid I made a mess," Emma said. "I leaked all over the floor."

"No problemo." Barbara dropped two towels onto the floor to sop up the moisture. "I'll clean it up in a bit." She took a deep breath and said soothingly, "Maybe a small problem. Your water has broken. You're in labor."

"I am not! I can't be. I'm not due yet."

"Close enough. Kicks is impatient. Remember, when you had the skunks, I told you animals pick the worst possible weather to deliver their babies, because the predators aren't out? This is the human equivalent."

"I can't have the baby. Seth's not here. Stephen will have to drive me to the hospital right now."

"The road's blocked, remember? I'll call 911 and tell them what's happening. They'll come as soon as they can."

"What do we do in the meantime? Play bridge?"

"We start by getting you dry and into my bed. Then I'll check how far along you are…"

Emma bent over and grabbed her belly. After a minute or so she relaxed. "Ow! That hurt!"

"Labor does hurt."

"You keep drugs. I want some."

"Horse drugs. I am an animal doctor."

"I am an animal."

"Not in the eyes of the United States government. I can't give you a thing except aspirin, and not much of that. You and Seth took the baby-prep classes, didn't you?"

"For all the good he's doing," she snarled. "Pulling stupid people off the ice. Why isn't he here to take me to the hospital?"

"Hold my hand and pant. Tell me when it passes, so we can get you situated. We should have plenty of time between contractions. This is early days."

"How long do I have to put up with this? And how did I get myself into this pickle?"

"Barbara?" Stephen's voice came from outside the bathroom door. "Is everything okay?"

"No, it is bloody well not!" Emma yelled. "Go away you—you man!

"Uh-oh. Barbara, am I hearing what I think I'm hearing?"

"Yes, Stephen, the dread and dangerous woman in labor. Open the door and help me get her into my bed, but first, put a thick layer of newspapers on the mattress."

"Newspapers?"

"Just do it. They're stacked by the fireplace."

"Coming right up."

Emma had another contraction when they

settled her in bed. "Pant," Barbara said. "Don't push—pant."

As Emma started to huff like a locomotive engine, Barbara signaled to Stephen to join her in the hall.

"That was less than twelve minutes from the last one," Barbara whispered. "If she keeps that up, she'll deliver before the ambulance can get here, even if the road is clear. I was in labor for twenty-six hours with both of mine. She's not going to take two."

"What do I do? Boil water?"

"Remember you said you were experienced with cleaning up messes?"

He nodded.

"Emma made a big one. The cleaning supplies are in the linen cupboard in the bathroom. Could you see what you can do?"

"Of course."

"I keep an emergency bag in the hall closet. Bring it to me, please.

"You can't deliver a baby."

"I pray I won't have to." She took his hand. "Stephen, I'm scared. She could hemorrhage, the baby could be breach or not breathing—oh, why on earth did I invite her to dinner?"

"You were doing a good deed for a tired pregnant lady who had days before she delivered. She could be sitting alone in a house with no husband, no heat and possibly no cell phone. I'll get your bag, call 911 again, try to get ahold of Seth—no, maybe not Seth. He might land in a ditch and kill himself trying to get here."

"Then come back and help me. Please."

As he turned away, she whispered to him, "I'm glad you're here."

Back in the bedroom, Barbara checked Emma's state and reported that she seemed to be progressing normally. But fast.

"This is normal? For who? An elephant? Bowling balls?" Emma snarled.

STEPHEN STOOD BACK in the shadows, where Emma couldn't see him to cuss him. He tried Seth despite his concern. He deserved to know what was happening. Voice mail. The landline was out, but the cell towers seemed to be working. The lights stayed on thanks to the good offices of Barbara's giant generator that came on automatically if the central power went off.

Barbara said softly to Stephen, "I think she's transitioning. With the next contraction, she'll start to push."

"Can't you stop her?"

"No more than I could stop a freight train with a hundred cars attached. With luck, all I have to do is rotate the baby's shoulders and stand by to catch."

"Ugghhh!" Emma shrieked.

"Here we go," Barbara said.

Behind her, the bedroom door opened and Seth loomed out of the shadows.

"You scared me half to death!" Barbara said. "Get out of the way. You're filthy."

"Oh, God, Em, are you all right?"

"Do I look all right?" Emma made a noise that sent Seth back to the corner beside Stephen.

"Whatever you do, don't faint," Stephen said. "Sit down or go into the hall, but stay out of the way."

"Come on, Emma, you're doing great," Barbara coaxed.

Seth gulped and fled to the hall. Stephen followed. Though he had been there for the births of his girls, he had been out of the action. At the time, he wished he'd been on the polar ice cap or the middle of Tasmania. He considered himself a coward for getting out of Barbara's bedroom, but he and Seth were the most useless beings on the planet.

Both men closed their eyes and leaned

against the wall at the next sound. Not a shout, not a scream—it was something primal, like a tiger or a bear.

Then silence. The two men stared into one another's eyes and each held their breath.

Then came what Stephen considered the most beautiful sound he'd ever heard. Actually, the third most beautiful. Anne and Elaine had given out the first two.

He opened the door a hair and peered in. Barbara was continuing to work on Emma. On her breast, wrapped in a towel, a naked human child mewled softly like a kitten.

Stephen had seen that same radiance on Nina's face when she saw her babies for the first time. Instant love. A chain that would never be broken. He had felt it, too. Tonight, he felt tears on his cheeks. He stole in far enough to lay his hand on Barbara's bent head. She nuzzled against it and whispered, "How about that?"

She sat up straight. "Now, go away. I've got an afterbirth to deal with," Barbara said. "Tell Seth to give me a few minutes, then I'll introduce him to his daughter."

Suddenly, the room was flooded with revolving colored lights and pierced by sirens.

Barbara lifted her eyes. "Now they show

up. Just like a man. Leave us to do the chores and then come claim all the credit."

As a precaution, the ambulance took Emma and Seth off to the small Williamston hospital to be checked out, although one of the responding EMTs congratulated Barbara before they drove away. "Nice midwifin', ma'am. She was lucky you was here. Mama and baby look to be in real good shape. Sorry we didn't get here sooner, but she was better off having that baby here instead of in the ambulance on the ice."

CHAPTER TWENTY-THREE

AFTER EMMA'S CORTEGE left for the hospital, Stephen cracked the bottle of champagne he had stashed in Barbara's refrigerator. It had originally been intended to celebrate their engagement, but this took precedence. They toasted Emma, Seth and Miss Kicks, for want of a better name. Stephen didn't realize how big a toll the delivery had taken on Barbara until she fell asleep on his shoulder.

Not one delivery, actually, but two—mare and mama. He thanked God that Emma had gone through a fast, uncomplicated delivery. He was also glad that Nina had chosen the hospital route. Oh, he'd heard all the stuff about delivering at home being best, but he had felt that the less chance he had of losing someone he loved, the better. He'd finally convinced her.

He swung Barbara around so that her feet were on the sofa, covered her with the tartan wool blanket from the recliner and went to the kitchen to make coffee and find something to fix for breakfast.

He had made a decision tonight. No more waiting for marriage. Barbara would accuse him of making decisions without consulting her again, but he considered it persuading. He was good at persuading, as his students could attest. He sat at the dining-room table, pulled out his notepad and began to make notes. Until his head hit the table with a resounding clunk. Then he moved to the recliner and slept immediately.

He awoke when he heard the shower running in the morning.

He checked his notes. It would work, his entire scheme. He fixed coffee for both of them, and wished he'd brought a toothbrush, a razor and some clean clothes to Barbara's the night before.

Tonight, he would do so. If all went well. It had to. It was the right thing to do and the perfect time to do it. Surely, he could convince her of that.

When she came out, she looked as fresh as though she'd slept all winter. God, he loved her!

He handed her a cup of coffee, then took

it away again before she threw it across the room, which she well might.

"Let's get married," he said.

"What? No. Not now, maybe not ever."

"Maybe's better than absolutely. I mean, let's get married today, right now."

"Impossible. No."

"It's not impossible. We can do it. We drive to Mississippi, pick up a license at the courthouse in Holly Springs, then my friend Walt can perform the ceremony at his church. He's an Episcopal priest. We'll be together for our first Christmas."

"Listen to yourself. Am I supposed to salute, say 'yes, sir,' and drive off into the sunset with you? Marrying is a big deal. We're not eloping teenagers being chased by Daddy with his shotgun loaded."

"Indeed, we are not. If you prefer, we could fly to Vegas, get married at one of those wedding chapels this afternoon, spend our first night in the fanciest bridal suite we can reserve, drink champagne and phone the children afterward. There are still seats on the afternoon plane and room at the Bellagio…"

"You checked? Tell me you didn't actually make reservations."

"Of course not, but I wanted to be sure it would work out, if that's what you wanted."

"What I wanted? Vegas? Really? What do we do for rings? Witnesses? What do I wear? Clean jeans? Will polishing my paddock boots turn our wedding into a formal affair? What on earth were you thinking?"

"That we're wasting our lives apart. Why miss even a single day?" He inhaled a deep breath, then took her hands. "Do you love me?"

She pulled away her hands. "I've told you I love you."

"Now, my next question. Do you want to marry me?"

"Our families aren't even reconciled to our being what you call an item. If we ran off and got married, we could start a feud. I could lose my children. You could lose yours and your grandchildren when and if you have them. We could split our families into warring factions. What is the rush?"

"When we're married, our families will come together, accept the situation."

"You can't know that. I don't want either of us to lose people we love—I want us to gain them together."

"And me? Do you still want to gain me?"

HIS VOICE SOUNDED TIGHT, as though he was fighting to keep his temper.

Barbara certainly was.

"I don't know any longer, Stephen. I do know I'm worn out with being blindsided by the wonderful plans you make for our lives without bothering to find out what I want. Have you always been a control freak, or have you turned into one since you met me?"

"I'm not a control freak. I want to take some of the burden off your shoulders."

"That's not what you've done. You have been trying to run my life, make me happy the way *you* want to make me happy. Never mind what I want."

"You want to be miserable?" he snapped.

"No, but I don't want to be goaded and pressured and second-guessed. If that's the sort of wife you want, find somebody else."

"You don't mean that. We love each other."

"Love alone is not good enough. Ever hear of respect?"

"Of course I respect you. What do you want from me?" He drove his hands through his short hair and turned his back on her.

"Look at me, Stephen. This is important."

He swiveled to face her but kept his fists in his pockets.

"Please stop acting like a one-man show! Stop making plans without discussing them with me first, stop making deals and setting up projects then standing back and expecting me to applaud. No more 'ta-da' moments. Ask me, Stephen, don't tell me. Big surprise—I've been making my own choices with a pretty high success rate for a long time." She could feel the tears streaming down her face. Not fair. Stephen wasn't crying. He looked as though he wanted to throw something or punch a wall.

She wanted to throw her arms around him and say, "There, there. It's all right." She didn't, because it wasn't. She held her ground, tears and all.

She felt sure he'd walk out. She could tell he was considering it.

He huffed like that bull at the fair getting ready to gore something. She'd never seen him angry before.

She waited for the explosion.

He stalked around the room. Once he headed for the front door, then turned and came back. Finally, he seemed to get hold of his emotions. The muscles in his shoulders loosened. He sank onto the couch and dropped his head in his hands. "That's not what I intended. I never saw my suggestions…"

She laughed. "Suggestions? How was the flight cage a suggestion?"

"It was supposed to be a surprise."

"It was that, all right. All I'm asking is that we work out solutions together, not Stephen presents and I accept."

"I like my 'ta-da' moments. I like presenting the people I love with something they want and don't have. Making their lives better."

"What you want them to have, you mean. Somehow the choices always turn out to be what *you* want. I've been alone too long. Maybe I'm better off staying that way."

He was on his feet in an instant. "No, you're not and neither am I. Before I met you, I figured I would spend the rest of my life alone, doing the same things with the same people. I was lonely and knew I would stay that way. Nothing in my life fulfilled me or even interested me much. Then I met you, and thanks to Orville, I got dragged into *your* life. You were a new world, right from the beginning. I watched you fight for Orville, and I thought, she makes me care about something other than my own grief."

"Just like that?"

"Just like that. Then I realized I wasn't dragging *you* anywhere. Talk about comfort zone. You were pulling me back into life. I wanted to return the favor."

"You like your ta-da, I like my comfort zone."

"I'm sorry I made you feel that way. If this is a deal breaker for you, then I have to stop doing it."

"Cold turkey?"

"I don't guarantee not to backslide, but I'll try. Call me on it when I start. I love you too much to risk losing you over my stupidity."

She took his hands but held him away from her so that she could look into his eyes, his beautiful eyes. At the moment they were anxious eyes.

"Stephen, most of the time I agree with what you propose, but ask me, don't tell me. Okay?" She tried to laugh, but it came out a sob. "And no surprises."

"If I stop prodding, then will you marry me? You say when, today or ten years from now. See, I'm asking, not telling."

She began to laugh. "Oh, Stephen, I do love you. I might as well marry you. With luck we'll have a long lifetime to work out our personal problems."

"How about today, before you lose your nerve?" He grinned. "Not Vegas. Hey, just kidding."

"Stephen, I'm scared."

"Me, too. Married we can be scared together. We can just make the license bureau in Holly Springs before they close for lunch."

"What about your priest friend?"

"I'll call Walt on the way. They must have at least one jeweler in Holly Springs, and surely at least one wedding band that will fit your finger." He glanced down at her left hand. "Unfortunately, you're still wearing your first wedding band."

"I'm not certain I can get it off, but jewelers have snipper things."

"Will you mind cutting it off if we have to?"

"I intend to wear it on a chain around my neck. Would that bother you?

"If you wear bananas on your head, I'll think they're a good look for you."

"You took *your* ring off," Barbara said. "Did you do it to get back in the dating game?"

"I did it because Elaine worried me into it. It's in my cuff-link box."

"Making your decisions for you? She must come by it naturally."

"She does think she knows best. Yes, maybe she did learn it from me. I should have remembered how much I resent it. Sorry, my love."

"Do you want another wedding ring?"

"If the jeweler has one big enough for me, then, yes, I do. I'm a great believer in symbols. I'll give you diamonds later."

"Oh, no, you won't! Diamonds do not mix well with horse liniment." She blew out a long breath. "Okay, Stephen. Let's go get married. Mary Frances and Heather can feed the animals. There's no surgery scheduled for today and no barn calls, but there can always be emergencies. I'm dropping Vince in at the deep end. I'll leave my phone charging in your truck. I never intended for Vince to start his first day without me. I can talk him through any unusual procedures over the phone."

"Bring your passport," Stephen called as she went to pack for her wedding.

She heard Stephen pour more coffee. She should have been hungry, but at the moment even the thought of coffee made her nauseous.

Barbara pulled out a winter white dress that her mother would have called a lady dress. Nope. White was for first weddings. Besides, it made her look washed out. She ended up choosing a red silk dress and a pair of red pumps that were not quite high enough to be dangerous. Maybe they could pick up some white roses in Holly Springs.

Now that she'd bought in to this craziness, she felt excited to be entering a life with Stephen. No doubt he'd still try to make her decisions sometimes. No doubt she wouldn't let him.

She'd been worrying herself sick trying to keep her world the same, immovable, unchanging. But most things changed on their own when you weren't looking. Now her life would never be the same again. It would be better.

They'd tell the children together.

Together was the operative word.

Eloping would do an end run around both their families and present them with a done deal. She was finally doing what she wanted, and what she wanted was Stephen. Not another minute of their life together would be wasted.

Men and women who loved one another made accommodations, confronted their problems together.

She'd so desperately tried to keep the single life she'd worked out for herself unchanged. Then Stephen had driven into her parking lot with Orville, and as good as blown the doors off her life.

When John had died and left her so suddenly, the animals had been her refuge. She had used them and their problems to avoid dealing with her own needs and emotions. But change happened even when your back was turned. What never changed decayed. Together, they would grow again.

First, they stopped at The Hovel so that Stephen could change into a suit, shave and pick up his passport for identification at the license bureau.

"Do you want a wedding gown?" he asked. "We can drive to Memphis and—"

"I just want you, Stephen."

STEPHEN CALLED THE small church in Holly Springs where his friend Walt was the priest.

When Barbara came out with her dress in a garment bag and carrying a small bag of shoes and accessories, she asked, "Did you get your friend? Will he do it?"

"His wife said he was out on a parish call. She'll give him my message to say we're on our way."

"What if he won't do it?"

"Then we'll find someone who will. Come

on, go check in with Dr. Peterson and tell Mary Frances where we're going."

Thirty minutes later, they were on the road to Holly Springs. After the excitement, they fell silent. Barbara kept her hand on Stephen's thigh, as though she needed the physical connection to give her an infusion of trust in this mad enterprise.

The ice had dissipated as quickly as it had accumulated. The roads were now clear with little evidence of broken trees. The tree that had blocked the road in front of the clinic seemed to be the largest victim. Twenty miles south, there was no evidence of the storm at all.

Stephen took back roads. With little traffic, he indulged his love of speed.

Barbara hoped they would not be stopped by the police, because Stephen looked as giddy as she felt. She had visions of having to take a Breathalyzer at ten in the morning. If they explained to the cop that they were eloping because their children didn't approve of their relationship, he would probably arrest them and toss them in the local jail as certified lunatics.

As Stephen's lawyer, Stephen's son-in-law, Roger, would have to come bail them out.

"Your friend Walt hasn't called back," Barbara said as they bowled through another mini-town.

"We'll go straight to the rectory. We won't make the license bureau by noon. By the way, I haven't asked what denomination you are or if you have one at all."

"I'm an Episcopalian. Not that I've done much about it since John died. For a long time I was furious at him for dying. Then I was too busy trying to grow a tiny practice that was barely breaking even. Will that matter to your friend?"

"Walt? I doubt it. He owes me. I got him through statistics and calculus at school. He does not have a mind for mathematics."

"Do *you*? I had no idea."

"There's a great deal we have to discover about one another. Once we're married, we'll have time."

"Am I going to discover that you are an axe murderer or a government hitman?"

"No, my dear. As one of my favorite cartoon characters says, 'I yam what I yam.' Are you?"

"No woman is. We just passed Red Banks. Only fifteen minutes to Holly Springs."

Ten minutes later, she spotted the small church nestled in a dell on the edge of town.

Stephen helped Barbara out of his truck and

they walked hand-in-hand up the brick path to the cottage that served as rectory.

Stephen rang a doorbell that chimed loudly somewhere back in the house. A moment later the front door was flung open so hard it bounced off the wall inside. "Hound dog!" The extraordinarily tall, thin, completely bald man threw his arms around Stephen and lifted him off his feet. "Martha told me you'd called. I tried to call back, but I got one of those out-of-range messages." He turned a smiling face on Barbara. "They're machines, so I can hate them without feeling sinful. Don't know how I'll handle artificial intelligence."

"Walt, this is Dr. Barbara Carew from Williamston."

"Come on in. We've got a fire in the den. Martha just stepped out to the grocery. She runs errands when she thinks she should stay out of the way." Walt took them into the den at the rear of the house and pointed to the sky-blue sofa by the fireplace. "What's the matter? I haven't seen much of you since…"

"Nina's funeral, I know. Barbara and I are going down to the courthouse to buy a marriage license."

"This afternoon?"

"We figured to talk to you first, then get the

license after lunch, then come back here and have you marry us."

Walt took a deep breath, peered from one to the other, and frowned at Stephen. "Not this afternoon."

"What? Too busy for an old friend?"

"Not that. Mississippi has a three-day waiting period. You can't pick up your license for three business days."

"I checked. They don't have a waiting period."

"Yes, they do. They changed the law not too long ago. The website probably hasn't been changed yet. They did get rid of the blood test, though. That's a good thing. What's the rush? Can't see an irate father after you with a shotgun. Barbara, this is an indelicate question, but I'm a priest. I get to ask this stuff. You wouldn't be expecting, would you?"

"Good grief, no!"

"A number of my parishioners discover they are carrying unexpected babies. Most are delighted. A few, however…" He waggled his hand back and forth.

"Barbara has two children, Walt. You've met mine."

Walt leaned back in his wing chair and crossed his legs. "So, what's the rush?"

Stephen took Barbara's hand and gave her a slight smile. "The thing is, Walt, when we announced at Thanksgiving that we were serious about one another…"

"It hit the fan? I'll bet. How long have you known each other?"

"Mid-September. I took up residence in a rental house two miles from Barbara's clinic and ran into an eagle."

Walt reared back in his chair. They heard the back door open and close. He called, "Martha, honey, Stephen MacDonald and his fiancée are here. Stephen's got a tale you should hear."

After introductions and greetings, over coffee and with a plate of homemade shortbread on the coffee table between them, Walt said, "Okay. Tell all."

Between the pair of them, they managed. After they finished the story, Walt blew out a breath. "Whew."

"Come on, Walt, don't go all old-fashioned on us. I recall you and Martha fell in love and got married in less time than that."

"Yeah, I had just gotten out of divinity school. I was afraid if I didn't snap her up, I would miss out on the perfect priest's wife." He reached across and took his wife's hand.

"I wasn't," Martha said. "But I am now. We probably should have waited, but at that age you want to charge into life, don't you?"

"May I use your bathroom?" Barbara asked. Martha took her. "I'll take my time, give them some privacy."

"Me, too. I'll go hide out in the kitchen. That's what I usually do when Walt has a parishioner that needs advice." She patted Barbara's arm. "Join me there."

BACK IN THE DEN, both men acknowledged that they'd been left alone on purpose.

"Even if you could come up with a Mississippi license today, which you can't, I couldn't marry you," Walt said.

"Don't tell me you have to publish banns or something medieval like that."

Walt shook his head. "A lot of people want them read, but I can choose to abrogate the necessity. No. It's not that. We have to have three counseling sessions—one with you and me, one with Barbara and me, and one with both of you together."

Stephen began to pace. "That's for kids, surely, not a widower and a widow. It's not our first time around. Just *say* we were counseled. Better yet, consider this as our counseling sessions. We're both here, after all. You're talking to me. I can go into the kitchen, then you can talk to her."

"Stephen, I might have been able to cheat my way through calculus, but you tutored me until I passed with a B. You do not skirt the law. Neither do I with my parishioners. Again, why the rush?"

Stephen leaned against the mantelpiece over the fireplace and stared down into the fire. "I don't want to give her time to get cold feet and back out."

"Stephen, I don't do kidnapped brides who want to back out. That's not your whole reason, surely?"

"Our children are trying to split us up. They'll keep trying until we're married. I don't want Barbara to have to spend her Christmas being sniped at by both sides. I can handle it. She shouldn't have to."

"Do they know you're trying to elope?"

"We are eloping, Walt. We're not *trying*."

"You are if you expect to do it this afternoon in my church. Sit down, Stephen, you're making me nervous."

"You're nervous? I'm a wreck. The one thing I'm sure of is that Barbara and I love one another and intend to become husband

and wife. I don't care if we're married by a shaman covered in ostrich plumes, so long as he has a valid license to marry and so do we. We're anxious to start living the rest of our lives, old friend. Not another wasted minute."

Walt peeled his six-foot-six-inch frame out of his chair. "Go in the kitchen. Drink more coffee, eat more cookies. Hug your fiancée. Heck, kiss your fiancée. I have to think."

"I put Barbara in the study," Martha said as Stephen entered the kitchen. She poured him a fresh cup of coffee. "Sugar and milk are on the counter along with another plate of cookies. Can I fix you a sandwich?"

"I may never eat again," Stephen said. "Getting married is not supposed to produce ulcers. Why did Barbara go into the study?"

"She's talking to her office on her cell phone. Sit, Stephen. It will all work out. I can count on the fingers of one hand the weddings Walt has done that have gone off without a hitch. Weddings and the people in them are always crazy. Walt never loses his cool."

"Did he ever lose one or both of the intended bride and groom?"

Martha burst out laughing. "Not recently, but yes. Are you worried Barbara will run away?"

"Isn't every man somewhere deep inside where he can't admit it even to himself?"

"We've had brides left waiting at the altar and grooms driving away alone in the wedding limousine complete with tin cans bouncing off the rear end." She bit into a cookie. "We've also had them call it off the day before the wedding. Walt says better to have to return the wedding presents than wind up in divorce court in six months."

"I honestly believe Barbara is as committed to me as I am to her." He hoped he was telling the truth. Barbara might be in Walt's office calling a cab to pick her up and take her back home for all he knew. She seemed certain, but was he doing that prodding thing again? He felt a chill up his backbone.

"She's a lovely girl, Stephen. After what you went through with Nina's death and then your accident, you deserve some happiness."

"So does she, but we don't always get what we deserve."

She looked up and smiled at Barbara as she walked into the kitchen. "More coffee?"

"I'm already on a caffeine high."

Stephen raised his eyebrows. "Well?"

Barbara shrugged, pulled out another

stool from the breakfast bar and slid onto it. "There's good news and bad news."

"Uh-oh," Martha whispered.

"The good news is that so far Mary Frances and Vince have successfully dealt with all the appointments and are not facing any off-site emergencies. They have proved they don't need me. They didn't even need to call Dr. Kirksey. Vince is so proud of himself he's like a dog with two tails and wagging both."

"So, what's the bad news?" Stephen asked tentatively.

"Elaine called the office looking for you when she couldn't get your cell phone. I didn't actually tell Mary Frances that where we were going was a secret…"

"She told Elaine." Stephen dropped his head into his hands.

"Yep. I get the feeling she might be coming after us." She covered Stephen's hand with hers.

"Alone?"

"Good grief, you don't think she'll round up a posse, do you?"

"I think it is a distinct possibility."

"I am not running from my crazy children."

"It looks as though we'll be coming home unmarried to face their united front," Stephen said.

"Then we will. If we intend to do this, Stephen, then they can join us for the ceremony. We're not running. I may take a while to make a decision, but once I know it's the right thing to do, I stick."

Walt leaned his lanky body against the door frame and stuck his hands in his pockets. "There is no waiting period in Tennessee. You do, however, have to procure a license in your own county. That means you'll have to drive back to Williamston, arrive before they close at four thirty—I checked that, as well—and then get yourself a public official to marry you in a civil ceremony."

"Barbara wants a church wedding. We both do."

"And you'll have one in January or February. Before Lent in any case. No weddings during Lent."

All three of the others started to speak, but he held his hands up. "Hush. Listen to me. A civil ceremony is perfectly valid. You will be legally married. That will give us time to jump through all the churchly hoops, like counseling sessions, at our leisure. That is, if you still want me to marry you."

"Of course we do," Barbara said. "But can you do that?"

"Yes. It's actually more of a blessing of your union, but it counts, I promise you. Stephen, you better move if you are going to make it to your courthouse before it closes."

"Don't tell him that! We'll end up in jail on reckless driving and speeding charges."

"If it's in Williamston County, the judge can marry you in jail."

"Come on, Barbara."

"Here's a thermos of coffee and all the rest of the cookies," Martha said, handing them a package wrapped in foil. "You don't have time to stop even at a fast-food place."

As they got in the truck and pulled away, Stephen said, "One short stop."

"Where?"

"We need gas, I need a bathroom and I have to call Seth."

CHAPTER TWENTY-FOUR

"HOW MUCH PULL do you have with city hall?" Stephen asked when he got Seth on his cell phone. He turned up the speaker so Barbara could listen as well.

"A fair amount. Depends on who you talk to. What's this about? Where are you?"

In the background Stephen heard the gaspy cries of a newborn. "Sorry if I woke Kicks up, Seth. When are you going to name her?"

"You didn't wake her up. She's hungry. She lets you know it." Silence. "There. Emma has her. The feeding frenzy has begun. We're still discussing names. Emma wanted her to have a personality before we named her. That's too New Agey for me. Emma wanted Artemis. I nixed that. She'd go through hell in school with a name like that. So we've pretty much agreed on the Roman version. She's going to be Diana, the goddess of the hunt."

"Good choice."

"Barbara, you there, too? What's this about? Are you two in trouble?"

"Sort of," Barbara said. "It's a long story."

"I need you to organize this situation, Seth," Stephen said. "Call Sonny Prather…"

"The *mayor*?"

"Beg him to keep the county clerk's office open until Barbara and I get there. Shouldn't be much later than they normally close. Tell him I'll pay for someone to stay late. Ask him to get a marriage certificate signed and sealed in the names of Stephen Magnus MacDonald—"

"Magnus?" Barbara guffawed.

"And Barbara—"

"I know her full name," Emma said in the background.

"We're on our way back to Williamston. We should be there in an hour and a half, maybe two. We'll sign everything when we get there. If they want money, please pay them. I'll reimburse you. Ask Mayor Prather to stay until we get there, then marry us in his office tonight. I'll pay him whatever he wants. Think you can manage that?"

"Who knows? I'll call you back and let you know."

"One final favor. Will you and Emma be our witnesses?"

"Stephen," Emma said from the background, "I love you both, but I just had a baby."

"Of course. Stupid of me."

"Laila's staying here to look after Diana for a couple of days. She's dying to get Diana all to herself. I don't promise, but depending on how I feel, we'll be there." She hesitated. "Have you told your kids?"

"No, and don't you, either," Barbara said. "We'll tell them when it's a *fait accompli*. This is nerve-wracking enough without having to battle our way into the mayor's office."

"Okay. Get off the phone and let me get to organizing," Seth said and broke the connection.

"Stephen, darling. This could work."

"It will work. Tonight, I intend to be a married man with a beautiful wife."

"Sounds like a plan."

CHAPTER TWENTY-FIVE

"WE CAN'T LET them do this." Elaine stomped around her overdecorated living room with her hands fisted at her sides. "Where is Roger? He was supposed to be home an hour ago."

"Daddy and Barbara aren't committing bank robbery or murder," Anne said. "They're eloping. They are both past the age of consent. It's none of our business." She curled her long legs under her.

Elaine didn't yell at her about it but gave her a dirty look instead.

"They are committing *scandal*!" Elaine snapped. "It's not enough that Daddy goes off into the back of beyond and rents a shack when he has a perfectly good house in town."

"I kind of like having our place to myself. Not that I'm there much, what with the horses."

"Those stupid horses. Anne, when will you grow up, take up a decent career and find a man who can support you?"

"If adulthood makes me like you, I'll stay immature. I have *some* happiness in my life. What do you have except a desperate need to make everyone around you miserable?"

"I have a husband who is trying to make partner in his law firm. Those people scrutinize everything we do. I try to keep everything perfect for him. I volunteer, I sit on boards, I spend hours at the gym. A man likes a woman who is well-groomed, well made-up—"

"Stop right there. My boots cost more than a dozen pairs of those fancy shoes of yours. And my britches cost more than your designer jeans and fit better, too."

"We are not discussing clothing choices. We are discussing my father's marrying this country woman who needs a professional haircut and a makeover."

"This country woman is a successful doctor."

"Animal doctor. Not a neurosurgeon. I'd accept a neurosurgeon. Why didn't he marry one of those women who have been after him since Mother's funeral? Why not Dahlia Leroy? She's beautiful, has more money than the president—"

"She's had more husbands than she's had plastic surgery."

"I'm on the symphony board with her. She's smart. She wouldn't bore him. What do he and that *woman* talk about? Having puppies? Big whoop."

Anne burst out laughing. "You haven't said that since high school. I wasn't so sure at first this would be a good thing. I've changed my mind. I like her."

"You would. Free vet care for your horses. Don't count on it. We'll never see him. He'll retire from the college so he can spend all his time with her. He'll sell the house out from under you, sister dear. You'll be living in a studio apartment in a bad neighborhood and getting your car stolen every other weekend. It's bad enough you tend bar."

"It's a very chic bar. I make enough money to afford a decent apartment in an excellent neighborhood, if I have to move."

"At least the horsey set is chic even if you aren't. Polo is fashionable."

"I don't play polo."

"But you go to parties with the polo crowd."

"Why are you such a snob? Mother was never a snob."

"She didn't have to be. She was perfect.

Her position in society was assured. Everyone adored her. Against all odds I keep trying to live up to her standards. Every time Daddy looks at me, he sees what she was and I'll never be."

"Now that is just silly! He does nothing of the sort."

"I try to be special, and I'm not."

"Of course you are. Here's Roger.

"Finally. Come on. Let's go stop this nonsense."

"Where, exactly, are we going?" Roger asked as he followed the two women back through the kitchen to the garage, where his Lexus was still warm after the drive from his law offices.

"I'll tell you on the way."

"I CALLED THE CLINIC this morning when I couldn't get hold of Dad," Elaine said. "The secretary person let slip that he and that woman are on their way to Holly Springs to get married. So I called Caitlyn and told her we had to do something to stop them."

"You what?" Roger turned to stare at her. A driver next to him honked at him to get back in his lane. "This is why you dragged me out of a meeting with a client?"

Elaine shrugged. "Caitlyn is no happier about this than we are. She said she was going to call her brother, Mark, then she planned to drive down and meet us at that little church in Holly Springs, where Daddy's friend officiates. Mark is in Nashville and can't get there in time. Just as well. He'll be no help. He's all for this—this misalliance."

"Elaine," Roger said reasonably, "I am not going to stop this wedding. If it actually takes place, I'm going to be a part of it."

"What?"

"If not a part, then at least a willing witness. I'm starting to think I should toss you into the nearest psychiatric facility, load you up with tranquilizers and go on a cruise until you're sane again. You have gone way overboard on this thing."

"Caitlyn agrees with me."

"Two out of five. You lose."

"He's right," Anne said from the back seat. "Roger, I'm proud of you."

"They have a right to get married when and how they like, whatever we think," Roger said. "Although they should probably have a well-planned wedding in the spring. In the meantime, we need to mend fences, not blow this thing up into a family feud."

"But—"

"You are so uptight about scandal," Anne said to Elaine. "Chasing after Daddy and Barbara is a much bigger story than their going off quietly to have an old friend marry them. Guess who the villain is in *this* one? You."

Elaine burst into tears. "I'm only trying to do the right thing. That's all I ever try to do. The way things look matters. People will laugh at us. Roger's partners will laugh at us. We won't be able to hush it up that they ran away like a pair of randy teenagers."

"Stop it," Anne said. She reached over the seat and patted Elaine's shoulder. "Don't take it so hard, sis. It could be worse. We mostly don't listen to you in the first place."

STEPHEN SLID HIS truck into a parking space right outside the main entrance at the Williamston County Courthouse and climbed out. Barbara met him on the sidewalk.

"We have ten minutes until they are scheduled to close," he said. "I can't believe we made it." He took her hand as they climbed the stairs and entered what Williamston considered a grand foyer. Stephen had never been inside before and found it a remarkably ugly amalgamation of fake Georgian and even faker

Victorian architecture spruced up with Georgia marble. By the double staircase hung a poster advising caution because of the slippery stairs.

"I can't believe we avoided getting locked up for speeding," Barbara said.

"The gods were with us and the highway patrol wasn't. Let's go."

The door to the county clerk's office was open, but no clients leaned on the counter. From behind an aged rolltop desk, an aged lady came to greet them. "May I help you?" Her tone was austere, but she burst into a grin when she recognized her customers. "Sonny said to wait for you, but you got here before we're supposed to close. Hey, Barbara. You finally getting married again? Took you long enough. Who is this cute thing you're marrying?" She simpered at Stephen.

Barbara introduced them. "Thank you for waiting, Janey. We just drove from Holly Springs at warp speed. Did you know they have a three-day waiting period for marriage licenses in Mississippi now?"

"Sure. Should have called me. I'd a saved you a trip. Come on around here and take a seat so we can get all this filled out and checked. Y'all got identification?"

Both handed over their passports.

"Y'all been married before? I know you have, Barbara, but you weren't married before John, were you? Never been divorced?"

They shook their heads.

"I need the names of your previous spouses for the record." She lifted her eyebrows at Stephen. "Who on earth named you Magnus?"

"My mother had Viking blood, or said she did. I keep it quiet."

"I think it's sort of cute. Now, let's get the rest of this stuff finished. Ever been convicted of a felony?" She continued with her questions.

When Barbara checked the clock on the wall, she saw they had been answering bureaucratic questions for what seemed like hours, but had been less than ten minutes.

"Sonny said for y'all to go on up to his office when you're ready," Janey said. "His office is right in front of you as you get to the top of the stairs. And watch the stairs. They're killers."

"Miss, uh, Janey, does Williamston have a jeweler?" Stephen asked.

"Two, actually."

"We need rings."

Janey's eyebrows lifted. "Put it off a little

late, didn't you? I'd try Gold and Son, right across the street. For a small-town jeweler, he has nice things, including some antiques."

"Will he be open?"

"Should be until six. I'll get this all typed up and stamped. You go buy your rings. You can pay me after the ceremony."

"Do you mind staying the extra time?" Barbara asked.

"Not if you let me come to your wedding."

Stephen thanked her. "We may actually need a witness, if Emma and Seth can't come."

"Now, y'all go get you a couple of rings. I'll be right here when you get back."

The jeweler's small shop was located in one of the narrow old brick buildings that faced the courthouse. Its old rose brick had recently been tuck pointed and its woodwork freshly painted robin's-egg-blue. When Barbara and Stephen came in, a bell over the door tinkled to announce them.

From the back came a young man, no more than thirty, with a well-groomed black beard.

"Mr. Gold?" asked Stephen.

"My dad's Mr. Gold. I'm 'Son.' Janey just called and said you were coming over for wedding rings." He glanced down at Barbara's hand. "Uh…"

"I'm not sure I can remove it," Barbara said.

"Here, let me give it a shot." He twisted her ring. It moved but refused to slide over Barbara's knuckle. "We can soak it in ice water for twenty minutes and use Vaseline to make it slippery. It'll probably slide off eventually. Can't guarantee it, though."

"Is there some faster way?" Barbara caught Stephen's eye. For a moment, she felt a wrench around her heart. This was the final tangible link to her marriage to John. If he could see her hesitate, he'd no doubt make a wisecrack about fat fingers. "Can you cut it off?"

"Sure. Give me a sec." He went to the back and returned with a minuscule pair of what looked to Barbara like ordinary tin snips. "Let me have your hand. I promise I won't carve you along with the ring."

His hand felt cool and smooth and very steady. Barbara closed her eyes at the sound the snip made, and felt the sudden release of the pressure that had been a part of her life for so long.

"We'll need a gold chain for it, and can it be welded on so that it doesn't slip off?" Stephen asked. He took Barbara's hand and held it hard. She returned the pressure.

I refuse to cry.

"Sure, pick out a chain. I've some nice thick gold ones. I suggest you add a chain slide so that the chain doesn't actually slide through the ring itself. If you do that, it'll never lie flat. Leave it with me, I'll polish it up, add a chain slide and have it ready tomorrow. Now let's check out the rings."

They picked out simple matching gold bands.

"Want me to engrave the date on the back?"

"Right now?"

"Sorry, no time tonight. You can pick them up with the chain."

"Unfortunately—no, make that fortunately—we need them right this minute."

"Okay. Say, y'all put this ring business off kinda late, didn't you?"

Stephen handed over his credit card. "Mr. Gold, you have no idea."

BARBARA WENT INTO the courthouse's unisex restroom, locked the door and changed to her wedding finery. Her stomach was doing such flips she couldn't concentrate on anything but zipping up the back of her dress and combing her wind-blown hair. She'd forgotten her hair spray. Nuts.

She'd eaten nothing but a bunch of homemade shortbread cookies and drunk far too much coffee. She felt certain that her stomach would give a massive rumble right in the middle of the vows.

She'd brought enough makeup to renew her eyeliner and her lipstick and to powder her nose. As a final touch, she threaded a pair of ruby earrings she'd inherited from her mother through her earlobes.

She looked at herself in the mirror. Not bad for a rush job. She wondered again that a man like Stephen loved her. Because he did. She knew that with her whole heart, her whole soul. As she loved him.

With any luck, they would have years and years together. They'd get their children back, have grandchildren, manage all the logistical nightmares they'd already gotten themselves into. Through it all they would manage to love one another and be happy together.

She longed to sleep in his arms, see him across the breakfast table, do all the ordinary things that married people took for granted. She vowed she would never, ever take Stephen for granted.

She patted herself down, took a deep breath, picked up her small bag and unlocked the door to the restroom. "Last chance," she said to the mirror. "I can still run. From this moment I am not a *me* any longer, I'm an *us*. Can I handle that?" She smiled at herself and nodded. "Damned straight I can."

Janey was locking the door to the county clerk's office and waved to Barbara as she walked down the hall. "Dr. MacDonald took the licenses up to Sonny's office. I told him he should wait there and not down here. Don't you look pretty! Red is definitely your color."

"Not very nuptial."

"It's the color of your heart's blood, isn't it? Isn't that what you're giving him? Your heart?"

"Why, Janey, I never knew you were a romantic!"

"The way I love on my cats? Of course I am a romantic. Now, come on, and don't fall up the stairs and break your ankle. Yoo-hoo, Sonny! We're here," Janey called through the partially open door of the mayor's office. She opened the door and shepherded Barbara ahead of her as though she didn't quite trust her not to run. Seth and Emma sat on the leather sofa under the windows. Seth stood up when the two women came in and hugged Barbara. Barbara bent over Emma and hugged her, as well.

"I can't believe you came," Barbara whispered.

"Actually, I'm sore but I feel pretty good," Emma said. "Fast labor and no drugs."

At the far end of the room, Stephen stood under the flags of Tennessee, Williamston County and the United States. Maybe it was the late afternoon shadows, but Barbara thought he looked ashen. He took a tentative step toward her but didn't get close enough to touch. "You're not really a kidnapped bride, are you?"

She laid her palm against his cheek. He captured her hand and held it.

"Not kidnapped, but yours. No more doubts."

He kissed her palm and let her go.

She turned back to Emma and Seth. "How is baby Diana?"

"She's great. I, on the other hand, have just had my first experience with a breast pump. Only for you, Barbara. I'm already starting to leak. Sonny, let's get this show on the road."

"Let's. Barbara, will you come take Stephen's right hand in your left. Fine."

The words of the ceremony were so familiar to them both from other weddings they had attended, yet the knowledge that they were creating a bond for themselves that they would never break felt other-worldly.

Sonny finished reading the preliminaries, then said, "Can anyone present give any reason why these two should not be joined in matrimony?"

"I can!"

Everyone froze as Elaine stormed into the room, panting from her run up the stairs from the lobby below, with Roger and Anne behind her.

"Elaine?"

"Daddy, you can't do this. You're ruining our lives, making us a laughingstock..."

"Elaine," Roger said softly, "shut up." He turned to Stephen and offered his hand. "Sorry about this. I didn't think she'd go this far. We called your priest friend when we were half-way to Holly Springs. He told us about the change of venue, so here we are."

"Oh, shoot," Sonny said with a bark of laughter. "I been marrying folks for over forty years. I've always wanted somebody to hop up and say *yes* but today's the first time it ever happened."

"Elaine," Stephen said, "you and Anne go stand over there." He kept his voice calm but so cold that Elaine gulped and backed away.

"No, you will not flounce off. You will remain and do as your husband says. Be quiet. Roger, I could use a best man."

"Got it." Roger stepped up beside Stephen.

Anne, with a single glare at her sister and without a word, stepped over to stand beside Barbara.

"Now, as I was saying…"

"Don't do this, Mother!" Caitlyn stormed into the room. "Elaine called me and told me you had gone crazy, but I didn't believe you could do this without asking us."

"Young lady, go stand over there in the corner with your soon-to-be sister-in-law and do not speak a word or I will have you both locked up for contempt of court."

Sonny leaned over and whispered to Janey, "Can I do that?"

She shrugged. "I have no idea, but then neither do they. Get on with it, Sonny, before the entire hundred-and-first airborne parachutes in for coffee."

Sonny cleared his throat. "Right."

The rings were produced and fitted onto Stephen and Barbara's fingers. At last, Sonny said, "Now, with the power vested in me…"

The ceremony finished without incident except for the occasional snuffle from the back of the room.

"Mother, I made it!" Mark charged into the room carrying an armload of white roses. "Here. You said you wanted white roses for your wedding. Am I too late? I decided to come at the last minute."

"Is this one for or against?" Sonny whispered.

"For, at least I think he is," Barbara said.

"Then for the second time, with the power vested in me—or it was the last time I checked—I now pronounce you husband and wife. You may kiss your bride. Whew. I'm glad that's over. Here, gimme your hands and turn around. May I introduce to you Mr.—uh, Doctor—and Mrs.—uh, Doctor. Oh, shoot, Dr. and Dr. Stephen MacDonald. Now, y'all stand back and behave yourselves while ol' Sonny kisses the bride."

EPILOGUE

"SNOW FLURRIES! Stephen darling, that's the last thing we need. We'll wind up sliding off into a ditch and missing our own wedding service."

"Only flurries, my sweet. What can you expect in January? No accumulation. No slick roads. Everyone will get to the church safely."

"After what happened at our wedding, I'd like this confirmation or affirmation of our vows, or whatever they call it, to be peaceable."

"It will be. Emma and Seth are bringing Diana. She may scream, but nobody else will."

Stephen pulled her into his lap, where she snuggled up with her head under his chin.

"Don't get too comfortable, darling," she whispered. "We have animals to feed before we dress and drive down."

"I married you for better or worse. I did not count on raccoons and foxes."

"Don't forget the baby beavers. We should

fill the kiddie pool in their enclosure down at Emma's tomorrow morning."

"Up, woman. Might as well get it done."

In the barn Stephen rubbed the nose of a big bay gelding recovering from a mild colic, and asked, "What have you done with Elaine, Barbara? I figure you've stashed her somewhere, and we're left with the clone. A marked improvement."

"Move, Mabel, drat it!" Barbara shoved the goose, who hissed at her, but moved out of her way. "All her friends were so fascinated by her version of our elopement, she's made herself into the heroine of the afternoon, smoothing the way for her daddy to marry his brilliant veterinarian wife."

"You're joking."

"Nope. Anne said she had lunch on Friday with Elaine and Caitlyn. They could barely finish their salads for all the ladies who stopped by the table and wanted to hear all about it. Elaine's thrilled. Anne says she's happier than she's seen her since she married Roger. She's stopped trying to impress everybody and is starting to make some friends.

"Then I asked her to make an appointment

with *her* hairdresser to get my hair cut and highlighted. Let's go get dressed. Don't want to be late to our second wedding."

On the drive down to Holly Springs, they discussed the construction of the new house they were planning together behind the clinic. Stephen swore the scheme was her idea. She laughed at that.

"I'm glad we decided to build our house in our own pasture rather than in Seth and Emma's," Barbara said. "Closer to the practice."

"Farther from the flight cage."

"We may have the occasional baby barn owl that needs rehab, but I hope that's the last Orville."

"I have not minded living in your apartment, although it's claustrophobic for you."

"Not as bad as I thought. I enjoy your company. And Vince loves The Hovel. He swears he's going to finish Emma's barn. No idea when he'll have the time."

"Still no girlfriend? You swore there'd be one."

"Not yet. He's bringing in new female clients who are young, attractive and unmarried. Not because of his skills, although those are good. I can't complain so long as they pay their vet bills."

THE LITTLE CHURCH was blooming with white roses and full of friends and clients.

As Mark took his place beside Stephen, Walt leaned over and whispered, "See, I told you between the two of you—and me—we could make this happen."

This time around Barbara wore a peach silk shantung dress with a short veil attached to a comb in her freshly styled hair.

Stephen wore a suit that really *had* been tailored for him in London.

The blessing ceremony at eleven o'clock in the morning on Friday went without a hitch or a glitch. When Walt queried the guests about "just impediments," Stephen spared a narrow-eyed glance at Elaine. She gave him a bland smile. She was a hundred-per-cent reconciled to her father's marriage and had discovered she really enjoyed smartening Barbara up.

The ceremony was short but moving. Even Caitlyn snuffled into her lace-edged handkerchief.

After the union was blessed, Walt said, "Join us in the parish hall for champagne, wedding cake, refreshments and dancing."

Sonny Prather leaned over and said to Stephen, "I did it better. He didn't have a bunch of hooligans trying to keep him from finishing up the ceremony."

"Sonny, you were magnificent," Stephen said and gave him a clap on the back nearly as hard as the ones Sonny gave other people.

After the toasts, the jazz combo struck up a waltz. Stephen led Barbara onto the floor.

Stephen had grown up in an era where kids took ballroom dancing and practiced something called deportment. He swooped into a waltz with Barbara, who managed to follow him without tripping. He hadn't used his cane for weeks.

"I'm letting you lead," Barbara whispered.

"Remember that when we get home tonight."

"Don't push your luck, husband."

He and Barbara both glowed when they looked at one another, as if they were lit from within. At least that's what everyone kept telling them.

"Come on, everyone," Stephen called over his shoulder. "Dance."

By dribs and drabs everyone did. When the floor was pleasantly full, Stephen and Barbara slipped out the door to the rector's study and put their arms around one another. "When did you know?" Barbara asked.

"That I loved you? Orville told me. Telepathy, you know. Plus, he screamed at me that I was an idiot if I let you go. All I really knew at first was that you were the most interesting woman I'd met in years. I figured the only way I could hold on to you was to marry you. So I did."

"I hope Orville found his mate," Barbara said.

"He deserves her. He found me mine."

* * * * *

Get 4 FREE REWARDS!

We'll send you 2 FREE Books plus 2 FREE Mystery Gifts.

Love Inspired® Suspense books feature Christian characters facing challenges to their faith... and lives.

FREE
Value Over
$20

YES! Please send me 2 FREE Love Inspired® Suspense novels and my 2 FREE mystery gifts (gifts are worth about $10 retail). After receiving them, if I don't wish to receive any more books, I can return the shipping statement marked "cancel." If I don't cancel, I will receive 4 brand-new novels every month and be billed just $5.24 each for the regular-print edition or $5.74 each for the larger-print edition in the U.S., or $5.74 each for the regular-print edition or $6.24 each for the larger-print edition in Canada. That's a savings of at least 13% off the cover price. It's quite a bargain! Shipping and handling is just 50¢ per book in the U.S. and 75¢ per book in Canada*. I understand that accepting the 2 free books and gifts places me under no obligation to buy anything. I can always return a shipment and cancel at any time. The free books and gifts are mine to keep no matter what I decide.

Choose one: ☐ **Love Inspired® Suspense**
Regular-Print
(153/353 IDN GMY5)

☐ **Love Inspired® Suspense**
Larger-Print
(107/307 IDN GMY5)

Name (please print)

Address   Apt. #

City   State/Province   Zip/Postal Code

Mail to the **Reader Service:**
IN U.S.A.: P.O. Box 1341, Buffalo, NY 14240-8531
IN CANADA: P.O. Box 603, Fort Erie, Ontario L2A 5X3

Want to try two free books from another series! Call 1-800-873-8635 or visit www.ReaderService.com.

---

*Terms and prices subject to change without notice. Prices do not include applicable taxes. Sales tax applicable in N.Y. Canadian residents will be charged applicable taxes. Offer not valid in Quebec. This offer is limited to one order per household. Books received may not be as shown. Not valid for current subscribers to Love Inspired Suspense books. All orders subject to approval. Credit or debit balances in a customer's account(s) may be offset by any other outstanding balance owed by or to the customer. Please allow 4 to 6 weeks for delivery. Offer available while quantities last.

Your Privacy—The Reader Service is committed to protecting your privacy. Our Privacy Policy is available online at www.ReaderService.com or upon request from the Reader Service. We make a portion of our mailing list available to reputable third parties that offer products we believe may interest you. If you prefer that we not exchange your name with third parties, or if you wish to clarify or modify your communication preferences, please visit us at www.ReaderService.com/consumerschoice or write to us at Reader Service Preference Service, P.O. Box 9062, Buffalo, NY 14240-9062. Include your complete name and address.

LIS18

HOME on the RANCH

HRCBPA18R

READERSERVICE.COM

Manage your account online!

- Review your order history
- Manage your payments
- Update your address

We've designed the Reader Service website just for you.

Enjoy all the features!

- Discover new series available to you, and read excerpts from any series.
- Respond to mailings and special monthly offers.
- Browse the Bonus Bucks catalog and online-only exculsives.
- Share your feedback.

Visit us at:
ReaderService.com